THE POLICE SURGEON

BOOKS BY GENE RONTAL

Sterile Justice

A Lethal Dose

The Cruelest Cut

A Pre-existing Condition

THE POLICE SURGEON

A Detective Ben Dailey, M.D. Mystery

GENE RONTAL

CAVEL
PRESS
Kenmore, WA

CAMEL PRESS

A Camel Press book published by Epicenter Press

Epicenter Press
6524 NE 181st St.
Suite 2
Kenmore, WA 98028

For more information go to:
www.Camelpress.com
www.Coffeetownpress.com
www.Epicenterpress.com
www.generontalbooks.com

This is a work of fiction. Names, characters, places, brands, media, and incidents are either the product of the author's imagination or are used fictitiously.

Design by Scott Book and Melissa Vail Coffman

Previously published by Sterling House

ISBN: 978-1-60381-740-0 (Trade Paper)
ISBN: 978-1-60381-742-4 (eBook)

Printed in the United States of America

To Joel and Gabriel

"There is a tide in the affairs of men,
Which, taken at the flood leads on to fortune;
Omitted, all the voyage of their life
Is bound in shallows and in miseries."

Julius Caesar, Act IV, Scene III

CHAPTER 1

I T WAS AN ANNOYING SOUND. Not terribly loud, but so relentless that not even the howling of an icy December wind could drown it out. In my dream I tried pulling a pillow over my head; it didn't work. The persistent noise pushed me to consciousness.

Wearily, I forced my eyes open and sidled up against the V-berth of my boat. A few more seconds of listening and I realized what the noise was: my bilge pump. For a liveaboard in a deserted winter marina, the sound was like an air raid siren. This was trouble.

I glanced at the clock. It was 4 a.m. Swinging my feet slowly over the edge of the berth, I stepped down and suddenly plunged into eighteen inches of icy water. It was like sticking my hand into an electrical light socket.

I jumped back to the safety of my bed, frantically rummaged through the shelf next to me, and flipped on a flashlight. My lungs gasped for air as I probed the spotlight around the cabin floor. To my horror, I could no longer see the battered teak and holly sole beneath the dark, murky water. Instead there were checkered seat cushions, cereal boxes, and life jackets floating around like large dominoes. My God, my boat was going down! What the hell was happening?

In the midst of my frenzied panic reason took over: water and a ship's batteries don't mix. Add a plugged-in battery charger from the shore power, and I had the potential of an electrical fire and my death, unless I could turn off the battery and get the hell out of here.

I scrambled into my corduroys and found my boots and heaviest sweater. Once dressed, I located my waterproof duffel and filled it with the things I might need: extra clothes, cell phone, and my emergency stash of money. I was about to zipper the bag, when I saw the large black folder with my name on it filled with photos, press clippings, and legal documents wedged into the corner of the shelf. On the outside cover it read "Trial" in large red letters. Without thinking I stuffed it inside.

My next task was to look for a way out. The first route of escape that came to me was to move upward through the Lexan hatch above my berth. I looked through the clouded plastic window. All I could see was the red neon sign proclaiming to all that this was "Beautiful Lake St. Clair, Michigan, The Gateway to the Great Lakes." Unlocking the handle and hunching over, I heaved my shoulders against the hatch. At six-three and two hundred and ten pounds, I'm no weakling, but I couldn't budge the ice of ten winter storms that had sealed it shut.

I looked around again. There was no other opening. I realized my only exit was through the icy deluge that filled the cabin. *Got to think, not panic.* Wallet, keys and Patagonia jacket. I jumped in with my duffel in hand. But my pep talk hadn't prepared me for the surge of frigid water. My legs could barely move. After a few steps, I fell face down into the turbid pool.

I had to get to the battery switch. I wanted to yell, but to whom? I was a captain going down with his ship, and I wasn't even at sea. Still hanging on to my bag, I clutched the edge of the chipped Formica dinette and managed to pull myself upright, two feet from the companionway steps. I saw the battery control next to the chart table. With the flashlight shaking in my hand, I turned it to turn it to the off position. The pump went silent.

As soon as I flipped off the battery, I lunged upward onto the worn, rubberized stair treads of the companionway, reaching a level just above the water. Even though I was shivering convulsively, I managed to bring my body to the sliding hatch and wrench the fiberglass cover back.

I poked my head outside and into a frigid squall. One more step up and I was immediately peppered with tiny ice pellets that stung my face as if they were shot from a BB gun. My lips and cheeks were already numb. I looked toward the bow and saw that the top edge of my boat was a foot below the edge of the dock.

I lurched out of the companionway and onto the ice-covered deck. With a sidearm heave, I threw my bag over the lifeline and onto the dock. Then I took a step forward in my wet boots. My feet started to slide on the deck, causing an accidental version of the moonwalk that threw me directly toward the lifeline. I hit it so hard with my thigh that I flipped over the plastic-coated wire.

Frantically grasping for anything to hold onto, I put a death grip on the mooring line and hauled myself toward the boarding ladder a fraction of a second before I went overboard. If I'd had an audience to my acrobatic escape act, they would have cheered loudly. But nobody knew and nobody cared.

I raised my body up to the dock and heard my frozen corduroys cracking like two large ice blocks. Somehow, I found my duffel in the blowing snow. Putting one hand on the strap, my legs stumbled forward at what seemed like an incredibly slow pace. The cold was so intense I could barely move. One more step and I fell down.

I don't know if it was delirium or an insightful vision, but as I lay on the dock, I suddenly had an epiphany. There in front of me was a tombstone. On it was my name: Benjamin Joseph Dailey, M.D.

I shook my head and came back to reality. I wasn't going to die like this, not without a fight. With what seemed to be incredible effort, I was able to bring first my right knee and then my left to a kneeling position. Moving on all fours and holding my duffel, I crawled fifty feet, collapsing on the snowbank adjoining the plowed blacktop. My breath was now coming in short gasps. I could think of only one thing—to get to my car.

I saw it in the distance, a rusted apparition of hope. Twenty feet more and I'd be there. With one last effort, I managed to drag my frozen body along the snow toward my fifteen-year-old heap. It was my only chance of survival.

My leg muscles tightened. Hypothermia was winning. My anesthetized hands found the keys in my pocket and extracted them, only for the metal ring to fall on the ground. Cursing and groping, I finally found them again, this time carefully picking the right key. I pulled on the unlocked door, and it sprang open. I threw my bag on the floor and struggled to the seat by grasping the rim of the steering wheel with my arm between the spokes. Slowly, I pulled myself up and onto the worn-out cloth seat.

My body was lying sideways, halfway into the car. I brought the ignition key up to my mouth, then forced it between the second and third fingers of my right hand. After two errant passes, I finally jammed the key against the cylinder. With one turn the engine mercifully growled to life. I managed to bring my legs inside, reach back to close the door, and fall, exhausted, onto the seat.

It seemed like only minutes that I had been lying there. Yet when I came to, the march to consciousness felt arduously slow. Wafts of warm air from the car's heater blew onto my body, eventually bringing with it an intense pain in my fingers as they began to thaw. It was a signal that my body temperature was starting to rise; my mind beginning to function. I had to get up.

Slowly, I lifted my cold, wet body from the seat and peered expectantly over the steering wheel. The first thing I saw was the half-submerged shape of my boat. Under the lights of the parking lot I looked at the boat's transom. There was the name *Judy D* and below it, *Detroit, Michigan*. A little deeper and she would be under. How could I have been such a fool to think I could live like a hermit on that beat-up old sailboat?

I didn't have an answer. Instead, the only thing that pervaded my senses was an intense and uncontrollable shivering. After twenty minutes of the heater blowing on my water-soaked clothes, the shaking stopped long enough that I could put the car in gear. I headed towards the emergency phone at the end of the driveway.

There's an old quip about my city. People always say they're from Detroit, but no one actually admits to living there. Whether it originated from embarrassment or indifference, it's unfortunately the truth. Having lived there all my life, I had come to realize that the attitude arose from constantly combating a collective melancholy bred from high unemployment, corrupt politicians, boarded-up, high crime neighborhoods, and the chronic hysteria of the press that has made the city's inhabitants feel like they live in a metropolitan *piñata*. Regardless of what Detroiters would say in rebuttal, calling the city a poster child for what has gone wrong with the American ethic is probably correct. Like I said, it's not easy to be a Detroiter.

A politician might have blamed the economy. A psychologist would have added that it would be easy to glom onto this depression and habitually feel sorry for one's self. But I'm neither; I'm a doctor, and I knew damn well that on a cold, sodden day in the middle of December, I couldn't blame the weight of distasteful public opinion for feeling like shit. The reason was much more visceral. With the loss of my boat, I was now officially homeless.

The thought was enough to paralyze me into inaction. I truly didn't know what to do. So instead of doing something positive, I found myself driving aimlessly through St. Clair Shores and Grosse Pointe, eventually winding up on Jefferson Avenue in the city's most populated area. Though I wouldn't have admitted it to anyone, subconsciously I was hoping that being around any kind of humanity would somehow ease the desolation that had overtaken me.

I parked across from the GM Building, trying to get my head together. Sitting there in the early morning dawn, I looked around at the empty eight-lane highway that represented the main drag along the waterfront of the city. My eyes moved toward the entrance of the building. There were two cops huddled together at the intersection, ear flaps down and thick gloves caressing their Styrofoam cups of coffee. They looked indifferently at me for a moment and then turned back to their steaming drinks. I was wrong—humanity didn't seem to care if I was in trouble or not.

I glanced up at the dominating five-tower, thirty-story structure that was built forty years ago to signal the rebirth of the city. The clouds were low enough to obscure the signature blue and white automaker's sign atop a roof that once beckoned the American dream. It only added to my confusion. I honestly didn't know what to do.

The fact that I had survived did little to lift my mood. I was nearly broke with no place to live and no future to look forward to. For a moment I wished I had gone overboard and drowned, putting myself out of my misery. But I knew that would never be an option.

That thought and my overall bewilderment were interrupted as the two policemen decided to get some exercise, instead of huddling against the cold. They started walking toward my car. When they were about twenty feet away, they pointed at the no parking sign I was under. Great. Seventy percent of the murders in the city went unsolved, and they were worried about me standing in a no parking zone on a street devoid of traffic.

I didn't argue, just saluted them as I pulled onto Jefferson. The action seemed to snap me out of my lethargy. I suddenly understood what my current problem was: I needed a warm place to stay, that was cheap and clean. That's when I recalled the small motel down from the marina, The Lazy Isles. I decided I would spend a little money to hole up there and dry out until I could figure what to do.

I CHECKED INTO THE MOTEL AROUND 9 A.M, and quickly changed out of my wet clothes. Looking around at my dingy, motel-plastic home, I couldn't wait to get outside.

When I reached the security of my Jeep, I slumped down behind the wheel for a moment. I was feeling weak with a fever-ridden soreness in every muscle of my body. But that discomfort couldn't compare to the pain and despair I felt over losing my home. I thought of my soggy half-submerged boat and realized that I couldn't just abandon the one thing that had kept me anchored to society. Without it I was truly adrift.

I picked up my cellphone and dialed the marina. The report was bad. While the boat wasn't completely ruined, they wanted eight hundred bucks to hoist it out. In a rash moment, I told them to go ahead. It wasn't until I hung up and checked my wallet that I realized just how short of money I was. That's when I picked the phone up and dialed Bruce Sanderson at Coastal Life Insurance Company. Luckily, he was in. When I needed coin of the realm, I usually paid him a visit.

I pulled out of the driveway, merged into rush hour traffic, and headed to Coastal's office. The remnants of last night's snow still covered the streets, making the going slow. As I sat waiting for the endless line of cars to merge onto the expressway, it occurred to me that I had a checkered relationship with the insurance industry, and with good reason.

While I was in practice, my agent had sold me a minimum medical liability policy, explaining that no one was taking out the max. When I lost my malpractice case and the plaintiff went after my personal assets and got them, my agent just shrugged in disbelief and said things like that never happened.

At one time I might have been justifiably accused of having a confident view of the profession. But after everything that has happened to me, much against my natural optimism, I've taken a sanguine view of life; the world is round, your worst enemy can turn into your best friend, and we all have to eat. So now, instead of berating those in the profession, I did their insurance physicals. According to most people who would give you an honest answer, such work occupied the lowest rung in the medical food chain.

Just to make sure that it's understood, working for an insurance company wasn't an easy adjustment. I used to be a real doctor—I was Chief of Staff at St. Vincent's Hospital, world authority on voice disorders, with referrals from all over the country. After enough people had told me I was good, I had even convinced myself.

But that was then and this was now. I had found out the hard way how fleeting public fame is. It lasts about as long as it takes to read a sensational front-page newspaper article outlining a horrific malpractice claim. At that point no one cares about what you used to be. They find someone else to prattle on about.

When my savings ran out and my ex-wife took me for all I was worth, I became desperate for some kind of work. Like a lot of people at the end of their rope, sacred principles really didn't matter anymore, so I approached Bruce Sanderson at Coastal Life. I had known him as a patient. Grasping at straws, I asked him for a job doing physical exams, hoping he wouldn't brush me off like everyone else. I was surprised and grateful when he said yes.

I shouldn't have been. It wasn't in Bruce's nature to throw people bones. He had a need, and I was available. I found out later that the insurance industry doesn't care about your bona fides. Talk about a misconception. It was all about the forms. They needed a certified body to fill out the paperwork. As long as the papers said M.D. on the bottom and you were licensed, they didn't care.

I thought about that as I dragged my aching body across the snow-covered parking lot and into to the seedy, one story stick and brick structure that housed Coastal Life Insurance Company. If the architecture of a building was meant to depict its inhabitants, inspiration and faith in the institution were not in the portrait.

My Maine guide boots, still wet from the salty slush of the parking lot, knocked against the darkly stained, hollow core door of the company's signature suite as I turned the knob. I don't know what I had been expecting, but nothing had changed in the two weeks since I had last been there. In the room were three cramped desks, a two-chair waiting alcove, and Sheila Pryzbycki, Coastal's tight-lipped, gum-snapping office scullion reading *People*.

There was no welcome mat, so I slogged forward, letting my boots drip dry on the brown stain already tattooed into the worn green carpeting in front of Sheila's desk. I'm not a small person, but Sheila did her best to ignore me. It was a game we had played over the past five years: how long would it take for her to make me mad? I think her disdain for me started when she found out my insurance work was all I did for a living. What kind of a doctor was I anyway? I'm sure that sentiment had crossed many people's minds over the years.

The thought brought out the worst in me, a stubborn streak that wouldn't give in to her irrelevant self-righteousness. In spite of my splitting headache and still-damp clothes, I was determined not to let her win this time. In retaliation, she gave her gum a few more clicks and leafed slowly through her pages until she realized I wasn't going to budge.

"Nice to see you made it in today, Ben," she said, putting the magazine between her Diet Coke and low-tar Virginia Slims. Sheila was a health nut. Then she looked up at me. "God, you look like hell."

I couldn't blame her. I must have looked like crap in my flannel shirt and wrinkled corduroys. Or maybe it was my brush with hypothermia. I felt like shit.

"Work is the curse of the middle class," I said weakly, curious whether I still rated that caste designation. "Is Bruce in?"

She nodded and pointed to the half-open door behind her. I didn't wait for follow-up conversation, just swiveled my way around her desk and pushed toward the executive office of the regional manager of the fifty-seventh biggest insurance company in America.

Bruce Sanderson was ensconced behind his desk, a three-piece belly in a two-piece suit. Spread before him was a half-open pastrami and cheese sandwich, two pickles, and a can of Sunkist orange soda. I hadn't had anything to eat and didn't feel like eating. I could feel a fever coming on. In my state the smell was almost overwhelming. When he saw me, he looked up and smiled. Bruce and I went way back.

"Welcome to the office, doctor. Once every two weeks isn't bad for the only medical consultant Coastal has in Detroit," he said, focusing his eyes on the triple-decker with mayo in front of him. Then he looked at me more carefully. "Jesus, what the hell happened to you?"

"I had a little problem with my boat last night. It tried to sink, and I tried not to follow suit," I said, trying not to sound too miserable.

"No kidding. Are you all right? Maybe you need to see a doctor," he laughed, holding the sides of his paunch. So much for the sympathy of Coastal Life.

I didn't mind. I was used to Bruce. "You got anything for me?" Right now money was my primary concern.

"Not much. Christmas is the slow time. Got this one physical on a PI attorney. Guy runs a legal mill, on the television all the time." I think he felt a little guilty as he handed me the file. "Other than that, there aren't any medical exams. This time of the year no one is interested in putting their dough into death benefits."

Shit. This was definitely bad karma.

Even Bruce must have recognized the look of dismay on my face. He rummaged through the mass of scattered papers on his desk. "Say, I do have one thing. You heard about Faye Donaldson, that woman who was shot and killed at the Veterans Hospital last week?" He had the look of a man who had just solved a nagging problem.

I coughed a couple of times. "Not really. What happened?"

He went on to explain that the woman was a local NIH administrator. She was found shot dead at her desk, the victim of a seemingly senseless killing. There was no evidence at the scene, no hint of who had committed the murder. All they had was the bullet from her head. He said no one had a clue why someone would kill her. Everyone seemed to have liked her.

"Turns out the victim had a policy with us," Sanderson continued. "She bought it thirty years ago when it was cheap."

"So shell out the premium and you're done," I replied indifferently. What the hell did he think I was, some kind of detective?

"It's not so simple. This woman's policy had an exclusionary clause for violent death as a Federal employee." He explained that according to the company's policy, if the policyholder is killed at work, the government assumes the responsibility for the payout. All we have to do is to make sure there are no other medical reasons for her death.

"If I were you," he added, "I would consider it free money, since we know she was murdered. The dead woman's husband is a rock-solid family man, hardworking, that kind of stuff. So is the rest of the family." As he spoke, he took another huge bite from his sandwich and washed it down with some soda. Amazingly, he was making me sick to my stomach *and* hungry at the same time.

"So if I find something, you're going to bless me with untold riches?"

"Believe it or not, Ben, this is a business. We hate the payout. Kind of gives us indigestion." I shouldn't have been surprised at his crass, unemotional viewpoint. After all, insurance agents were the quintessential salesmen in three-piece suits, bargaining your life for cash. Bean counters with multi-colored tables, telling you exactly when you were going to check out, and how much you were going to leave behind.

However, if Bruce was truly worried about this case giving him dyspepsia, it didn't show. Instead of contemplating the victim's fate, he again looked down at the food in front of him. Picking up the kosher dill, he wiped the juice from his chin with his hand, and then heaved a *grepps*. My confusion clarified, I decided that watching him gorge himself was definitely making me sick.

"What do I have to do?"

"Just check out the facts, talk to her husband, and fill out this form. You know, find out if there were other medical problems, including depression or psychiatric disease." He handed me a three-page questionnaire with Coastal's logo at the top. "Oh, and one other thing. I've checked with the police and the Feds. They'll give you all the help you need."

"The Feds? What's the deal?"

"The shooting was at the Veterans Hospital. That makes it a federal crime." As he spoke, he handed me a slip of paper with a name on it.

I read the name: Jordan Dalkind, Assistant Federal Attorney, Southeastern Michigan. Shit, I didn't want to do this. I had enough problems without getting involved in some dead lady's insurance policy. "What do I get for all my effort, Bruce?"

"The company pays big time for stuff like this. Hundred bucks a day, plus expenses. If you don't want it, I can call someone else."

I quickly added up my bank account balance. It looked like the scorecard at a Tigers game. Then I thought about my boat.

"Let me look it over. If it's not for me, I'll let you know. Hundred dollars a day, right?" I asked again. With Bruce, you had to make the deal stick.

He nodded. "Don't wait too long to get back to me. We only got a couple of days to close it down, okay? Coastal employs me to get this done expeditiously. This is not an open-ended job." Then he stopped for a moment, let out another belch, as if he was relieving his brain of excess tension, and picked up two tickets that he somehow retrieved from the mess on his desk.

"Say, you're a sports nut, aren't you?"

I was going to explain to him that a lot of people thought I was just plain nuts, but that explanation might not sound good to my employer, so I merely shrugged and asked why.

"Some guy at the bank that we do business with gave me these tickets to the Pistons game next week. He said they were real good seats. You interested?"

I thought for a moment. Even if I didn't go, I could sell them. They were the hottest ticket in town. "Sure, Bruce." He handed me the tickets and smiled. There was a large piece of pastrami caught between his teeth. It made him look like one of those clowns with a blacked-out tooth. I wanted to laugh, but I couldn't bite the hand that fed me, so I thanked him and pocketed the tickets.

As I walked out, I didn't even bother to serenade Sheila with my version of "Take This Job and Shove it". I just made for the safety of my car in the parking lot.

Inside the sunlit warmth of my fifteen-year-old Wagoneer, I felt a sense of grateful security. Aside from my boat, this hulk was now my only real possession. So instead of my usual grind-it-till-it-starts routine, I gently jiggled the ignition. The car roared to life almost in appreciation of my soft touch. I sat there waiting for the heater to kick in, as the throaty sound of my partially blown muffler echoed embarrassingly down the street. All I could think of was the mess I was in.

A hundred bucks a day. I needed the money. Should I feel guilty? Hardly what I had worked so hard for when I'd gone to medical school . But then, I hadn't bargained for a lot of the changes that had come my way. Every time I thought about them I became dizzy, like I was in a freefall.

CHAPTER 2

I SAT AT THE CURB, STARING OUT THE FRONT WINDSHIELD at the cars mushing their way through the wet, early winter snow, and pondered Sanderson's offer. It occurred to me that, in an intriguing way, it might be interesting to take on the case. It was certainly a welcome change from doing physical exams on rich lawyers and businessmen. It was close to 12:30. I'd take a quick lunch and then swing by the Federal Building—almost like being at work again.

Something was still gnawing at me. It took me a moment to realize what it was. Money—or lack thereof—was beginning to control my life. Look at me. Some innocent bystander gets shot, and I'm making a living off it. *What the hell am I doing? I'm still a doctor, am I not?* I looked around at my beat-up car, my shabby clothes and the realization of how far I had fallen. The answer didn't come easily. Yeah, I was still a doctor, but I was hanging on by a thread.

I shivered and shook my head as if the act would keep me from feeling sorry for myself. The only solace I could find was in the thought that it could have been me they were doing the insurance investigation on.

I shivered again, and this time it occurred to me that it wasn't just fear that was making me tremble. A nearly lethal bout of frigid Midwestern winter had lowered my resistance—I now had a cough and maybe even a little fever. I turned up the heater and started to shiver. It was an unpleasant reminder of just how close I had come to earning an epitaph.

A horn blared from behind me, and I suddenly snapped out of my reverie. Someone wanted my parking space. I dropped the folder back on the seat, put the car in gear, and looked over at the clock. I quickly decided that, whatever my emotional state, I wasn't ready to check out just yet. Especially since Bruce Sanderson was guaranteeing me a C-note.

THE GOVERNMENT DIDN'T MAKE ITS HOME EASY TO FIND, especially in this weather and this economy. If I wanted to ask for directions, I would have been screwed. There was no one on the street and no one in the plants. Having grown up with a pride in the city, the mantras of "what's good for Detroit is good for America" and "The Motor Capitol of the World" now seemed like the shallow, lingering bluster of an old soldier at the VFW hall, reveling in the past. Bankruptcy, layoffs, and an uncertain future were all that Detroiters had to look forward to.

The McNamara Federal Building was on Fort Street. In another city, its Bauhaus architecture might have been appealing. But stuck as it was on this woebegone street that dead-ended in downtown Detroit, it was definitely out of place. Finding Jordan Dalkind's office was even tougher. Jordan. I figured he'd been some preppy, eastern school guy, probably Harvard or Yale, working to make a reputation and then move up into some high-paying, corporate litigation job, or maybe even politics. Three receptionists, two secretaries, and fifteen minutes later, I finally found the floor.

The foyer at the elevator split into two paths of gray carpeting that ran in opposite directions around the floor's perimeter. Off the sides of each, small, glass-windowed cubicles sprang like branches from a tree. I took the empty halls to mean that either my tax dollars were being well spent in diligent effort, or our public servants were having the largest coffee break in the history of the world.

Making the turn at the first corner and past an open door, I could hear a woman shouting in the corridor. Curious, I peered down the hall and saw two uniformed policemen holding a struggling, middle-aged woman by the arms.

"Let go of me, you baboons. I have my rights." I could see that her lipstick was smeared, and her running mascara had made her face gray from crying.

"Sure, lady," one of the blue coats replied. "Take it easy and we'll get you out of here."

The woman looked back through an open office door. "All you governmental pencil pushers are the same. I demand justice for my sister. You people are doing nothing. As a taxpaying citizen, I demand that you find that out." Sounded like a dead-end argument to me. Hell, I paid taxes and look what I got.

I didn't hear the reply. Whoever was speaking from inside the office was obviously demonstrating more self-control than this woman.

Finally, the woman yelled back the final epithet so common in most conversations with bureaucrats, of whatever make or model. "I'll be back, and the next time it'll be with a letter from my congressman."

With that, the woman, red-faced and frowning, kicked her foot against the door, slamming it shut. The officers escorted her to the elevators, as I in turn moved cautiously down the corridor. That's when I saw the name, Jordan Dalkind, Assistant United States Attorney. At least I had found the right office.

I knocked on the door and waited for a response. After that outburst in the hallway, I was anticipating a stiff reception. Instead, I got the one thing I didn't expect—an attractive woman dressed in a tailored gray suit coming to the entrance. Nice legs, athletic body.

"Another relative?" She gave me a quick once-over. It made me want to know what she thought.

I smiled back. "Nope, just a few questions from Coastal Life."

She hesitated a moment, then went back to her desk, found the slip of paper, and read it. "Oh, you're the guy that Mr. Sanderson's office called about."

I smiled again. It was hard not to smile at a face that beautiful. Light green eyes, auburn hair, freckles, probably early thirties. "Ben Dailey is the name." I held out my hand. I liked shaking hands with people; it told me what they were like, especially women.

What I got back was a lot: the smooth, firm, warm handshake of someone used to being in charge. And no ring on her fourth finger. I had learned to notice these things since I had returned to the ranks of the unmarried.

"Jordan Dalkind. And it's too bad you weren't here a few minutes earlier. You would have seen some angry people who want the same information you do. Maybe it would have saved some time."

With my per diem on the insurance company's chit, I wasn't looking for shortcuts.

"No problem. I've got lots of time." I glanced at her again. She was tall with slim hips and lots of leg. I was finding it hard to quit staring at her, so I looked around the room. Sligh desk, a credenza with a Sarouk runner, Waterford crystal on top. I remembered all this stuff. My ex-wife used to brag about crap like that to her friends. There was also a great view through the window behind the credenza, looking south toward Lake Erie. For a second I forgot the ice floes and saw myself sailing toward Sandusky with a following wind. It was only a short moment before I remembered the *Judy D* on the hoist and why I was down here.

I did some more looking. A few photos on the walls, mostly of a muscular man next to a variety of toys: sailboard, sea kayak, and skis. Not a bad office for a government worker type. In one photo, the same guy was in a SWAT team outfit and had his arm around Jordan. He looked like more than just a friend.

If Ms. Dalkind noticed my scrutiny of her office, she didn't say anything. Instead she made her way behind the desk and motioned to me to sit down in the leather side chair. "Mr. Sanderson said you wanted to ask me a few questions about the murder."

I was a little embarrassed at my nervousness with someone who appeared so professional. With a little effort I managed to pull myself together and explain that I was there to get information as to whether there was any job-related connection between the victim and the murder.

"I guess we'd have to find the killer first, wouldn't we?" she said.

My face reddened. "Like I said, I'm no detective. Mainly, I'm interested in the medical things."

"Why? Are you a doctor?" Nothing like cutting through the bullshit.

I nodded. But for some reason I had to make more of this. "I'm basically retired. I do this to keep myself busy."

"Well, I can tell you that there was nothing in the crime scene work-up to link anyone to the killer. As far as the police are concerned, it's an open and shut case. Guy comes in, pulls out a .357 Magnum, and fires." Her eyes narrowed in anger as she spoke.

I asked her why the government was involved, and she brushed the question aside with the "happened on Federal property" routine. There was a definite hardness to her voice when she spoke about it.

"Do you know what the bullet hit?"

"They tried to explain things to me, but I couldn't understand it. You know lawyers. They're all would-be medical students who couldn't stand the sight of blood." She smiled softly when she said it. She had a nice smile, and white teeth.

I noticed that as she spoke, she looked at me closely, fidgeting with the black Waterman fountain pen on her desk. My nose was running like a faucet, and I took out my blue workman's handkerchief. I figured my runny nose was making me look even less attractive than I felt.

"I see your point." I gave my red nose a good honk and put the handkerchief back in my pocket.

"Bad cold?" She backed away slightly. If I were in her shoes, I would have wanted to reach for a mask.

"Yeah, caught it the other day. Sorry, I didn't mean to bring my germs here, but Bruce wanted the information right away."

"Don't worry. I took the flu shot. Listen, not to change the subject, but is this all you do?" she asked, looking me over the same way I had checked out her office.

"What do you mean?" I countered, embarrassed by her scrutiny.

"I mean, do you work at another job?"

"Only other thing I do is play the piano at the Pipeline once in a while." Not a real job, but it was maybe the only thing that had kept my sanity intact.

She snapped her fingers. "You do the intermission sets, don't you?"

"Yeah, that's me, the filler-man."

"I knew I had seen you before. I go down there once in a while. You've got a nice style, kind of like Oscar Peterson."

I should be so lucky. "Yeah, well I sound like a lot of people when I play their music. But they've got the record contracts, and I don't."

"Maybe I'll come down and check it out again."

"Yeah, that would be great. What do you like?"

"Dizzy, Duke, Sonny Rollins."

"For a young person, you have old taste."

"Not really. Just good jazz." She hesitated a moment. I took it to mean the conversation was drawing to a close.

But she spoke again. "By the way, what hospital did you work at when you were practicing?"

"St. Vincent's. Why?"

"Oh, nothing." The way she said it made me wonder. She seemed on the verge of asking me something else when the phone rang.

I didn't know whether I should leave or stay. Then I thought I noticed her eyes narrow and her lips purse. A few nods. I took my cue, lip-synched my thanks, and started to walk out. From the look in her eyes, I almost thought she was motioning for me to stay.

I walked back out the long corridor. Boy, how I hated legal offices. You only need one brush with the legal institution and the decision of a jury of your peers to realize how vulnerable you are. It was five years ago, but as I remembered it, it seemed like yesterday.

The judge was looking down imperiously over his half-glasses with a gaze of self-importance. "Bailiff, will you please read the verdict."

There was an impenetrable silence, like the world had stopped moving. I stared straight ahead, hoping no one was watching me, knowing that they were.

"The jury finds in favor of the plaintiff, your honor."

I could still feel that horrific moment of freefall, a life in suspension, not ready to accept what had been said. There was a shout of victory from behind me, yelling from newsmen and the ricocheting sound of the judge's gavel cracking against a wooden stand. There was the family shouting and pointing their fingers at me. One of them, in a moment of delirium, even shook my attorney's hand. Then the words processed, and I felt my whole body sag in the sudden realization of what had just happened. It was as if the air had come out of a tire.

I wondered if Jordan Dalkind knew what kind of a failure I was, if it even mattered. I felt stupid. She saw right through me. A physician doing a medical investigation: I had loser spelled all over me. Most doctors in their forties would be at their peak, doing big cases, collecting big fees, attending charity balls. They would definitely not be chasing after murder evidence.

CHAPTER 3

I WASN'T FEELING MUCH BETTER THE NEXT MORNING. The Lazy Isles, the run-down motel that I was staying at, didn't help matters much. Their charge-by-the-hour policy and paper-thin walls kept me awake most of the night. Nothing like hearing some guy loping his mule to give you a restful night's sleep.

At about seven p.m. I got out of the rickety bed, took a deep breath and immediately went into a spasm of deep throaty coughs. It was enough to convince me that my minor cold had now become a significant bronchitis. Like most doctors, I was a bad patient, a fact aggravated by my lack of health insurance. My mind rationalized that all I needed was a little food. I had to feel better so I could get paid.

The thought was a sufficient impetus for me to dressed and get the hell out of there. A quick check in the mirror, as I brushed back my hair, and I was semi-presentable.

I found a diner down at the corner that served decent food. Hot tea and oatmeal for two dollars and fifty cents. Not bad. In fact, I almost felt human after I finished. Or at least I did until I got back to my car and started into another paroxysm of coughing. Antibiotics cost eighty dollars for a ten-day supply. Funny, when I was in practice, I had never thought twice about the cost. The drug companies were glad to hand samples out. Now I was seeing how the other half lived. I had to scramble for anything and get my care where I could. My best solution was the Beacon Street Clinic.

I had helped set the clinic up several years ago, when I was Chief of Staff at St. Vincent's. It was an inner-city outreach program to help disadvantaged people. The fact that it still existed gave me a good measure of pride. But that was purely personal gratification. No one knew me there anymore.

Occasionally I would go there, do a little clerical work, filing and that kind of thing, and trade my efforts for medical care if I needed some. Nobody said much on the occasions that I came in; they were used to volunteers coming and going. The nurses were only too glad to give out free advice in return. After listening to me cough for an hour, it didn't take much persuading for the nurse practitioner to give me some samples of Zithromax when I asked for them. As I swallowed the first pill, I remembered what was said about a physician who treats himself, something about a fool for a doctor. At this point, it was all word salad. Without health insurance, I was the only doctor I could afford.

It was close to one o'clock by the time I made my way from the clinic to my car. My head ached and my throat felt raw, but, even worse, my stomach was growling again in protest. I found a bagel shop just before my intestinal tract could make the decision to sabotage me.

Sitting down in a booth in the warmth of the deli, I saw a used copy of the morning edition of the paper lying on the table next to me. I glanced at it for a moment and felt the blood rush from my face. The headline read: "Young Man, Victim of Malpractice, Dies." I read further.

James Scotten was found dead from an apparent suicide at his home last night. Scotten was the victim in a sensational malpractice trial that received national attention five years ago. At the trial, Dr. Benjamin Dailey was found guilty of negligence. In a multimillion dollar settlement, Dailey, former Chief of Staff at St. Vincent's Hospital, was sanctioned by the state medical society and dismissed from the hospital staff.

I stared at the words with more remorse and sadness than I had ever known. After a few moments, I threw the paper back on the seat with a combination of anger and sorrow. Anger for once more getting an unwanted reminder of what had happened to me. I felt sorrow for the death of Jimmy Scotten.

I sat there wondering why I ever picked the paper up in the first place. I hated the local rags—they always brought me bad news. During the trial, the writers took my initials, B. J., and called me "Botched Job" Dailey. It didn't stop there. My colleagues referred to me as B.J. behind my back. Then I thought about Jimmy. What difference did it make how I felt? Jimmy was dead, and it was my fault.

I suddenly experienced an urgent need to get out of the deli. The waitress came over to fill my cup. I shook my head without speaking. I saw her glance at me and wondered what she thought about this derelict sitting in the booth.

I knew that feeling sorry for myself was not an option. The past five years held enough self-deprecation and depression to last a lifetime. When I finally came out of that slump, I was determined to live my life in anonymity. Getting the headline once again was like getting touched with a hot poker.

Reluctantly, I picked up the paper, left the deli, and went back to my room at the Lazy Isles. Without taking off my jacket, I sat down in the thin plastic chair near the window and stared out at the grimy traffic moving up and down the street. Occasionally, a car would hit the large puddle of wet slush in front of the motel, covering several cars in the parking lot.

I remained there motionless for a few minutes, seemingly stuck to the seat, and then did what I had always done every time this feeling of depression had engulfed me; I reached for the black folder from my duffel and started reading the records of the trial. This time I re-read for the hundredth time the copy of Chip Thornton's operation, even the nurses' notes, trying to find some chink in the legal armor that encased my guilt. Once again I found nothing, so I put the folder back in my bag and returned to my post, watching the traffic. Tears started streaming down my cheeks. Jimmy Scotten was dead.

I'm not sure how long I remained fixed in that position, but aside from watching the afternoon sun set, nothing had changed; the cars were still moving, and the same spray was hitting the parking lot. I stirred for a moment and glanced at my watch, trying to persuade myself that I had things to do. My sadness meant nothing to my debtors. I set the paper aside and looked around for a phone. No telling how long I was going to feel well enough to stay on the job. I called Faye Donaldson's husband and arranged to meet him at his house.

When I was done, I picked up the paper and read the article again. The funeral was scheduled for the day after tomorrow.

CHAPTER 4

I FOLLOWED THE STREAM OF CARS into Clovervale Cemetery. A slow, monotonous drizzle soaked everything with a dreariness only a cemetery could match. Parking at the end of the line of cars, I got out, pulled up the collar of my worn Patagonia jacket, and opened an umbrella from the backseat. Being noticed was not an option I wanted to contemplate.

As I walked slowly behind the line of mourners, a cold mist penetrated the lining of my jacket like sharp icicles. I drifted into the back of a wide semicircle as the clergyman spoke. Droplets of water fell off the twigs of barren trees, thumping out a dull drumroll as if God was marking the time until Jimmy reached his final destination.

"We give our brother, James Scotten, back to the earth, back to God. Perhaps he will now find the peace he never experienced in life."

As he spoke, I looked at the family I had known so well. There was Jimmy's father, Terrence, his face drawn, looking down at the ground. I remembered the last time we had met. It was after the verdict, and I was standing next to my attorney. I turned around and there was Scotten.

"I'll ruin you, you bastard," he hissed, as he stuck his forefinger in my face. "You think the money means anything to me? I want you finished. And I'll do it. By the time I'm through with you, there will be nothing left of you, your practice, or your life."

I actually couldn't blame him. The operation I had performed on his son had ruined the boy's life. If that had been my child, I probably would have felt the same way in his place. Looking back, he had meant what he had said. I was already ruined. Now the death of his son only made it worse.

I listened until the sermon was over and then started walking back to my truck. I was just about to open the door when I felt a tap on my shoulder. I turned around quickly.

"Dailey, right?"

I looked at the man in front of me. He had a microphone and there was a bright light in my face from a TV camera.

I nodded and tried to get inside. By that time the reporter had insinuated himself between me and the door.

"Are you here out of curiosity or guilt?"

I could feel my face redden and my fists tighten. Then I remembered what my old man would say when he got into a tight situation: never let them see you sweat. So I forced myself to stay calm and looked directly into the camera.

"This day is not about me. It is about the tragedy of this young man and his family. For that I am deeply saddened." Without saying anything else, I pushed him aside, got in my car, and drove away.

I maneuvered around the expressways that circled Detroit for what seemed like an eternity. I couldn't seem to focus. Nothing made sense—the wrong diagnosis, the trial, my life. After five years of trying to dig myself out of a tunnel to see the light, it was suddenly dark again.

I stopped at a drug store nearby, bought some aspirin, and popped ten grains in my mouth. It wasn't until then that I remembered I was supposed to check out my boat. Considering the way I felt, I needed a diversion.

I drove through Grosse Pointe and past the huge lakefront houses of the auto barons, the large leafless oaks exposing the otherwise secluded, magnificent homes to scrutiny. The drive gave me time to think. Unfortunately, all I could focus on now was Jimmy Scotten and the cruel fate that had befallen him. I must have been concentrating too much on what happened, because I didn't notice I was nearing the marina until I had almost passed it.

I blinked my eyes back into focus as I saw the flashing lights, storage sheds, and wooden-piered marinas, signifying the edge of the largest inland freshwater yacht basin in the world, the resting place of the only shelter on earth I could honestly call home. The place looked desolate this time of the year; boats in cradles and a few liveaboards like me were scattered among the mostly empty docks.

Driving to the outer harbor, I pulled up to the lonely dock where my boat was moored and got out. Amazingly, they had pumped out the boat and reconnected the shore power. Surveying the worn-out craft for a moment in the fading rays of the late winter afternoon, I realized how beaten up it looked. I got out of the car and walked down the gray, wooden dock that only a few days ago had almost been my last resting place. I climbed up the boarding steps, held onto the stanchion, and carefully made my way into the cockpit of the old Islander 37.

I grabbed onto the wheel pulpit and stepped toward the back railing, where I was greeted by the droning sound of the bubbler, announcing its relentless effort to keep the water around the boat from freezing. The temperature must have dropped into the low twenties.

My body shivered in the damp cold, so I moved forward, slid open the cabin hatch, and climbed down into the cabin, looking for warmth inside. Instead, I shivered again. That's when I saw the layer of frost covering the inside of the porthole.

The place was a soaking mess. The guys from the marina had left a portable heater going, but it wasn't availing much against the cold outside. It was going to be a while before this tub was habitable again.

If only that circuit breaker hadn't popped. That's what they said had caused it. With no heat, ice formed on the thru-hull, causing a crack, and that was that.

I went over to the instrument panel and picked up the small penlight lying on the chart table next to it. Flipping the light on, I held on to the latch on the front cover and jerked it open. In the maze of electronics, I could see that the red circuit breaker for the heater had flipped. Reaching inside, I spread apart the intertwined mass of spaghetti-like wire, groped for the switch, and pushed it over. There was a brief dimming of the lights in the cabin, then a rush of warm air came out of the vent beneath the companionway steps.

I stood in front of the flow, holding my hands in front of me, sucking in the warmth as I tried to clear my head. Just as quickly as it appeared, I heard the click of the breaker again and the hot air disappeared. I surveyed the circuit board and realized I had two choices: play Mr. Fixit and replace the bad breaker or call Easy Ed from the marina to do it. Actually, it wasn't much of a choice. With my bank account running on empty, Mr. Fixit won by a landslide.

CHAPTER 5

MY SLEEP AT THE LAZY ISLES MOTEL was fitful, alternating between shivering and watching the clock next to the bed. I had a fever, and from the way I was sweating, my temperature must have been a hundred and two or three degrees. At about four in the morning it broke, leaving me uncomfortably clammy and exhausted. Yet no matter what I did, I couldn't fall asleep. Letting my mind wander over my meeting with Jordan Dalkind might not have helped my efforts to drop off, but at least it made the night pass with something akin to pleasure.

I was grateful when seven o'clock illuminated the dial, so I could tell myself it was time to get up. Slowly, I pushed the covers aside and shakily sat at the edge of the bed. I tried to muster my strength; it took me a few moments to recognize that the aching in my muscles and the hurt in my throat were better.

There was a coffee pot sitting on an imitation wood coffee table in the corner. Next to it was a paper plate with a couple of packets of instant coffee and a jar of powdered cream. Moving like an automaton, I turned on the pot, then powered up the TV in the corner. It wasn't long before the water came to a boil.

Martha Stewart would have been proud of the way I poured hot water into the casually washed plastic mug, mixed one and a half teaspoonfuls of instant coffee, and added the imitation cream. I took a sip, grimaced at the taste, and downed another pill.

I sat down on the plastic chair next to the table just in time for the news. At first I didn't pay much attention; then my unwanted interview appeared on the screen. I quickly snapped the set off, slumped back in the chair in dismay, and stared through the grimy window at the parking lot. As he had in life, the ghost of Jimmy Scotten seemed destined to haunt me forever.

It wasn't until noon that I was ready to continue my foray into the world of boat repair. Naturally, the Ace Hardware near me didn't have the part. Typical, so I tried the one across town. It took me three hours to get it.

Ace Hardware to me, was like a mysterious castle, full of strange and puzzling reading that I knew I could never decipher in a lifetime of manual reading, full of solutions to a whole world of problems I could never solve. But the man behind the counter did give me one piece of advice in changing a circuit breaker: "Turn off the juice. Ground to black and live to red." I should have written it down, but I didn't have a pen.

I had just enough time to get back to the motel, change, and get something to eat before going to the Pipeline. I could miss a lot of things now that I was no longer practicing, but my weekly piano gig wasn't one of them.

Most people who knew me were usually surprised to find out that I played. That was because they didn't know me when I played in the high school band between halves. They only heard that I was an all-state tight end.

But until recently I hadn't played very often—too much medicine and not enough time. Until my legal troubles. Since then, things had been different. No patient demands, no night calls, and a need to be with people. That's why I sought out Sid Blanton for a job as the intermission guy.

Actually, in an eccentric way, it was comforting to know that no matter what, I had a job if I needed it. It was like a kind of late-night, last resort security blanket. Believe it or not, business stayed good while I played. Tonight, the joint was packed.

The Pipeline was at the end of a small street near the River Place development. Usually after eight o'clock the cars were lined up and down the narrow back street. In the summer, Sid would put out chairs on the sidewalk and the sound of his cool jazz would echo down to the river. But not in the winter. Even the parking attendant was huddled inside the front door.

I parked in the back and entered the smoke-filled bar through the rear door, shaking the cold out of my arms. As I warmed up, I gazed at the packed house and listened to the boys wail out the last few stanzas of Brubeck's "Rotterdam Blues." I must have been intent on the number count, because I didn't see Sid sidling up to me.

"Cold weather, hot jazz. Opposites attract, don't they, Doc?" he said hoarsely. I had saved Sid's life ten years earlier, diagnosing a cancer of his larynx and taking it out before it spread. The gravely voice that remained became his trademark, with a Louis Armstrong meets Joe Williams delivery that kept his bar filled on the weekends.

I turned and looked at him, dressed in a bright fuchsia jacket, black pants and open neck white shirt. "I get it, Sid. In the summer it's hot weather and cool jazz. That's why you wear dark clothes when it's hot, and bright clothes when it's cold, right?"

He laughed. "Got to look good for my crowd, get them in the mood."

I looked down at my own threads—not much of a contest. Sid must have noticed my self-scrutiny, because he grinned. "Don't worry, Doc. It's only me that dresses like this. You're fine, just fine."

"You know how to make a guy feel wanted."

"Needed, Doc, needed. They put wanted guys on posters."

By this time the band had put their instruments down and dispersed to the four corners of the bar. Leaving Sid, I walked behind the counter, dropped my jacket on a chair, and made my way to the empty stage. There was an increasing murmur of voices and a rising sound of clinking glasses as the hundred or so people started their conversational dance, in recognition that the main show was taking a rest.

What did I care? I knew my place: Ben Dailey, the filler man. So I adjusted the seat at the piano to my height, stretched my fingers, and started in on my Duke Ellington medley. By the time I had gotten through "Satin Doll," the clinking had subsided. A "Mood Indigo" and "Caravan" and the murmuring was gone too. There I was, a three-number marvel.

I finished with my own version of "You Can't Always Get What You Want." It was the Stones, but it still made for good jazz, especially with a little improvisation. The whole piece took about five minutes, and earned me a long round of applause from the crowd. I was getting what I needed.

I got up, went over to the bar, and Charlie gave me the Dailey Special, Labatt Blue in a frozen shell. It was crowded around the counter, enough so that my usual political conversation with Charlie would have to wait. I was about to make my way to the back of the place when a hand lightly touched my shoulder. I turned around, and there was Jordan Dalkind.

"Nice playing," she said softly.

I looked at her for a moment. No business armor. Soft, mohair sweater clinging to her full chest, and shiny, auburn hair pulled back in a single, inlaid silvery turquoise clip. Maybe my luck was finally changing.

"Are you a listener or a player?"

"Just a listener. I've never had the patience to practice. It used to drive my mother crazy. Say, do you have a table we could sit down at?"

I didn't get passes made at me too often, so I managed to hustle the boss's table near the bar and get her a chair. Charlie must have seen me with her, because he quickly shifted over to get her order. Charlie was a connoisseur of good-looking women. He asked her what she wanted. She asked for a Stella, no glass.

"Recognize that last piece?" I asked her.

"Sure, originally performed by the only rocker ever to attend the London School of Economics."

"Besides Sid, the boys, and me, you're probably the only person here who knows that little-known fact," I observed, sipping my drink.

"I'm one of those trivia freaks. I was almost on *Jeopardy* once."

"For real?"

"Truth." She wiped the sweat off of the bottle and stared at it for a moment. "If you're going to make it big, you'd have to get some kind of funky name like Lockjaw or Satchmo. A plain Irish name like Dailey doesn't seem to cut it."

"Not Irish. The name is a fake." I was having a hard time not staring at her.

"What do you mean?"

"My family calls it the cottage cheese thing." As I spoke, I set my drink down and angled a little closer to her.

"Cottage cheese?" She didn't seem to mind my getting closer.

"My grandparents came off the boat at Ellis Island in the '30s to escape Hitler. The immigration officer asked my grandfather his name. He didn't understand and simply shook his finger at a billboard to tell him he didn't speak English."

"And the sign read . . ." Jordan had her back to the bar now as she leaned against her chair with her chest sticking out.

"Dailey's Cottage Cheese," I said, trying not to stare at her breasts. It had definitely been too long.

"Therefore, the Dailey family." She laughed. It was a full sound, the kind you hear from people who truly enjoy life.

"That's us, a bunch of hardworking stiffs from the old country." There was a pause in the conversation.

"You were a voice surgeon once, weren't you?" *A used-to-be doctor. Shit, here it comes.* I should have known it wasn't my looks that had dragged her out to the bar in the middle of the week.

"How'd you know?" I was now on the edge of surly.

"I saw your interview on television last night."

"Anything else?"

Her eyes had turned a little harder. Definitely a business look. "I Googled you and found out that at one time you were one of the best voice surgeons in the country."

"You must have been reading about one of my relatives." I was looking around the bar. Maybe Sid would conveniently need me for something. "Look, if you came down to drag up old stories, I'm out of here." I got up to leave, then I felt the warmth of her hand on mine.

"Please, don't leave," she pleaded. I hesitated and sat back down. "I'm not here to annoy you. I read about what happened. Is there any truth to it?"

"Why are you so interested?"

'I want to know."

I stared at her for moment. Something about the way she said it seemed honest, not like idle curiosity. I had never talked to anyone about Jimmy Scotten. Good or bad, it was my life. But somehow this seemed different. They say it is sometimes easier to open up to a stranger than someone you know. I fell for it.

"I operated on the wrong patient. Then he had complications from a sponge left in his neck. The rest of it turned into a lawsuit, a newspaper and television circus, and my expulsion from the hospital staff."

The shocked look on her face made me feel like shit. "How could that happen? I thought they had checks against that." She spoke earnestly, no guile in her voice, only real interest.

I studied her again. Her eyes were focused on me, she seemed to care. It suddenly mattered what someone thought of me. In front of this woman, I didn't want to be that second-rate, would-be professional the papers claimed I was. I didn't want to be the depressed guy who had been ostracized from his life. I decided to tell her the whole story.

I initially gave her the short version. The patient was asleep when I entered the operating room. There was a mix-up in the pre-op holding area. Two of my patients of the same age and same appearance came in on the same day. The charts got presented to the wrong patient. They got banded with the wrong bracelet.

Once I started the surgery I couldn't stop. I explained how I had performed an operation for a paralyzed vocal cord on the wrong patient. It was a delicate operation that can cause airway problems. In this case it did, requiring a tracheotomy. To make matters worse, when they called in Chip Thornton, Chief of Surgery, to do the corrective operation, he found a sponge in the neck. It seemed as if anything that could have gone wrong did, and the rest is history. I waited to see what she would say.

Jordan stared pensively at her drink and then took a long pull. "Isn't that a hospital problem?"

"It is if the hospital doesn't settle out of court. The nurses made the mistakes but, technically, I was the captain of the ship. I was the last one standing—a poster boy for incompetent doctors. It didn't help that the father had connections with every media person in the city and was determined to see justice done."

I could see her wince momentarily as I explained what had happened. That small grimace made it seem that much worse. "Two days ago, the boy was found dead in his room. The word is that it was a suicide."

Her eyes saddened, and she said she was sorry. It didn't take long for the lawyer in her to return. "There has to be some explanation. You don't look like the kind of doctor that would let that happen."

I wanted to tell her that she was right, but the facts were clear. I had done everything I was accused of. How could anyone deny the facts?

Then there was the boy's father. I knew he wanted to get even with me, I just didn't anticipate how far he would carry it. He was relentless, promising to go after my personal assets. He was true to his word. By the time the lawyers were done, I was financially ruined.

"Isn't that unusual?"

"Like I used to tell patients, it might be unusual, but if it happens to you, it's a hundred percent. But that's not the worst of it."

I told her that, as if it wasn't enough, there was a public outcry—or maybe I should call it a mob lynching. First were the series of op-ed articles in the newspaper, intimately describing how I had ruined young Jimmy Scotten's life by carelessly disregarding the trust I had been given. It highlighted poor medical care and neglectful abuses, including the sponge left in the wound. Then there were the stories in the national news almost every day. It even made the *Today Show*.

As far as the hospital was concerned, my years of service meant nothing. They wanted me out, and they weren't going to make any mistakes doing it. There were the meetings of the various committees at the hospital, namely Quality Assurance, Medical Legal, the staff executive committee, and finally the board of trustees. Then they kicked me off of the staff.

It was at that point that my mind shut down. I couldn't talk about that last meeting with the board of trustees and make myself that vulnerable in front of anyone. It was the most humiliating moment of my life, my confrontation with the Chairman of the Board: Charles Thornton.

Now there's a name I would never forget. Haughty, arrogant, and despotic. A fancy guy from the 'burbs with fancy friends, fancy cars, fancy clubs, and more influence than I'd have in a thousand lifetimes.

As Chief of Staff of the hospital, I fought many battles with Thornton and his board trying to raise the quality of care at the hospital. All they could see was the bottom line. And now that he had a chance to get rid of me, he wasn't about to let go of the opportunity.

I could still see Thornton standing at the end of a highly polished oval table. He was perfectly dressed in a blue pinstripe suit with a regimental striped tie, matching red pocket square, and highly polished black cap toes, the epitome of corporate America, haughty and arrogant and imperious to a fault. Next to him was his son, Chip, sun-tanned, fit, the George Hamilton of general surgery, smiling confidently. There were fifteen other board members present. Some of them were my colleagues, men I used to call my friends.

"Dr. Dailey," he said in his deepest stentorian voice, "it is the decision of the board of trustees that your presence on the staff of St. Vincent's is deleterious to the reputation of the hospital. We have decided to terminate your appointment."

I could feel the heat of anger swelling in my head. I wanted to rip Thronton's face off. "Deleterious to the hospital" were the words he used. Fifty scientific publications, a national reputation in the treatment of voice disorders, and a professorship at the medical school, and I was deleterious to St. Vincent's? I felt like jumping across the twenty-foot table and giving him a forearm shiver, just like my college coach had taught me. But I quickly saw that this was not a trial; it was a final judgment passed by the high court. I wasn't going to beg for mercy. I wasn't going to let them see my pain. Instead I swallowed my anger and got up. Without looking back I strode out of the room, slamming the huge oak paneled door loud enough that the sound resonated like a cannon shot down the empty hallway.

I blinked my eyes and stared back at Jordan Dalkind. She was talking. "Are you all right?"

"Yeah, I'm okay," I lied.

She sat quietly for a moment and then said, "But you're still a doctor. You could still practice."

"Listen, whatever you think, that's not the public view. Every place I tried to go some kind of smear campaign suddenly appeared. I didn't have a chance against Terrance Scotten.

"What about the hospital?"

"As far as the hospital was concerned, I was an avaricious, self-centered egotist who cut corners and got himself in trouble."

"I'm not that naive, Ben. I've been around long enough to know that a judgment in a civil case doesn't mean guilt. Especially in malpractice." Her eyes had an intensity I couldn't look away from.

"Tell that to my referral sources and my patients. There was enough press on my case to fill a novel. Once I was suspended, I didn't have a chance. I bet my whole practice on St. Vincent's managed care program. And the boy's father was relentless. He was determined to ruin me."

She stared at me for a moment, but I could tell her mind was elsewhere. "But you could still practice. There are other hospitals, aren't there?"

"Same story. They want to know if you have ever been dismissed from a hospital staff. Try and explain your way out of that one. When St. Vincent's gave me the boot, nobody else would take me, except maybe some small town in Alaska."

"I don't know you very well, but you don't look like someone who would give up that easily. Why didn't you fight back? Restore your life."

It all sounded so simple, didn't it? Like some kind of movie where the good guy resurrects himself. Unfortunately, real life is different.

"Divorce, public disgrace, depression. It'll do that to you," I replied. "By the time it was over, I was finished." It was a peek into my inner self, and I instantly regretted saying it. Why was I telling her this? Admitting my failures to someone I didn't know. I was beginning to feel like a fool. That's when I fell back on my usual defense: It doesn't make any difference and I'm not into hand wringing. I'll deal with what I've got. There it was. I put the wall down again so no one could get in and changed the subject. I should have never opened up to some stranger. "Listen, I'm sick of talking about this. You're too smart to come down here just for a chat about my past. What do you want?"

She seemed taken aback. There was a hint of hurt in her eyes. "You're right, I do need your help," she said, now in a business voice.

"Me? I'm not even practicing."

"I'm not talking about a live patient," she shot back, setting her drink back on the bar.

I told her to quit beating around the bush. She explained that she felt that Faye Donaldson's death was more than just a random murder. Based on its isolated nature, she said this death had the features of a planned execution.

This was great. Every red-blooded man in the bar was figuring I was in some hot conversation with this beautiful chick to get her in the sack. And here we were, talking about murder.

I put my hands on the bar, palms up. "So how could I possibly help you?"

"There was a copy of a newspaper on Faye Donaldson's desk with the article about that Scotten kid. The paper was crumpled but your name was at the top of the page."

I thought about Faye Donaldson. I had never heard of her and wondered what that underline meant. Apparently, the FBI had questioned Faye Donaldson's husband, but he had no information. They thought he knew more. When I asked her why I should interview him, she said as a Federal prosecutor, she had spoken with the agent in charge of the case. It was his thought that her husband might open up to someone besides the police. Then she unsnapped her purse and handed me a slip of paper with his name underlined in the card.

"What do you think I'll find?" I asked, assuming that some idiot at the bar looking at us must be figuring I was scoring her phone number.

"Nobody knows for sure, but it's our only lead."

"Not to be mercenary about this, but what's in it for me?" She probably wanted this as a favor. Flash her smile, stick out her chest, and I was hers. Forget it. Then I had a pang of regret as I realized I had once again fallen for the money.

"Two hundred dollars a day. Standard fare for experts on the Federal tab," she said in a very business-like way.

"Are you serious?" I didn't want to seem too anxious, but in my present state that seemed like a lot of money.

She nodded. "Absolutely serious."

Working for the government—my new career move. The weird thing was that the prospect didn't seem so bad. Especially at two big ones a day, plus something else: a feeling of worth I hadn't known for a while.

"I'll look into it. If there's nothing I can do, I'll tell you." I spoke the words flatly and without emotion. But inside I was troubled. Was this altruism, a need for the money, or strictly my attraction to this gorgeous woman in a bar? One thing was for sure: I'd never been a good judge of women.

"If you decide to do the job, call this guy, Lieutenant George Sennett, Detroit Homicide. He has some information on the case." She wrote the number down on one of her cards. I looked at it for a moment. There was another number below it. It was her cell.

CHAPTER 6

I CALLED GEORGE STANSBURY SENNETT THE NEXT DAY and met him around eleven. His office was at the Detroit Police Headquarters on Beaubien Street, just across from the city courthouse. I made my way to his office through a gaggle of criminals, lawyers, and overweight sergeants drinking coffee and eating doughnuts.

Once I was on the third floor, I found his nondescript office sandwiched between identical rooms, each with a small dirty window overlooking the street below. His aide, Sergeant Knudsen, a brush-cut, freckle faced forty year old, was seated in a small cubicle guarding his lair. I told him who I was, and he ushered me inside the room.

Sitting at his desk reading a newspaper was a burly African American man with huge shoulders, a square jaw, and a smooth dark skin that made him look like a middle linebacker in a dress shirt. He put down the newspaper and looked up at me with steely gray eyes under thick black eyebrows that gave him a warrior's fierce look. A man to be reckoned with. I came to learn that it was his work face only.

I looked at the paper; he was reading the sports section. It was a good start. I introduced myself, and he stuck out his hand. He had a beefy vise-like grip. Considering his occupation, I figured it was like that from either exercise or working the streets.

"You're the doctor that the Federal prosecutor sent over, right?" he asked in a deep baritone. I nodded. "You do this for a living?"

I immediately said no. But I was a little taken back. It was the first time anyone had ever said that. It kind of shook me up. It was that doctor-thing raising its head again.

"Jordan told me you were interested in the Donaldson case." I nodded again. He then proceeded to tell me that they found a few items on Faye Donaldson, none of which made any sense.

"For one thing, on her desk was a newspaper article about a kid named Jimmy Scotten. According to the story, you had some contact with the boy."

"You might say that. I was involved in a malpractice suit, nothing else." I looked around the room as he spoke. Papers strewn on his desk, a pair of hand-cuffs looped over a pen set, and a holstered gun resting on the edge of his desk. It made the homicide department feel very real.

"She had underlined your name in the article. Did you ever meet her, or have you heard of her?" The question startled me. It almost seemed like I was under suspicion.

"I never met her or knew of her until I was sent on the case by the insurance company." I had to explain the situation to him, and it made me feel uncomfortable. I wasn't a detective, I wasn't a doctor, I just worked for an insurance company. After I said it, I quickly changed the subject. "Was there anything else?" I asked.

He went on to describe what was on her computer: There was a bunch of office business and then a few pages that looked like a school writing project, "The Life and Times of Henry David Thoreau," an essay by Mary Lou Donaldson for Mrs. Carmichael, 11th grade, Sterling Heights High School. He said it wasn't uncommon to see schoolwork like that on office computers. Computers were expensive.

"All of the rest of the computer program was devoted to FDA applications, with the exception of a complaint file," he said. "There were twenty or so names. Apparently, these were individuals who were unhappy with some type of action by the FDA."

I studied the list. None of them had any significance to me. "What about her family?" I asked.

Sennett said that she lived in Sterling Heights with her husband. They had two grown children. He said they seemed to have the perfect middle class life, complete with all the toys.

"I know it looks strange in today's economy," Sennett said, "but I see that a lot in guys that work at the plant. Before the downturn in the auto industry, they were making seventy-five to a hundred bucks working overtime. They bought boats, RV's, second homes. Now they're working just to keep themselves alive. With fifteen percent unemployment, they haven't got a choice. Work or starve, and be glad you have a job."

I knew how it felt. Sterling Heights was a hard-working, middle class suburb north of Detroit. These were the swing voters, the Reagan democrats. Now half of them were unemployed and the other half were taking buyouts. They were disposable people, with too high an hourly wage without the skill to earn it. That's why for sale signs littered their front yards.

"From what we can tell she worked for the FDA doing clerical stuff. You know, typing forms, filing papers. She did a lot of work with grants for the National Institute of Health. A pretty benign job. Just another dead-end in what appears to be a random murder. But I'll tell you one thing: I wouldn't want to be the killer and meet up with her husband."

"Why?'

"He told me he hoped we'd 'catch the sonofabitch and fry his balls.' His words."

Looking at Sennett, I figured what Donaldson's husband had said must have been pretty intense to shake him up.

I was about to leave when Sennett looked at his watch. He said he was going to lunch at a Chinese place around the corner, and asked me if I wanted to come along. My stomach agreed. We walked out of the headquarters building and down the street to a little joint called the Jade Glade. The hostess sat us at a corner table. Sennett must have gone there often, because the waitress called him Mr. Lieutenant.

I examined the menu and decided on the cashew chicken; it seemed safe. When I was done ordering, I handed the menu back to the waitress and then looked up at Sennett. "You look like you could have played football."

Sennett laughed. "That was when I was a kid. I wasn't big enough to go any further, but I played some college ball. How about you?"

"I mostly played on the practice squad at Ann Arbor. I got into a couple of games when it didn't mean anything. I made my mind up to go to medical school about halfway through my sophomore year, after I played on the scout team and got hit a few times. Besides, there aren't too many Jewish boys in the hall of fame."

We both had a good laugh.

I liked Sennett. He was plain spoken and friendly. I could tell he was the kind of guy who would always have your back. I decided to ask him why he became a cop. He said there wasn't much future for a slow, five-eleven, two-hundred and ten pound linebacker in the pros, and he had always liked enforcing something. In the department he had found his life's mission.

It wasn't long before the waitress brought over our food. Sennett turned out to be a whiz with chopsticks, handling his moo shu pork like an artist handling a brush. He told me he was an Army brat. Part of his father's tour was in Japan. You either learned to use chopsticks or starved.

I found out a few other things about him. He believed in justice and loved the city of Detroit. The city was a tough place, with gangs, drive-by shootings, and poverty. He said nothing made him feel better than making some small inroad in the pervasive lawlessness of the city.

By the time we finished, I had almost started to begin believing in the law, too. The only trouble was, I had seen it from the other side. For me, justice was a pretty hollow word.

Our conversation was interrupted as the waitress brought us a couple of fortune cookies. I'm not superstitious, but I like reading the little pieces of paper inside. I opened it and, to my dismay, pulled out a blank sheet.

What the hell? I signaled the waitress as we paid the bill. She was just about to leave with the money when I stopped her. "Say, what does it mean when you get a blank piece of paper in a fortune cookie?"

She stared at me with a look of consternation. "Do you really want to know?"

I nodded. "Sure."

"Well, one of the girls that worked here told me it's very bad luck. She said she got one and going home she had an auto accident and wrecked her car."

CHAPTER 7

AFTER SENNETT LEFT, I SAT IN THE BOOTH for moment, trying to delay venturing out into the cold Detroit winter. I saw a used copy of the morning edition of the paper lying on the table next to me. I thought about my last experience of picking up someone else's paper and figured nothing could be worse than that, so I began to read. The lead story was about the shooting of Faye Donaldson: "Hospital killer remains a mystery," it read. The rest of the article was a statement about random violence and a proclamation by the police department that they were working hard to solve the case. I reminded myself again that I had to quit reading newspapers. It was enough to take your appetite away.

Setting the paper aside, I pulled out my cell phone. Thankfully, it didn't take me long to get Faye Donaldson's husband on the line and tell him that I was on my way over. As I hung up, I reflected on the possibility that Bruce's dough might not be sufficient to numb me to what I was about to do.

I drove for about twenty minutes until I reached Willard Donaldson's house. He lived in a farm colonial in a quiet neighborhood of identical homes, one of those thirty-year-old subdivisions that had suddenly sprung up in the suburbs when cross-district bussing and riots erupted in the sixties. I saw an eighteen-foot Bayliner in the driveway. Next to it was a shiny new Airstream. I pulled up in front of his house, got out of the car slowly, and walked to the front door.

Donaldson was waiting for me as I walked up. A huge man, the kind you'd see in the auto plants around Detroit; he was around fifty-five, with an open collar, plain wool shirt, gray work pants, and a worn black cap with a Caterpillar emblem. A no-nonsense, stand-up kind of guy. I wasn't sure what this interview was going to entail, but from the guarded look emanating from beneath his bushy eyebrows, it was going to be all business.

I took my boots off, left them in the small foyer, and followed him into an immaculate living room. He motioned me to sit down in the flowery, upholstered easy chair next to him. As I did, I looked at a photograph above the sofa; it showed a trim, neatly dressed woman and two kids.

"That's my wife in the center and those are my two children around her," he said gruffly. "She did everything for those kids. She always said education was the key to success. That's why she worked for the government, to pay for their schooling. Parochial school, college, and then she started on the grandkids."

"It's a shame what happened, Mr. Donaldson. I'm sure this isn't easy, having me come into the house like this. But the insurance company needs the medical information before you can getting the insurance money." I felt like an undertaker, taking money from the dead.

"Guess it's gotta be done. What is it you need to know?" he asked humbly.

"Her insurance company, Coastal Life, sent me here to ask you about her medical history. As I understand it, it's purely a formality." I pulled the questionnaire out of my jacket and started reading from it. Thirty-odd standard questions, blood pressure problems, heart disease, et cetera. Near the end there were some particulars about the killing. I had a feeling this wasn't going to be easy.

"Any relationship that you know of to the killer?" I asked.

"What do you mean?"

"Do you think she knew him?"

"I doubt it. She never mentioned any problems."

"How about you? Were there any family problems that might have triggered something?"

"What the hell do you mean by that? That's a helluva thing to ask someone who just lost his wife," he challenged. A malignant look soured his face, changing him from the upset victim's husband to a downright scary, vengeance-seeking thug.

"I'm sorry. I don't mean anything by it. This is a standard form that the company sends out." I hated playing bureaucrat, but I could see how it walled your brain off from having to deal with emotion.

Donaldson looked down at the carpeting for a moment and seemed to recant his anger. "Yeah, I know you're only doing a job. No, other than the usual things married people go through, we were happily married for thirty years. But I've already said that to the police."

"Any conflicts with the people at work?" The question wasn't on the list, but I was curious just the same.

He explained that the police had gone through everything in her desk at work and here at home. There didn't appear to be a connection to any kind of trouble with her job. As far as he knew, his wife did clerical work for the FDA. When I asked him the nature of her employment, he quickly brushed it off, saying she was just a secretary.

"Do the police have any leads?" I asked.

"They said they're working on it," he replied, seeming to get agitated again the more I questioned him. I could see his enormous hands clench and unclench in front of me. I quickly thought of Sennett and what he said about Joey and the boys being crushed by Donaldson's hands. It gave me the shivers.

"It's been tough," he continued. "I was laid off for a while from the Rouge Plant last year. I worked in the construction division. With the downturn in the economy we started demolition projects. Pretty soon I worked myself out of a job. Thank God we had Faye's income. She handled all the bills."

I thought about the Bayliner and the Airstream in the driveway. Too much debt and not enough income. Detroit on a dollar a day. It was once the birthplace of the middle class, but now it was the new America. I looked down at the questionnaire. There was nothing more to ask and nothing else to know. As far as I could see, Coastal was off the hook and that was that.

"I guess we're finished," I declared. "I wish there was something else I could do," I added dejectedly.

As I spoke, I glanced at a photo on the side table of the sofa. It was a picture of a good-looking blond with big hair and a leather vest with lots of cleavage standing next to a Harley. Donaldson must have seen me staring at the photo.

"That's my daughter, Jill," he said, his face reddening slightly.

"Nice bike," I said. There was an awkward pause. I decided the least I could do for him was make the insurance part of it go away. "Don't worry about this paperwork. I'll send it to headquarters. If you think of anything further, give me a call." I handed him the Coastal Life card that I carried around, and he looked at it for a moment, as if deciding on something.

Donaldson followed me to the front door as I put on my boots.

"Listen, I know this sounds stupid, but I'd give my wife's life insurance as a reward if they could find this guy." Tears misted his eyes as he spoke.

I got up to leave and stopped. I don't know why I opened my big mouth, but the doctor in me wanted to say something to comfort him. "Trust me, I'm going to make some more calls for the insurance company, maybe I can find out something. I know the police officer on the case. I'll try and follow up." The blank stare that he returned told me he had heard this advice before.

Even I had to admit it sounded pretty thin. But my ego must have gotten the best of me, because I told him what I told all my patients: I try not to quit until I find an answer. He looked at me a little strangely, as if he really believed me now. It made me regret what I had just said. In a way I felt committed.

I walked out of the house. Talk about being in the wrong job and feeling useless. The next time Sanderson handed me an investigation, I'd pass. Especially a murder. The money really wasn't worth it.

By the time I had made that decision I was already behind the wheel. That's when I remembered about the attorney and his physical. I was feeling lousy and not in the mood to see another lawyer. *Screw it, I'll do it tomorrow. No loss except to him. It'll only be one day less he'll be able to avoid paying taxes.*

I stopped at a drug store nearby, bought some decongestants, and found a pay phone. After popping a pill, I called the lawyer's secretary, told her I was tied up at the hospital in surgery, and mentioned something about seeing him tomorrow. One advantage to being a doctor is that there are always a million excuses for not being somewhere.

CHAPTER 8

I T WASN'T UNTIL LATE FRIDAY AFTERNOON that I was able to get back to my boat. I had it all planned out. Install the circuit breaker on the seat next to me, take my time with the panel, and I was back in business. I felt confident as I walked back to the boat. As I got to the dock, I saw a beat-up red F-150 pull up. It was Easy Ed Flannagan, head man at the Shore Garden Marina. Somebody once told me he got his name because of the way he separated his customers from their money.

When he got close enough, he yelled, "What you up to, Doc? You gonna fix that heater?" I knew what he was thinking: I was cheating him out of a job.

"I think it's pretty simple, Easy, just change a couple of wires, and I'm back in business." I held up my circuit tester and breaker to show him I was no amateur.

"Sure you don't want us to fix it?" The bored tone of his voice told me he had seen this play before.

I could see the dollar signs lighting up his face, so I simply shook my head in defiance. I continued down to the dock until I reached the boat. Once inside, I was careful to shut off the AC service. There was enough light coming in from outside so that, along with my flashlight, I could see the breaker clearly. All I had to remember were the electronic guru's words: red in ground and black in live and turn off the juice.

It worked like a charm. Small screwdriver, perfect fit, and the wires changed in less than ten minutes. Looking at the finished product, I had a great sense of pride at my workmanship. I had shown Easy and all those other mercenary river rats that I could do it. I knew he was smirking somewhere on shore, waiting for me to fuck up.

Triumphantly, I switched the AC back on and flipped the circuit breaker for the heater, waiting for the warm air of the heater to plume through the boat. Instead there was a dimming of the lights overhead and a crackling sound. Before I could reach in to shut the breaker off, all the power went out. I pulled the panel back. Smoke was coming out of the board. Shit, what the hell had gone wrong? *Wait until I get my hands on the Ace Hardware guru. I'm going to ream him a new asshole.*

I stumbled out of the boat, humiliated, pissed, and facing another two-hundred-dollar problem from not installing a dollar-fifty part correctly. Easy was standing by the banged-up door of his truck. I think he could tell by the look on my face that everything wasn't great.

"Fix'er up, Doc?" he asked insolently.

"Forget the small talk, Easy. Just do the job and add it to my tab," I said morosely.

He looked at me and snapped his fingers. "I almost forgot. A guy stopped by and left this message for you."

He handed me the folded note. I read it slowly. *Meet me at the Plain View tonight. 8 PM. Frank Scotten.* After all that had gone on, I was shocked. What the hell was this all about?

I hung around a while watching Easy's engineering dilettantes minister to my boat. It was around seven o'clock when I finally left and made my way down I-94 toward the airport to visit the Plain View Lounge. By that time, it had started snowing again. They say if you don't like the weather in Detroit, just wait a few minutes.

IT TOOK ME HALF AN HOUR TO GET THERE, which was surprising in view of the snow. The salt trucks were having trouble keeping up with the weather, but the traffic was light. Besides, I had a four by four. It felt good pushing the snow aside in high range until I hit a patch of ice. Nothing works on ice except cautious driving. I righted the wheels and backed off the accelerator.

I found the Plain View about a mile south of the airport. It had a large flashing sign of a naked woman emblazoned in red and straddling a 747. A strip bar. Just what I needed on a cold night in Detroit. I parked in the nearly filled lot and made it past the bouncer at the front door. It was a nice homey place, they were even playing Christmas music through the outside speakers.

The bar was pretty much the way I had seen them in the movies. There were two large brass poles at either end of a large rectangular room on elevated stages. Slithering around the poles, as if they were some type of giant phalluses, were two bare-chested women in what could be loosely called a thong. Their faces appeared to be in various stages of ecstasy. I was having a hard time understanding how a brass pole could be that exciting.

At the base of the stage were a dozen men with drinks, a mélange of gel crusted hair, leather jackets, and boastful laughing. They all had a common goal—trying see the promised land as the girls spread their legs. The dancers, for their part, didn't try to hide anything, coming close to the edge to receive the dollars bills the men shoved inside their strings.

Strange place to meet Frank Scotten, I thought, but I supposed everyone is entitled to their entertainment. I shouldered my way through a throng of men, toward the long bar at the end of the room. I was almost at the counter when a woman with bright red hair in tight ringlets approached me. She was about five-ten, long-legged and topless, with incredibly large breasts and mahogany nipples that seemed to point to the moon. She seemed just old enough to have a driver's license.

"My name is Irina. Are you interested in a dance?" she asked in a thick accent that was foreign, probably Eastern European.

I looked around for a dance floor, but didn't see any.

"Where do you dance?"

She pointed to any empty chair near the stage.

"I dance for you." As she stood in front of me, she gyrated her hips a few times.

I might be old and slow, but I got the idea. "Not right now, thank you."

She didn't seem too disappointed. Business is business. "Maybe you want something else? I can rent you space in my cock garage."

After surveying her voluptuous body, I decided I wasn't against the something else. The only problem was that it violated Dailey's first law of social integration: I never paid for sex. So I just shook my head, made my way to the end of the bar, and ordered a Labatt. I looked over the entire scene in front of me. It was like some kind of live, soft-porn stage show.

I couldn't imagine getting excited in a public place like this, but most of the men I saw had smiles on their faces. Who was I to be judgmental? Las Vegas was built on the concept. I looked around again to see if there was anyone coming toward me. That's when I felt a tap on my shoulder. I turned to see a medium-built man in his mid-twenties with an angular face, high cheek bones, and the sallow complexion of someone who had spent too much time indoors. The family resemblance was hard to miss. Frank Scotten had his brother's cleft chin, upturned nose, and broad forehead. There was also the same quizzical look, as if he had just awoken from a deep sleep.

"Frank Scotten," the voice stated firmly. His hand was extended from his leather jacket.

I shook his hand cautiously. It was the soft and clammy handshake of someone who was nervous. "I would like to say I'm pleased to see you, but after all that's happened, I'm not sure that's possible."

Scotten nodded as if he understood. "I saw you on television after my brother's funeral."

I thought to myself that everyone in the city must have seen my appearance. I glanced around the room. To say this was a weird place to have this kind of discussion was an understatement.

Scotten must have noticed. "Sorry. It's my family's business. My father owns three of these places. I rarely come here, so I thought we could meet here and not be recognized."

I nodded indifferently. "Different strokes."

When I told him business must be good, he shrugged his shoulders, as if he didn't care.

"My father started out in the car repair business. Somewhere along the way he got into these strip clubs from some customer of his. It's not for me. I'm working on my PhD in acoustical engineering at Ann Arbor. He wished I was more into it. It's the macho in him, if you know what I mean."

He went on to explain that his father loved cars and that's how he got started. I could understand that. Detroiters have a love affair with the internal combustion engine that's almost cultural.

"How about your brother? Did he love cars too?"

"No, he was into electronics and music." He hesitated a moment, staring off vacantly at the two naked women thrusting their pelvises at the eager men below them. "After he got sick he spent a lot of time listening to music. He loved stereo equipment, turntables, all kinds of gadgets."

Well, at least I had some things in common with Frank Scotten: we were both scorned by his father, and we both went to the same schools. But that didn't explain why he had asked me to meet him.

"Jimmy and I were very close." He hesitated for a moment, as if thinking about what he was going to say. "I want you to know that Jimmy liked you even though he thought you might have made a mistake," Frank blurted out.

I lifted my eyebrows and stared at him. "Well, he must not have listened to the evidence. Even I thought I was guilty."

"I'm not talking about guilt, I'm talking about you. He liked you. He even told my father that. The mere thought that Jimmy didn't hate you made the old man crazy."

"I knew how your dad hated me. Just looking into his eyes you could tell. He would have killed me if he had the chance."

Scotten sipped at his Diet Coke slowly. Two new girls had climbed onto the stage. They were both lying on their backs with their hands on the pole and their legs lifted and spread apart. In a weird way it reminded me of a gynecologic exam being performed to music. I glanced at Scotten for a moment. It was curious to see how disinterested he was in his surroundings. For a twenty-year-old kid, I would have thought the ladies would be irresistible.

He must have realized I was looking. "It could be mesmerizing," he said.

"What?"

"These girls. Breasts hanging out, legs spread apart, something you read about on porn sites. It's hard not to believe it's real."

"Is it?"

"Not really. These girls are well-trained mercenaries. They follow the money and couldn't care less if it's your dick or someone else's, as long as they get paid. That's the joke. All these guys think they're for real, that they're studs and these girls want them."

"You didn't ask me here to discuss the psychological mindset of your family's business, did you?" I asked.

He shook his head. "I wanted to show you this," he said, pulling a piece of paper from his pocket and setting it on the bar in front of me. I picked it up and looked at it, reading it carefully: *New York Times, 1/15/95, implants, and Dr. Dailey.*

"What's this mean?"

"I'm not sure. I found the note while I was rummaging through some papers on his desk. Jimmy was onto something. He was obsessed about what had happened to him. He read everything in the hospital chart, everything in the depositions, and all the trial transcripts. It never left his mind." I thought about the black folder in my duffel. Two people with the same purpose coming from different directions.

"Okay, but why are you giving this to me now, after all this time?"

"Like I said, Jimmy always liked you. It was my dad who could never let it go. Ever since the trial was over, it bothered me. I felt guilty. If Jimmy had some information, I thought he would want you to have it."

I took the paper and slid it into my jacket pocket. As I did, I looked around for a moment, thinking about the incongruity of watching naked girls humping a brass pole while listening to Frank Scotten's outpouring of goodwill.

"I like to think that I'm not a cynic, Frank, but after everything that happened to me, I don't take rides on the bullshit train anymore."

Frank didn't look surprised. "Jimmy knew something. He told my dad it wasn't your fault."

"What did your father say?"

"'You're not old enough to understand,'" he said, sadly defiant.

"Did your brother ever mention a woman named Faye Donaldson to you?"

"Never heard of her," he said, shaking his head. "Why?"

"Just a name that someone gave me." I looked around at the scene in front of me. I'd had enough. "Listen, I appreciate the information. I haven't a clue what it means. I'll check it out and call you if I find out anything."

He asked me where he could get hold of me, so I wrote down the number of the Lazy Isles and handed it to him. I was suspicious enough not to give him my cell phone number. As he stuffed it in his pocket, I got up from the barstool and quietly turned around. I didn't trust him or anyone else in his family. I'd look at Jimmy Scotten's note in my own time and in my own way.

By this time the gaggle of men around the stage were yelling obscenities at the two naked ladies on the pole. I saw the vacant look in their eyes. They didn't understand either.

I was just about to exit the joint, wondering what the hell this was all about, when a large man in a Hawaiian shirt brushed against me. He stared at me in a moment of recognition.

"What the fuck do you think you're doing here?" a growling voice grated at me.

I gazed into the face of James Terrance "Terry" Scotten Sr. So much for the safest place Frank Scotten could think of. The word "set-up" crossed my mind, but I didn't have time to ponder it. Scotten's eyes were lit with a coal fire of hate burning at me. He was a large man, six-one, maybe two hundred and forty pounds, with an Irish temper. I thought about his son, Frank. Then I knew I'd been set up.

"Just passing through. I thought I might express my condolences on your son's death."

Being kind was apparently not going to work, because he grabbed me by my jacket and threw me against the wall.

"You fucking cocksucker," he hissed, breathing Jim Beam in my face. "You killed my son. I'll never forget that. You'll get yours someday. Trust me, you'll get yours. Now get the fuck out of here."

I was going to say something about how I may already have, but at that moment the two bouncers at the door came at me. This didn't look like a pat-me-on-the-back kind of exit.

The smaller of the two men was short and burly with a shaved head and a bristling soul patch beneath his lip. He had a thick ridge of bone above his dull wide set eyes that gave him a Neanderthal appearance.

"Take him, Jake," the bigger man said.

He came at me slowly, rocking his weightlifter's shoulders from side to side in anticipation of kicking my butt.

I'm not a small man, and when I played tight end at Michigan, a few of the guys even said I was tough. I'm also not stupid. This guy was probably training for one of those mixed martial arts fights on TV. I looked for a place to escape, but with Scotten behind me there was no where to go. I had no choice now.

My look must have given Mr. Short an extra load of confidence, because he dropped his hands and started sauntering toward me. My position coach always told me that's when a guy is most vulnerable. He was about two feet from me when I suddenly fell to my knees and then lunged forward in the same way I would take on a middle linebacker.

The move caught him by surprise. He stood upright, another bad mistake on the offensive line. I leveraged my body and hurtled at him, lowering my shoulder into his midsection. I heard a grunt as I knocked the wind out of him. I had him now. With my shoulder in his belly, I lifted him upright and threw him over the bar and into a row of partially opened bottles. There was a scream as he crashed to the floor. Blood started trickling down his face.

I looked behind me. His taller buddy was rushing toward me. He grabbed me by the arm and lifted me up. Looking at his raised fist I didn't think I was going to be as lucky with this guy. He was about to decapitate me when Frank Scotten stepped between us.

"Stop, now!" Frank commanded. Mr. Tall let me down and watched as Terry Scotten moved toward his son.

"This is the guy that killed your brother," Scotten growled, his face turning a bluish red as he spoke.

"It won't bring Jimmy back," Frank retorted. "Now let him go!"

There was a moment when it could have gone either way. Then Terry Scotten raised his hands in the air in a what-can-I-do type of gesture and walked away.

I took it as my cue and stepped past Mr. Tall, just close enough to land hard on his foot and then dig my elbow into his ribs. I heard him wheeze with pain, but didn't stay around to make a clinical diagnosis. As I walked out, I heard *Deck the Halls* coming through the outside speaker. It was the holiday season all right, and I just got my lump of coal.

CHAPTER 9

I DIDN'T SLEEP WELL THAT NIGHT. A doctor involved in a bar fight. How low had I fallen? Still, when I woke up the next morning, two things occurred to me. First, in spite of everything that had happened to me, I wasn't dead yet, and, even more importantly, I could still take care of myself. I had to admit it was a good feeling. Second, there was a gnawing curiosity that lingered in my head about what Frank Scotten had told me. Add to this my newfound debt and I was doubly motivated. That was why I was in my car at 7:30 in the morning. Nothing like spending the day working on this case and realizing everything I earned was going to Easy Ed Flanagan and his marina.

From the Lazy Isles it was a fifteen minute drive to the Detroit Public Library in what is known as the cultural center of Detroit, across from the Detroit Art Institute and next to the Detroit Historical Museum. Considering the problems the city had incurred over the past forty years, a cultural center in Detroit seemed like an oxymoron. Fortunately, it was true—they were the crown jewels of a bankrupt city. Entering the brick and stone portal, I set my jacket down at a bare wooden table and went to find the librarian. Immediately upon reaching the desk, my eyes caught the keyboard data information sign. I was about to ask someone what that meant when I realized the whole place was computerized now. Light years from my time in medical school.

I put my request slip on the desk and waited. Soon a studious-looking, middle-aged lady from behind a computer picked it up. It took a moment before she looked up at me. That's all the time she needed to figure it was easier to print up the article list than try to explain the program to a computer ignoramus like me. They must be able to spot my type from a mile away.

She punched in a few lines and pretty soon a short list of references came up. I scanned the books until I found the one I wanted. The librarian pointed me in the right direction while giving me the distinct feeling she was glad to get me out of her hair.

I started thumbing through the paper. The *New York Times* on January 15, 1995 had approximately 300 different articles ranging from the NHL contract dispute to banning the "fresh" label on poultry. On page A13, in the middle of the page, was an article by William K. Stevens, "New Study of Electromagnetism Clouds Hunt for Cancer Link."

"In a study that further muddles the issue of whether electrical transmission lines affect human health, researchers have found that electric utility workers exposed to high levels of magnetic radiation face a greater risk of dying from brain cancer than workers exposed to lower levels.

The study to be published in the American Journal of Epidemiology *further goes on to say that "Low frequency electric and magnetic radiation is emitted by all kinds of everyday electrical conductors, from appliances and household wiring to high energy transmission lines . . . the findings strengthen the idea that electromagnetic fields produce some risk of cancer."*

I read it again and wondered what the hell it meant. On the way out I felt I should to call my employer. When I told him what I had found, Sanderson seemed non-plussed. I could almost hear the cash register ringing up as he listened to my explanation. As long as Coastal wasn't involved, he didn't care.

"What do I do, Bruce?" I asked. "Fold up or finish this out?"

"It would be nice to find out for sure the identity of Frances Donaldson's killer. But that's not our job. As long as it remains a governmental responsibility, I don't know what to make of this article. And you know, if I keep paying for your investigation without a good reason, my ass is grass. This company audits everything. I'm going to give you another two days. That's all I'm authorizing. After that, we've done our due diligence."

"I'm impressed by your ecumenical attitude." I didn't want to sound like a sycophant, but I was grateful that I was still on the dole.

"My what?" Bruce asked.

"Nothing, it's just a saying," I replied.

"All I've got to do is produce enough to exonerate my policyholder and keep the company fiscally responsible," he said.

"Are you reading from a manual, Bruce?" To be honest, even though they were paying my bill, Coastal Life's well-being wasn't high on my list of concerns.

"No, but remember this, Ben, after a certain point I don't need you to play detective on the company's time."

I had a momentary pang of conscience. Should I tell him about my meeting with Jordan Dalkind? No. He was the one who wanted me to call her.

"I'll try not to let you down, Bruce."

The phone didn't have a chance to cool down before I dialed Jordan Dalkind at her office.

It took a moment of fighting the bureaucracy, but I finally I got through to her. "It's probably harder to get to you than it is to reach the President," I said.

"The Federal system was designed that way, so that the caller feels like they're getting their money's worth for all their tax dollars," she replied.

We both laughed for a moment and then I told her about my meeting with Frank Scotten.

"Scotten? Is that the same family as the dead boy I read about in the paper?" she asked.

I told her it was and that we met at their family business. I left out the part about the strip club and my run-in with Scotten's heavies. When I finished my description of the meeting, she said it was interesting but beyond that she didn't seem to have any insight as to what it meant.

She told me she had to run and then gave me her private line so I wouldn't have to wait the next time. As I reached into my pocket for a pen, I felt the tickets that Bruce had given me. That's when I asked her to the Piston's game.

Oddly enough, she accepted.

CHAPTER 10

WHEN I RETURNED TO THE LAZY ISLES that night, a message was waiting for me from Frank Scotten. Despite my confrontation with his father, I was curious enough about the information he had given me to call him back. He apologized for what had happened at the Plain View, saying that his father wasn't supposed to be there. Besides, he never guessed his father would resort to violence. He seemed sincere enough, but when it came to the Scotten family, trust was a hard word to define. I told him I would get back to him if I found out anything. He gave me his phone number.

When I hung up, I stood there for a moment, thinking about our meeting. I pulled out his note again and focused on the word *implant*. I wondered what it meant. My name was next to it, but the only implants I had ever performed were in the voice box and had nothing to do with Jimmy Scotten.

I shrugged my shoulders and put the note back in my pocket, along with Frank Scotten's phone number. My meeting with Sennett and now with Scotten had somehow depressed me. It took a while for me to realize why. It was the smoldering idea that I was no longer considered to be a physician; an insurance rep or investigator maybe, but not a doctor. It bothered me enough that I began to think about going back into the medical business.

For me the mere thought was a big change. I had long ago forgotten about practicing medicine. Anger and depression will do that. But my loss of self-respect was beginning to bother me. Another thought crossed my mind. I wondered whether meeting Jordan Dalkind and wanting her approval had something to do with that. The real question was whether my past history would block my return to the medical community.

The next morning I went to the medical library and pulled out some specialty journals. There were usually advertisements for available jobs. I thumbed through the notices. Oddly enough, there was a job opening at Great Lakes Medical Center in Detroit. It said, "Contact Phillip Pennington."

I had heard of Pennington. He was the chief of the department at the medical school and had taken over a few years ago after the retirement of an old friend of mine, Walter Synkowski. That was shortly after my dismissal from St. Vincent's. Walt was a good man and a fine teacher.

I decided to call him at his home in Florida just to find out what Pennington was like. I knew Walt was a little embarrassed for me, because of my lawsuit and what had happened to my career. When he answered, the hesitancy in his voice made me wonder if I had made a mistake calling him, but after a few moments of conversation it became cordial. In fact, when he heard I was thinking about going back into practice, his voice became more animated. He thought the University would be a good fit for me. As far as Pennington was concerned, he said he didn't have much contact with him. He explained that he wasn't involved in the search committee when Pennington came in, but he had a few meetings with him during the transition. He knew Pennington had a big reputation as an ear surgeon and was an expert in cochlear implants. Walt was too smart to speak ill of anyone, but I had the distinct feeling from the way he spoke that he was damning Pennington with faint praise. We spoke for quite a while, and then I heard his wife in the background. He grumbled something about retirement and having to do chores around the house. I told him I would keep in touch.

I set the phone back on the hook and waited for a moment. Something about what he had said bothered me. It took me a couple of minutes, but I realized it was on Jimmy Scotten's note that his brother had given me. I pulled it out again and stared at the word "implants." I wondered if there was a connection. It was a long shot, but it was all I had to go on.

It seemed that I was destined to learn more about Phillip Pennington. In spite of the fact that we practiced in the same city while I was in practice, I had rarely been at the Great Lakes Medical Center. I think it wasn't just geography. I knew I shouldn't be making generalizations, because I trained in an academic institution and had many good friends who still taught and worked at universities, but for me it was a square peg in a round hole. I had been widely published, but only because I wanted to be. In academic medicine there exists a publish-or-perish ethic destined to help facilitate a doctor's path to a tenured position. Along with endless committees, a stagnant bureaucracy, and the omnipresent realization of being somebody else's boy, I had become soured on academics early in my career. Now I was knocking on their door. It was strange.

I went to the stacks and found some articles that Phillip Pennington had published. According to the literature I reviewed, he ran the largest cochlear implant program in the country. Then I looked at his research. Most of it was unintelligible articles filled with the three-line formulas that only a physicist would understand.

I was curious, both because it might have to do with the note that Frank Scotten had given me and the fact that I might be interviewing for a job. I suddenly began to doubt myself again. How could I compete with people who actually understood this stuff?

But I was trying to be realistic. I was a clinician, not a PhD. I wanted back in, and maybe my skills as a doctor would open the door. So I swallowed my fear, called Pennington's secretary for an interview, and made an appointment for the following afternoon. To paraphrase the old line, necessity makes strange bedfellows.

The whole idea seemed odd. Government and hospitals were the most oppressive bureaucracies in the world. Now I was working for one and trying to get a job with the other.

I needed to look presentable, so I stopped at a discount clothing store and bought a corduroy jacket, a tie, and a dress shirt for under a hundred bucks. When I got dressed, I looked at myself in the mirror. There was a brief moment when I actually thought I saw Ben Dailey, M.D.

THE FOLLOWING AFTERNOON TURNED BRIGHT AND SUNNY, with a slight wisp of a wind coming from the northeast. That usually meant something was brewing. But considering the lousy weather we had been having, I'd take the sun any day.

It only took me a few minutes to find a parking space in front of the medical center, which surprised me. I didn't know if it was the recession or just a lack of people in the city. I walked from my car, stopped at the front entrance to the Great Lakes Medical Center, and looked around at the medical school.

It had a hodgepodge appearance with its random disorganization of buildings, both old and new, surrounding the main 1000-bed hospital. The visual effect was a subliminal undercurrent of disquiet. Around the medical campus were neighborhoods of dilapidated stores, low cost apartment housing, and empty fields where homes had once stood. If I were a patient, I certainly would have questioned my safety. But regardless of its appearance, it wasn't going anywhere. Great Lakes Medical Center was the largest single employer in the city.

Twenty minutes later I was reading magazines in Phillip Pennington's outer waiting room for the department offices. After an hour, I politely asked the secretary again when I could see Dr. Pennington. She told me that Dr. Pennington was tied up with an emergency, but would be down shortly.

That "shortly" turned into another hour. At about four o'clock the secretary called me into his office. Phillip Pennington was sitting behind a modern desk in the corner of a large room with corner windows. One might have described it as a power office, but I wasn't trying to prejudice my opinion. Striding across the thick wool carpeting seemed somewhat intimidating until I realized that was his goal.

Pennington was seated at his desk, reading what appeared to be a medical record. His coat was off, and his black braces stood out sharply against his starched white shirt and red and black paisley tie. He had straight, combed-back, black hair and a pencil thin mustache. He didn't look up.

I studied his desk. Other than a pen set and a stainless steel model of the inner ear, it was devoid of any clutter, including photographs. After a few moments of standing there, I began to feel stupid, so I cleared my throat. He must have heard me, because he put the paper down.

"I was just reading about your past, Dr. Dailey. Quite unusual." There was no introduction, no hello, no "thank you for coming." His voice was crisp and impersonal. I was an expert on voices, and I read his loud and clear: academic arrogance.

"Well, I've been around for a while."

"And now you are looking for a job."

I told him that I felt I was ready to make a return. I missed the practice of medicine.

He seemed unfazed. "Why did you pick the medical center?"

"I had heard that you were looking for a laryngologist. I've also read about your work with cochlear implants."

At the mention of cochlear implants, his eyebrows raised, not much, but enough for me to see that he had registered something. He asked me why. I had gone over Pennington's CV before I came for the interview, so I told him I was interested in studying the effect of profound hearing loss on the development of speech. It was a total lie, but it sounded good. Good enough to get a response from him.

"Maybe you would like to see our research area?"

I had touched the right button. Who was I to say no? He put on his two-button jacket, arranged his pocket square, and escorted me through the outer office. He didn't say much as we wandered through the clinic, looking at rooms and checking out equipment. When we got to the private examining area, he pointed out mechanized chairs, a videostroboscopy unit, and gleaming cabinets filled with every instrument a laryngologist could dream of. The latest and greatest. Whatever was happening with the economics of medicine, it hadn't affected Phillip Pennington's service.

We made it through the tour in short order: clinic, administrative offices, and then the research lab. When we got there, he seemed to change. His eyes widened, and he actually seemed excited. Frankly, I was surprised at the size of the space, which occupied a whole floor of the research building.

Looking at the people in white coats scurrying around and the maze of electronic equipment, it was hard to believe there was any shortage of research money at the University Medical Center. We stopped in one room. Inside were two technicians and a couple of live chipmunk-like animals with electrodes on their skulls.

"This is our chinchilla lab," he said, pausing to look at the furry animals in small wire cages. "Their inner ears are the closest thing in a research animal to the human ear. Right now, we're testing the effect of certain antibiotic medications on the hair cells of the inner ear."

He was obviously proud, because he suddenly took on the mantle of higher authority. As he began to lecture me about his research, I could see his chest puff out and his jaw jut forward. This man was a supreme egotist, and it showed.

Finally, after listening to him talk for about ten minutes, I looked at the animals breathing regularly under the anesthetic that had been administered. They had wires poking out of their skulls. "What happens when you've finished with them? Fur coats?"

His face turned black. It was obvious he didn't enjoy my joke. "Not hardly, doctor. We're not a haberdashery. These are pioneering experiments. Those electrodes are inserted into the animal's auditory center of the brain. We're measuring their response to inner ear stimulation. This lab is big on veterinary experiments," he said paternally.

The phrase struck me as odd the way he said it. When we were residents, some of the guys would joke around when we were performing a new procedure on someone and called it a "veterinary experiment." It was gallows humor, not meant for publication. But the way he said it, I got the feeling it was meant for more than just operating on chinchillas.

He seemed unfazed by his comment. "We run the largest cochlear implant program in the country. Our success rate is higher than any other implant clinic. I have personally done over a thousand of these procedures, many of them right here at Great Lakes Medical Center." He was blowing so hard I thought he was going to lift himself off the ground.

I listened to him pontificate for a few more minutes as we walked through several more labs and computer rooms. Finally, we made our way back to the department offices.

We stopped just outside the entrance. He paused for a moment and looked at his Cartier watch. "I have another appointment that I can't miss. I'll tell my secretary that we met, and she'll get back with you if we need any other information." There was no "thank you for coming," only the "don't call me, I'll call you" salutation.

Before I had a chance to ask him another question, he had turned and walked back inside his office. The door closed behind him. My first interview for a job, and it was a bust.

CHAPTER 11

INSTINCTIVELY, I DISLIKED PHILLIP PENNINGTON. I had seen his type of academic snob before. His arrogance made me angry. An arrogant doctor is okay, as long as things go well. But when a procedure goes bad, they usually want no part of the complication. Maybe Phillip Pennington wasn't God, and not everything was as perfect as he said it was. I wanted to find out more about his implant program.

When I left his office, I stopped at a pay phone and called Jordan. I told her about my meeting and said I wanted to look at some records at Great Lakes Medical Center. She asked why, and I explained that Jimmy Scotten's notes mentioned implants. While the word implant could mean a lot of things, I wondered if there was a remote connection to Phillip Pennington's program.

Jordan thought I was stretching the investigator thing a little, but then relented. She saw no harm in looking and said she'd get me into the hospital, alluding to someone at Great Lakes who owed her a favor for a drug sting the prosecutor's office played on five unsuspecting pharmacists. Thirty minutes later she called back and told me that they would make the badge at the employment office.

I thanked her. "Are we still on for the basketball game tomorrow night?"

"Wouldn't miss it for anything." Anything? Maybe she really did like basketball.

I was at Great Lakes Medical Center early the next morning. After quickly locating the employment office on the first floor, I cooled my heels outside for an hour until Jordan's contact appeared. A lot of apologies, a digital mug shot, and twenty minutes later I was out in the hall with an official badge. Benjamin Dailey, M.D., Administrative Staff. I was now part of the bureaucracy.

When I was in the hallway, I looked at my picture. I mentally compared it to the other picture badges I had worn: a little grayer, a little more wrinkled. But it said *doctor* on the badge, didn't it?

I shook off my ego and decided that my first search would be in the records room. My theory was that in this part of the country, Phillip Pennington was the wizard of implantable hearing aids. The procedure wasn't done at every community hospital. Hell, even in a place as big as St. Vincent's, we hadn't done it. If there were a source of records on implantable hearing aids, I'd bank on finding it near Pennington.

I finally made my way to the basement office that housed the medical records. Admittance was by ID card only. My first bureaucratic barrier. I slipped my card through the sliding entrance scanner and the door unlocked with a click. Opening the metal door, I entered a huge fluorescent-lit room filled with stacks of metal files, computers, and mounds of charts everywhere. It bothered me a little that access with a card, no matter how phony, could get you anywhere in the hospital, as long as it said M.D. on it.

I walked into the large file room. Beneath the check-in sign were two women in front of five or six plain green metal racks stacked floor to ceiling with hospital charts. One of the women in front of the stacks looked up. She had three pencils coming out of her gray, coiled hair and a look of exasperation on her face.

"What can I do for you, doctor?" The word "doctor" was spoken like a challenge.

I explained carefully to her that I was doing a research project on cochlear implants and needed to look over some old charts. Instead of demanding service, I described the nature of the study and how it might help some people. I felt bad for giving her a phony line, but what the hell, that's what detectives did, isn't it?

Her hard exterior softened a little. After punching a few keys on the computer, she found that I wasn't on her uncompleted chart list. That's when she looked up the two-hundred-some patients, complete with names, addresses and phone numbers. Taking the list with her, she disappeared into the file racks. About half an hour later she returned with a shopping cart full of records.

"Sorry," she said, "but I had to go back in the file room for the records. Especially some of these old charts."

"Why's that?"

"Some of them were pretty old. We don't keep them all up here. After five years, we put them on microfiche. We simply don't have the room."

"I appreciate the effort." Two hundred charts. She might as well have given me a thousand. I'd be here all day. "Is there a place I can look at them?"

"Over in the carrel in the corner."

I wheeled my little cart over to the small enclosure and sat down with a pad and pencil. I'd written enough research papers to understand the drill of a good chart analysis—separate the items and try to find a pattern.

Undaunted, I started with names, dates, telephone numbers, and addresses. It didn't take long to identify the patients. Some kids and some adults, relatively evenly split between males and females, and all operated upon by Phillip Pennington. I looked at the dates. Pennington had done most of his cases when he'd first arrived, followed by a period when he'd done very few.

I decided to examine the medical records to see if there was something that distinguished one from another in terms of their disease processes. This turned out to be tedious: histories, physical examinations, x-ray reports and lab studies. I made four new columns and entered the data. After writing it up and looking at it, nothing seemed any clearer. All of them were patients who had decent auditory function at one time and then totally lost their hearing. Meningitis was the most common cause, along with a few progressive hearing losses on a congenital basis.

I noticed that the last five cases were tagged with a red sticker. The information appeared different, with only a face sheet of rudimentary demographics and no histories or physicals. There were some hearing tests that looked like before and after results. From what I could determine, the results were excellent for the nerve hearing loss they had. Aside from that there wasn't anything else, not even phone numbers or addresses.

I didn't know what to do to find these cases, so I called Sennett's office and spoke with Knudsen to see if he could find them. He told me it would take some time. I looked at my watch and realized that waiting there another hour wouldn't accomplish much. I told him I would call back.

I was about to leave when I heard some voices at the front desk. I looked up and saw Phillip Pennington with what appeared to be several residents, interns, and medical students. I did not want him to see me, so I took the charts to a copy machine hidden from the front desk. I proceeded to copy the face sheet with the patients' names, insurance, and intake data and the operative registration sheet of each of the five patients. When I was done, I put the copies in an empty folder and hid the charts in a corner of the carrel, behind some phone books and papers. I knew how the record room worked. I was safe.

I looked around the corner and saw that Pennington was still there, so I ducked behind a metal rack and listened as he berated what appeared to be one of his residents for not completing a chart. It was a cruel dressing down of a young man who had probably been up half the night.

I knew what Pennington was doing and I hated it. Belittling someone in public didn't appeal to me. I thought it did nothing for teaching except to make the chief look like an ass and the residents appear too afraid to ask questions.

The other residents looked at each other nervously as their boss walked over to the record desk and waited for my pencil-haired lady to appear.

"Madam, excuse me. I wonder if you would pull all of the charts for Dr. Pennington, please?"

I watched as she looked at him strangely. "Certainly." Within minutes she had a list of thirty cases. The computer retched them out. Pennington passed the discharge over to the resident he had just chastised.

"I grew up the hard way, doctor. Working nights to make money, student loans, used books. Don't tell me you don't have time. Hard work is an ethic. I want everything done by tonight, doctor. History and physicals, operating room reports, and discharge summaries. Maybe the next time you won't forget to look up the pathology slides. We make rounds at six tomorrow morning. I want you to show me everything."

The unfortunate resident merely nodded in submission. From the look on his face it was clear that he wasn't going to get away from here for another three hours. I suppose it could be argued that Pennington's response was a just punishment. Discipline is important. But public humiliation is another thing. Take away a man's pride and he has nothing. I should know.

After they left, I walked back to the records desk. "Rough crowd you deal with here," I remarked to the file clerk.

"I really felt sorry for that young man. These residents earn what they get when they finish."

I was about to give her my commentary about never crapping on the ladder of success, but she had already disappeared behind her stacks of charts. I made up my mind that even if Pennington offered me the job, I wasn't available.

CHAPTER 12

I SPENT THE NEXT DAY DEALING WITH an edge of anticipation. This detective work was interesting, maybe even alluring. But I knew that what I had uncovered wasn't the reason. It was my date with Jordan Dalkind that evening.

I had never met anyone like her. She was certainly nothing like my first wife, Judy. Some marriage, I thought. For her, it wasn't love, it was really about money. My ex had gotten used to the high life. Now, after the lawsuit, she proclaimed me an inveterate low-life as all of her dreams faded with my practice.

I remember coming home that night with a feeling of deep despair after Thornton had ex-communicated me from St. Vincent's. Judy was waiting for me in the living room; surprisingly she was dressed to go out. I told her that today was the last straw. We were going to have to make plans to move or downsize. I couldn't support our lifestyle without an income. I wasn't expecting sympathy, just understanding.

She merely stood there, her perfectly toned, personally-trained body next to a set of antique Giacometti chairs that had cost me a fortune. Her arms were folded across her five hundred dollar cashmere sweater, and a scowl was permanently etched onto her forehead. When she spoke, her words cut through me with the indifference of a guillotine. "I don't think that it's going to make much of difference, Ben."

"Why?"

"I'm filing for divorce."

What was I going to do? I should have seen it coming, should have realized why she never wanted children. I was stupid. Too honest to think my wife was cheating on me, too absorbed with my work to think about it. A month later I saw her on the society page in the *Free Press* with Jeffrey Rembertson, Grosse Pointe socialite and CEO of one of Detroit's largest banks.

Now I had met Jordan Dalkind and for the first time in a long while, I felt renewed. The old fire in my belly had started. I tried to check myself, warn myself about failure, but like a castaway found on a deserted island after so many years, the touch of humanity was irresistible.

I picked Jordan up at the Federal Center. She was inside the entrance, waiting. I got out of the car. When she saw me, she opened the door and walked down the steps. She was in a long, black overcoat with a fur collar pulled up on her neck. The steam from her breath followed her down the steps, the streetlamps illuminating her head like a halo.

When she got in the car, I asked her where she wanted to eat, and she suggested Gus's Diner. She said she had heard about the place, and liked the idea of trying someplace new. My kind of woman.

We arrived just in time to beat the early dinner crowd that filled Gus's place before they hit the casinos. Gus's Diner and the chili he served were a legend with Detroiters.

We walked in, and I immediately saw Gus Katsopopoulos at the counter, checking the till. Gus was the master of Detroit's answer to the Philly Cheesesteak: the Coney Island hot dog, the name stolen from New York, smothered in chili, onions, and mustard. In Detroit, Gus was an institution. He was short and round, with thick black curly hair, a perpetual five o'clock shadow, and a grin from ear to ear. His infectious personality made him an instant attraction. When he saw me walk in, he jumped up. He seemed excited.

"How you doing, doc?" he offered. He scanned Jordan for a moment. "Bringing new business for me, huh? Nice looking girl."

I looked over at Jordan, and she blushed for a moment.

"Meet Jordan Dalkind, Gus," I announced.

Jordan smiled and extended her hand, as Gus wiped his palms off on his apron. "You coming down here because you like a Coney or for the doc's company?" As he said it, he ushered us to a booth next to the window. I could see people walking in and out of the Greektown Casino, but there weren't many.

She laughed. "We're on our way to the basketball game. Ben asked me where I wanted to go, and I told him I'm a big Coney fan. So make it extra hot, lots of onions."

Gus smiled again. "My kind of woman, doc. You want the same?"

What was I going to say? I had to show my manhood. "Make it two for me," I said, sitting down across from her.

We chatted for a few minutes. When the door to the kitchen suddenly snapped open, we looked over and saw Gus walking down the aisle with two large plates resting on one of his thick arms. The other hand carried two bottles of hot sauce.

Gus reached our table and set the plates down. Then he placed the bottles of hot sauce in front of Jordan and gave her a wink.

"What's that?" she asked as she picked up one of the bottles and studied its contents.

"That's Jamaican Red Sauce, the hottest we've got."

Jordan studied the label for a minute then opened the cap and poured this red stuff over her Mr. K Special. Not wanting to seem out of place, I did the same. She looked at me and smiled as she took a large bite. I put the food in my mouth, and suddenly it was as if my throat was being stung by a thousand hot pins. My eyes were watering, as I reached for my water glass and started chugging as fast as I could.

"Milk works the best," she said laughingly. "I thought you ate here regularly."

"I do, but Gus has never given me the sauce before," I gasped.

"I cultivated a taste for hot sauce when I was in Miami. I was worse than you when I first tried it."

We both started laughing, and I suddenly felt the anxiety that had clouded my day disappear. We talked about football, politics, and even sailing. It turned out she was from Boston and that her father was crazy about boats. She had been on one type of sailboat or another since she was a kid.

Gus came up to the table while we were talking.

"Did you say you're going to the game tonight?" I nodded. "You know that guy that plays guard for them? I forget his name." When I told him Jenkins, he snapped his fingers. "Well, I don't like the guy. I see him in the casino all the time. Comes with a big stretch limo, even on game nights. They say he's injured, but I know he's just collecting a big paycheck."

"It's Detroit, Gus. Remember, this is the place where the auto companies originated the jobs bank; get paid for not working."

"Well, it reminds me of a guy from the old country. He made lots of money selling fish, or so he says, until the cops nab him for running a numbers racket. You never know what a guy really does for money." Gus looked at his watch. "Say, if you don't leave now, you'll miss the game."

"Come on, Gus, you know you only need to see the last five minutes of a basketball game." I wish I had taken my own advice.

GOING TO SEE PROFESSIONAL SPORTS IN DETROIT always carries a tinge of anxiety: is it safe to venture into the city? Personally, it never bothered me, but I always heard my colleagues at the hospital tell me they would rather see a basketball game at the suburban Palace of Auburn Hills than watch football, baseball or hockey in Detroit.

Obviously, the owners of the Palace felt the same way. It is a beautiful, fan-friendly venue, about forty miles from the city's downtown. I pulled into the entrance and handed the attendant the pre-paid parking pass. Bruce was sending me in style.

I didn't realize how much style until I gave the usher my tickets, and he led Jordan and me down to the bottom of the arena. We had front row floor seats at center court.

As we sat down, Jordan nudged me with her elbow. "I didn't know you were such a shooter."

"I'm not. I got the tickets from a friend of mine." I didn't want to tell her I got them from Bruce.

I had been to the Palace a few times before. When I went with my friends, these were referred to as the "leather pants" seats: reserved for guys with slicked-back hair and open collared shirts, and made-up women in tight leather pants.

The Pistons were playing the Cavaliers, a cross-lake rivalry that usually stirred up a big crowd. The place was filled except for the two seats next to us. But it was still early; a lot of people didn't show up until the start of the second quarter.

The game was close and the fans were especially raucous. I could tell that Jordan was having a good time. With about five minutes left in the half, a couple walked over to the empty seats next to us. It was annoying, so I looked up at them. I thought I had seen the girl before, I just couldn't recall where. Hard to miss her huge breasts in a buttoned sweater cut down to her navel and, as my friends would have predicted, tight leather pants that gathered at her crotch. Neither did the overhead television cameras in the arena that projected onto the middle of the court jumbotron or the crowd in the stadium. When I saw the guy she was with, there was no mistaking the face. It was Charles "Chip" Thornton, Jr., Chief of Surgery at St. Vincent's and son of the man who had dismissed me from the staff.

Shit. Couldn't I ever get away from these guys? Bruce's gift now looked like a Trojan horse. I didn't say anything to Jordan. There was no sense in involving her in my problem, but it sure changed my mood.

Thornton was so intent on the girl that he didn't see me. They had a couple of drinks in hand and must have had a few before, because they were loud and obnoxious. Chip Thornton was a blowhard. His incompetence as a doctor was equaled only by the esteem he felt for himself.

As soon as he sat down, he began yelling jibes at the Cleveland players. Each time he did he would grope his girlfriend. After a few outbursts, his antics were becoming insufferable, enough so that one of the refs gave him a look and then a warning. The admonition prompted him to glance around for support. That's when he saw me.

"Well, I'll be a sonofabitch," he yelled. It's "Botched Job" Dailey. How the hell did they let you in here?"

I didn't say anything and kept looking at the court. I had the feeling this evening wasn't going to turn out well. The next thing I knew he was on his feet and turning toward the people behind me.

"Hey, remember that doctor that operated on the wrong patient?" he asked loudly to anyone who could hear. "He's right here, "Botched Job" Dailey." Then he started convulsing with laughter.

If I had been somewhere else, I might have punched his lights out. But in front of all these people and with Jordan, I didn't know what to do. I just sat there, mortified. That's when Jordan got up.

"Why don't you sit down and enjoy the game instead of making a fool of yourself?" she yelled at him.

"Fool? Who the hell are you to say that considering the jackass you're with?"

That was it, I was going finish him off. Before I could do anything else, a guy behind us, who apparently had seen the whole affair developing, jumped up and signaled for the usher. I looked at the man, and he was nothing to mess with, bulging biceps in a tight Under Armor long sleeve shirt. He had professional athlete written all over him.

People were all standing now, trying to see what was happening. The ushers and a police officer rushed over and quickly confronted Thornton. In spite of being drunk, Thornton was still smart enough to recognize what was happening. He quickly got up with his bimbo and made his way to the stairs. I watched him until he entered a suite above the court just as the half ended.

I turned dejectedly to Jordan. "I think I've had enough basketball for tonight."

"No, we haven't," she said firmly. "I don't want to let a jerk like that ruin our night."

"It's hard to forget a guy like Chip Thornton."

I explained who he was and his relationship to St. Vincent's. As the son of the Chairman of the Board, it was a short trip to Chief Surgeon. On paper he looked good, Harvard educated and a residency at the Brigham. However, his resume outperformed his abilities, and everyone knew it. He also had a nasty streak in the operating room that made him disliked by almost everyone he worked with. Needless to say, we weren't close.

"The more reason why we should stay."

So we did and Jordan actually seemed to enjoy the rest of the game. Before we left, I got up and thanked the man behind us. It turned out he played middle linebacker for the Lions. I guess he had seen his share of derogatory comments and must have known how I felt.

In spite of staying, I left the game with an empty feeling. I couldn't shake my past, no matter where I went. I tried to be upbeat, but it wasn't working. I drove

Jordan to her home. We paused on her front porch. I had just said goodnight and turned to leave, when Jordan put her hand on my shoulder.

"I had a great time, Ben." By this time her arms were around my neck. She looked up at me and slowly I felt the warmth of her lips on mine. We stayed like that for a moment, then I pulled away.

"So did I," I exhaled. I wanted to say something else, maybe something stupid. So I stood almost paralyzed for a moment, not knowing what to do. Finally, I responded like I always did and said, "I'll call you." She looked disappointed, but in my mind it was too late. So I walked away, wondering how I could be depressed and exhilarated at the same time.

When I got back to the Lazy Isles it was late, and I was in a foul mood. I wished I had been quicker, slammed Thornton with a quick repartee or maybe just slammed him physically. Instead, my date did it for me and the big guy behind cleaned up. I felt inadequate, ashamed, and depressed. Jordan was starting to mean something to me. I wanted to resurrect my life, but my past always seemed to get in the way.

I sat down on the bed and looked around the dump I was staying in. That didn't help either. There was a small, rickety desk along the wall with a cheap lamp on top. I emptied my pockets on the table, including the ticket from the game and the papers I had copied at the hospital. I stared at the ticket, then threw it in the trash.

After undressing I slipped under the threadbare covers, hoping I could sleep my bad mood off. Unfortunately, my mind was still racing. Following another hour of tossing around, I got up and turned on the small TV in the corner. There was an old John Wayne movie, *True Grit*, playing on the classic film channel.

As I sat in the chair next to the desk watching the TV, I half-heartedly picked up the papers and thumbed through the pages, just looking at the names and addresses. Frank Strickland, Jack Hazeltine, Walter Trudeau, and Albert Henderson. When I picked up the last page, my eyes focused on the last patient for a moment. I stared at the name, Ralph Gernowski. I had seen it before, I just didn't know where.

The television was playing in the background. I watched John Wayne on his horse, spinning his rifle as he galloped up to confront the bad guys. Some cynics would call his performance corny, but it was his classic role, the ultimate good guy in a world of bad people. No one could play that role like he could. Shots rang out and the bad guys went down. For some reason it made me think of Faye Donaldson, and that's when I recalled when I had seen the name. I decided to call Sennett in the morning.

CHAPTER 13

IT TOOK ME TEN MINUTES ON THE PHONE the next day with Sennett to confirm that Ralph Gernowski's name had been on Faye Donaldson's computer. He asked me what was happening, and I explained that I had found his name on some charts I had been studying at the University. I told him I had spoken to Sergeant Knudsen and he was supposed to get me some information on the patients.

I waited on the line for a couple of minutes until Sennett returned. He had some partial information. Strickland and Trudeau were deceased. Hazeltine was at a nursing home. Henderson was in a motel near downtown Detroit, and Gernowski was living west of town near Ann Arbor. Sennett was cooperative, but I could tell he had enough on his plate, and I wasn't going to get much more from him.

I hung up the phone, realizing I was too curious to let it go. What the hell, someone had already asked me if I was an investigator. Even if I wasn't a detective, I decided to play the role.

The Jeep cranked up a little slower than usual but finally rumbled to life. As it warmed up, I looked at the remaining names on the list and picked Albert Henderson's place first, as it was the closest. It was around four o'clock when I reached his address. A wave of gloom came over me, mostly because the place looked a lot like the dump where I was staying. The only difference was that instead of a rent-by-the-hour bedroom, his place was one of those inner city, one-story motels that had been converted into efficiency apartment units.

I parked in the lot near the vacancy sign and knocked on the door of the caretaker's apartment. After a few moments, a scruffy, bearded man in his late twenties opened the door, wearing a sleeveless undershirt and boxer shorts. He looked upset that I was interrupting him. From his appearance I decided that whatever he was doing, I didn't want to know.

I did stay long enough to find out about Albert Henderson. He had lived here for the past three years. According to the manager, he hadn't seen him for two days, which apparently wasn't too unusual. Mr. Henderson had a tendency to go on a binge once in a while. So much for that lead. In five minutes, I was on the road and headed to the suburbs west of town. One more stop and I was done.

It was around six o'clock when I finally reached the western suburb of Dixboro, where Ralph Gernowski lived. The early winter twilight of the Midwest gave just enough illumination to let me see the shadows of the open, rolling countryside of Washtenaw County. I looked around at the lights on scattered houses that dotted the landscape and imagined the independent people that lived inside. They probably spent endless hours with their neighbors, drinking coffee and talking about how to stave off the urban sprawl that constantly gnawed at their fence lines. Nobody told them it would be a hopeless fight.

I kept driving, looking for road signs. The absence of streetlights made it that much harder to see the occasional signpost. A couple of wrong turns, a trip to a gas station for directions, and finally the address on Prospect Road.

The house had a winding drive that seemed to shrink away from my headlights in the deepening ground fog. I don't know if it was the dismal mist or the isolation of the house, but the name John Norman Collins flashed across my brain. He had lived out here in the late sixties. A nice-looking guy who killed college coeds for enjoyment. Even though they put him away, the thought of him gave me the creeps.

I've never been big on superstition, or for that matter common sense, so I drove up the gravel path for about fifty yards and then swung to the left. About halfway down the drive I hit a pothole and bottomed out on the springs. Thank God I was driving this beast.

Ahead, there was the house, or should I say, the former house. It was burnt bare to the ground. I fumbled in the glove compartment for a flashlight and got out of the car. Shining my Maglite slowly to the right and left, I saw nothing except the charred remains of the foundation, a few crumbled bricks, and the remnants of an overhanging porch. Even the garage was gone. I had a tremendous urge to leave, but my curiosity wouldn't let go. Suddenly a noise scratched from behind me. I whirled, shining my light on a cat running across the backyard.

I knew I should get out of there. Swinging the flashlight from side to side again, I headed back toward the car. As I did, the light reflected off an object lying near the stump of an old tree. Reaching down to pick it up, I realized that my great discovery was one of a number of old electric motors, the kind used in washing machines and dryers.

Looking around the rusting machinery again, my light hit on something else, a metallic object in the base of a tree stump. I looked at the stump for a moment, then reached in my pocket and took out the Swiss Army knife attached to my key ring. I dug the blade into the rotted wood and extracted the metal object. It looked like a bullet slug.

I had just finished when I heard another rustling in the bushes behind the garage. A cold shiver went through me. Stray cat or not, I was getting the hell out of there.

I stuffed the slug in my pants pocket, ran toward the Jeep, and jumped behind the wheel. My key quickly turned the ignition, and the engine sparked to life. Once in gear, I laid on the accelerator and waited as the wheels spun in the soft snow and then found traction. I didn't breathe a sigh of relief until the tires hit the main road.

A half mile down the highway, I sought sanctuary in the lights of Hal's Country Store. After parking, I walked in and headed straight for the three-hour old pot of coffee. I filled a Styrofoam cup with the mud, added three sugars, and took a sip, hoping the stuff wouldn't kill me.

"Rough day?" the counterman asked me as I reached in my pocket for the money.

"Yeah, kinda." I grimaced as I swallowed the sludge. "Say, you know the house up the street, the one that burned down?"

"Sure do, crazy old man Gernowski's place," he said.

"You knew him?" I asked.

"Yeah. He used to come in here, buy cigarettes. Ain't seen hide nor hair of him since his place burnt down."

"You said he was crazy. Why'd you call him that?" I pursued casually.

"Strange guy. Fixed old machinery for a living. I don't know how he managed to make out, especially with his hearing problem."

"Had he been hard of hearing ever since you knew him?" I asked.

The counterman nodded. "I think everyone around here thought he was, you know, mental, 'cause he never spoke. Then he up and gets this hearing aid, suddenly he's talking. Damndest thing I ever saw."

"Changed his life, I bet," I said, abandoning the Styrofoam cup on the countertop.

"For awhile. Then he kinda got funny again."

"What do you mean?"

"Pretty bad, huh?" I looked at him strangely. "I mean the coffee."

"I've had worse."

"Wait a minute. I'll make another pot. You wanna wait?"

I nodded, and he came out from behind the counter. He had a friendly smile, thinning gray hair, a full open face, and bushy white eyebrows that would have looked good in combination with a Santa Claus suit. As he made fresh coffee, he went on speaking.

"Gernowski was a weird guy, always firing them damn guns. The police were called out there several times because of the racket. I guess he never heard it anyway." It didn't take long before the Bunn coffee maker was spitting out a fresh brew.

"How long ago did you see him?"

"Been several weeks. Usually he'd come by and get two twelve-packs of Budweiser. That would last him a week. Say, why all the questions?"

"Oh, nothing in particular. I've been driving around the area, looking for property. You know, the suburbs are going to be here sooner than you think."

He poured another cup and handed it to me. "Well, let me know when they're coming, because I'll be long gone." His voice had an edge of defiance to it.

"I can see what you mean. Pretty peaceful around here." As I spoke, I put a dollar on the counter.

"You can say that again." He reached for the bill and handed it back to me. "Coffee's on me. Anyone comes out on a night like this deserves it."

I thanked him, picked up the cup, and walked back to my car. While I'd been inside, the mist had gotten a little worse, the fog a little denser. I knew the weather was deteriorating, because I slipped as I was getting into the Jeep.

I started the car up and sat inside the cab, finishing the coffee. It wasn't going to be a fun ride back to the city. But there was nothing more to do, so I put the Jeep in gear and pulled out into the street. At the end of the driveway, I stopped, looked around for a moment, and then proceeded out onto the road. I checked the rearview mirror. There was no one except a single car coming down the highway behind me.

CHAPTER 14

I PROCEEDED DOWN FORD ROAD looking through the mist for the entrance onto the M-14 connector between Ann Arbor and Detroit. This unlit stretch of highway under normal circumstances would have been the new tech corridor for the Detroit area. However, even the lure of the University of Michigan couldn't alter the drop in the economy. Instead of bright neon signs lighting up the darkness, I saw only scattered subdivisions stuck amidst acres of empty farmland and an almost impenetrable darkness.

As I entered the service ramp I felt apprehensive, and I didn't know why. I think the whole experience at Gernowski's house had put me on edge. Merging onto the expressway, I saw the car that was behind me speed in front of me and then suddenly slow down. My foot hit the brakes. Nothing happened.

Frantically, I pumped the pedal. Nothing. All I could feel was the touch of the metal against the firewall. My mind panicked, realizing that at fifty-five miles an hour and without brakes, I was guaranteed to hit the slowly moving car ahead of me. I quickly punched the accelerator and passed the vehicle on the other side. Once my car edged by, I slowed down, but there were other cars ahead. I had absolutely no way to stop.

Three autos up ahead were lined across the road diagonally. There was nothing I could do except to swing the Wagoneer toward the shoulder. I hit the shoulder, hoping not to crash into the razor-sharp guardrail along the side of the freeway. That's when I saw the bridge abutment.

I knew the Wagoneer was going to hit it. In a fraction of a second I swung the wheel back to the left and the Jeep veered over on its two left tires. As it did, it hit a patch of ice on the shoulder and started to spin toward the middle of the four-lane expressway.

I was totally out of control as I moved sideways down the center of the road. Out of sheer panic I kept pressing my foot on the brakes, trying to regain control of the Jeep. I could see the cars around me speed ahead, trying to avoid my vehicle, as the tail of my Wagoneer headed directly for the concrete of the bridge. I was about to hit the abutment when I jammed my foot down on the accelerator again. It was all I could do.

The engine gunned, making the wheels spin, but there was just enough traction to maintain forward movement. I saw the pillars of the abutment pass as I swerved back into the middle lane, missing the two cars next to me. My eyes picked up the terror in the face of one of the drivers. It was like being in a widescreen movie, as the Jeep completed its three-sixty. My hands were shaking as I clutched the wheel. Finally, my car slowed down enough so that I could drive up the now gently sloped embankment.

After 500 feet I came to a complete stop in the wet snow. My trembling hands turned the engine off. I just sat there, staring straight ahead.

No one stopped. To the passing cars, I was merely another disabled vehicle. Ben Dailey, now part of the flotsam and jetsam littering the expressways of Detroit. I sat there, stunned from my near-death experience and enveloped by a depression so deep I felt I would never get out. What else could possibly happen to me?

I must have been sitting like that for a long time when the flashing light of a State Police car broke through the darkness. It was another twenty minutes before a tow truck had me hooked up and on the way to a garage.

The mechanic at the service station pushed my hunk of metal through an open bay and onto the ramp of a hoist. Within minutes he was looking at the bottom of my car. His grease-smudged face announced that he had found the problem. From a distance I could see a trace of fluid dripping down onto the floor of the garage.

The mechanic reached his blackened hand forward and pulled on the hose. "Here's what almost killed you, boss. Broken brake line," he said, holding up the two ends of the metal pipe. "Worn clean through. If I didn't know better, I would say it'd been cut."

"Probably worn out," I said weakly. "It's an old car." Then I remembered the pothole at Gernowski's house. I told the mechanic about it.

He shrugged his shoulders. "Like you say, it's an old car. Something was bound to happen. You were damn lucky."

I went back to the waiting area, got a couple of cheese crackers from the vending machine, and sat down. As I waited there, legs crossed, I happened to look at the bottom of my shoes. Brake fluid on my soles. It must have been what I slipped on getting into the car outside the convenience store. I thought again about the hose being cut. Maybe my depression was giving way to paranoia.

The mechanic told me he would have my car ready the next morning morning. It was two a.m., and I had nowhere to go and no way to get there. I felt alone and destitute, both financially and emotionally. When the mechanic said he would have one of his boys drive me home, I was too embarrassed to tell him I didn't have one. Then, for reasons I still don't quite understand, I gave him Jordan's address in Birmingham.

I scooped up my papers from the seat of the Wagoneer and climbed into the tow truck. When the driver dropped me off at Jordan's doorstep, I waved as if I belonged there. Then I sat down on the front step under the lamp and pondered what to do next. It was cold, and I started shivering. I wanted to ring the bell, but I was too proud to knock on the door. I don't think I had ever felt so alone. At one point in my life I might have been smart and resourceful, but now I was a rudderless ship with no destination.

I must have been sitting there for twenty minutes when I saw the search beam from a passing car. It lit up the front of the house and then focused on me. I was paralyzed from the cold and from the indecision that tormented me.

A uniformed policeman came out of the car, a Maglite in one hand and the other on his holster.

"Stay where you are and don't move," he shouted. I had never been arrested, but I assumed any sudden move on my part and I was dead, so I raised my hands. "Now turn around and put your hands on the brick wall next to the door."

I did as I was told. He came from behind me and frisked me for weapons. When he was sure I was unarmed, he asked me to turn around. I slowly turned to face him. He was a big man with crooked teeth and a pink-cheeked, ruddy Irish complexion. By now his gun was drawn, and he was reaching for his cuffs. As he did, a second light came on above the portico and the door opened. A couple of seconds later Jordan peeked around the door and stared at the scene in front of her.

"Ben! What the hell is going on, and why is this officer cuffing you?"

Before I could explain anything, Irish told her that he had found me sitting on her front doorstep and was going to arrest me for vagrancy.

"Let him go, Rich. He's a friend of mine. I'll take care of him."

"Are you sure, Ms. Dalkind?" he asked.

She nodded, and Irish backed off.

"Come on in, Ben."

Obediently, I followed her inside her townhouse. The rush of warm air clung to me like a down blanket. I shivered again.

I stood on what I assumed was an expensive oriental rug and looked into the wrought iron framed mirror in the hallway. Under the light I looked at myself, unshaven, unkempt, and haggard from my experience.

"Before you tell me what you were doing on my front porch, I am going to make you some tea and get you warmed up."

We walked into the kitchen. It was modern but cozy. Stained wood floors contrasted with dark granite counter tops and light wood and glass cabinets. There was a small circular glass table in front of a sliding door. In the middle of the table was a vase filled with bright blue irises.

Jordan put a kettle of water on the stove and within a couple of minutes it was boiling. She put out two mugs and two tea bags of Earl Grey.

"Sugar?" she asked. I nodded and put two cubes in the mug.

After I had taken a sip of the tea, she slid a couple of oatmeal cookies in front of me.

"You better eat something. You look terrible."

"Not like the piano player at the Pipeline?"

She laughed. "Kind of what I look like without makeup." I stared at her and wondered how much more beautiful she could be. "Now, do you want to tell me what you were doing on my front porch at two in the morning?"

I told her about Gernowski and my conversation with Sennett.

"What did you think you were going to accomplish?"

I shook my head. "I needed to do something positive instead of just sitting and waiting for something to happen. I know I'm no detective, but there is some relationship between Gernowski and Faye Donaldson." Almost as an afterthought I pulled out the bullet slug from my pants and put it on the table. "It probably was a fool's errand, but I found this in a tree stump. Maybe it has some significance."

"C'mon, Ben, that's for CSI on television, not the real police world."

I handed her the bullet. "Do me a favor and see if there is a connection."

She took the bullet and placed it in a plastic bag. "I'll give it to Sennett in the morning. But don't expect anything."

Then I explained what had happened to me on the expressway and the recounting of the mechanic's opinion that my brake line might have been cut. The rest of it was hard to admit, but I said that I was nearly broke and had nowhere to go. I couldn't confess to anyone that I was on the verge of being homeless. That's why I gave the mechanic her address. Once there I couldn't bring myself to knock on her door.

She stared at me quizzically. "Why, did you think I wouldn't help you?"

"After last night, you never know. I didn't want to interfere with your life." Then I blurted out, "I guess I had too much pride to admit I needed help."

"We all need help, Ben, in one way or another."

I sat down on the sofa, exhausted, both mentally and physically. I heard her ask whether this was due to something related to the Scotten family. I wanted to respond, but nothing came out. Moments later I was asleep.

I woke up the next morning, awakened by bright sunshine pouring through a window onto my face. My head was on a pillow, and I was covered with a blanket. I heard the clinking of glasses in the kitchen and turned around in time to see Jordan pouring coffee into a mug. Suddenly everything came back to me from last night.

"How'd you sleep?" she asked.

"Like the dead. Sorry about last night." I felt ashamed and beholden. I was in unfamiliar territory.

She must have sensed it, because she changed the subject. "I thought about what you said. Your personal problems have no merit either for the local or federal authorities. But that doesn't mean there isn't some truth to what you said. Terry Scotten may be involved." As she spoke, she popped two slices of multi-grain bread into the toaster.

"It's a logical line of thinking. He hates me for what happened to his son, we had an altercation, and he used to run an automotive repair shop. What else do you need?" The idea that my own thoughts might not just be paranoia sent a chill through me that I hadn't felt since Charles Thornton had given me the death sentence. "Maybe I've stirred something up, and now someone thinks I know something."

"Or maybe you're just paranoid." She took the toast from the toaster and put it on two plates. "Butter, jam, or plain?"

"Butter." By this time I had made my way to the kitchen and sat at the table. I was sore and stiff from last night's adventure.

"What do you know about these hearing aids?" she asked.

"Not a lot. From what I understand they are amazing."

"Didn't you say there were NIH grant papers?"

"I have them with me. I took them from my car when I left the mechanic last night."

Jordan sat down across from me as I opened the folder and scanned the papers. "I'll look them over later."

"Tell me, how did the cops know I was on your front porch?"

She told me that, since she was a federal prosecutor, the police routinely drove by her house. As she spoke, I got up and looked for my coat.

"Where are you going?" she asked.

"I'm going to call Easy at the marina. I'll see if my boat is ready."

"You could stay with me." From the tone of her voice I knew she meant it.

"What if I am a target? I'm only bringing you into my problem."

"Maybe I don't mind. Listen, you showed up at my house last night. You can't just walk out."

"There isn't a long line of people out there waiting to be my friend. As strange as it sounds, you were the only person I thought of."

"I'm honored."

Then from the depths of the Dailey Book of Stupid Things to Say, I blurted out, "You know, I could like you a lot. But I'm no fool. I'm in my forties and on the ropes." I was surprised that she didn't laugh in my face.

"Don't be so close minded as to believe you are the only one who could get hurt." Tears welled at the corner of her eyes. I didn't know what she meant, but it was obvious that there was a pain in her that ran deep.

I gently reached down, pulled her up from the chair, and held her against me. Her head rested against my chest. I smelled the sweet scent of her hair, felt her breath first come out in short heaves and then settle into a regular rhythm. It was intoxicating. I felt myself get excited as I held her in my arms. She must have noticed, because she pressed her pelvis close to me. I was about to kiss her when the phone rang. My luck.

She raised her forefinger to tell me to wait and reached over for the phone on the wall. I could see her eyes narrow as a scowl came across her face. Then she hung up.

"That was my office. This corporate fraud case I've been working on has gotten hot. The judge may release a wiretap and they need me to go over the papers. Sorry. I'll drive you back to the repair shop." She and I both knew the moment had passed.

Jordan drove me back to the mechanic's shop. On the way over she told me she was going to give Sennett the slug. They should have an answer as to whether or not it was something of interest soon. When she began to insist again that I stay with her, I told her I would call her later.

I hesitated to open the door and then got out.

"Don't forget to call me," she said through her open window.

I said I would, lingered with indecision for a moment, and then walked into the Farmington Brake Shop. At the door I made up my mind I wanted to stay with her, so I turned around. I was too late, her car had already left.

I stood inside the shop, looking at her car disappear in the distance and wishing I hadn't been so indecisive. The smell of rubber and grease permeated the air, and her perfume was a distant memory. I must have looked a little bewildered, because the salesman behind the counter asked if he could help me.

When I told him I was the guy from last night with the broken brake line, he told me they were working on my car now, but it was taking longer than they had expected and asked me to wait. I sat down and waited like a relative of a patient anticipating the report from the surgeon. To pass the time, I pulled out the NIH paper from Phillip Pennington. It was devoted to the development of a new, high-power implantable hearing aid and the studies related to laboratory animals. The aid was inserted through the ear canal and placed adjacent to the ear drum. The findings showed that in experimental animals, this aid was far superior to any other amplifier ever developed.

I had just finished when I was told it was going to be a $200 brake job. I was working now just to stay even. Could be worse, I rationalized. I could be dead.

Naturally, there was a two-day wait for parts. I needed to get out of the shop, but other than a cab I couldn't afford, there was no mass transit in Detroit. The auto barons in the forties and fifties had planned it that way: keep the workers in Detroit and live like princes in the 'burbs. Now it was too expensive to correct the mistake.

Being stranded without a vehicle in Detroit was like being on a desert island without a boat. I asked the guy behind the counter about a rental car, but all he had was the thirty-two fifty model from Hertz. That was outside my budget. It wasn't in my nature to stay holed up, so I thumbed through the Yellow Pages for rental cars, and after a few calls, I got the nineteen fifty per day special at the rent-a-wreck place down the strip: an unadorned ten-year-old Ford Escort with 75,000 miles. They even made me sign an insurance waiver on the thing.

At least it had wheels. It didn't go fast, but fifty-five miles an hour is still fifty-five, no matter what you're driving. And that was good enough to get me around on my next-to-last day on the Coastal's payroll.

By the time I left it was almost dark. I decided that I needed to review the chart of Ralph Gernowski more carefully. Fortunately, Great Lakes Medical Center was near the expressway.

The plow trucks were working overtime to keep the driveways open, but the wind was making the main parking lots a drifted mess. Instead of fighting the deep snow, I found a small sheltered area to the side of the main entrance. Then, hunching against the wind, I trudged the hundred yards to the large revolving doors of the hospital. Once there I pinned on my Jordan Dalkind-issued ID badge.

The guard nodded me through. I went down the rear stairs, made my way back to the records room, and slid my ID card into the access slot. The hospital kept the place open all night just in case some diligent physician wanted to find some four-year-old chart at two in the morning.

I walked into the brightly lit area and headed to the rear carrel. I hoped the charts were still squirreled away where I had left them underneath the phone books. My karma must have been improving, because they were still there.

I picked the last five charts and rifled through them again. I studied the names carefully: Strickland, Henderson, Trudeau, Hazeltine, and, lastly, Ralph Gernowski. I combed over Gernowski's chart. Lab tests, x-rays, clinic notes, hearing tests—all the same. The only thing missing were the operative reports.

It was quiet in the records room. Eerily quiet. I thought I heard a creaking noise behind me. I got up and carefully walked to the end of the aisle to see if anything was there. The room was empty.

Cautiously, I slipped back to the carrel, picked up the charts, and looked at them one more time. Nothing. I looked at my watch with a feeling of frustration. I had spent three hours going over the records and the only thing I had found that was unusual was the absence of operative reports. Was it a coincidence or was there some other explanation? At this point it was inexplicable.

I decided to give the clinic notes one more review. Pennington's charts were typed instead of handwritten. The notes were mostly the same. Patient doing well, hearing improved, that kind of thing. It wasn't until I looked at the registration sheets that I noticed a difference. Unlike the other charts, the last five bore a large rubber-stamped name: *Phillip Pennington/SVH.* I wondered what it meant. Nothing made sense.

I checked my watch again. It was getting late, and I had promised Jordan that I would call her. This detective work was for the birds. I'd much rather be challenged by a medical problem that I had a fighting chance to figure out than something as obtuse as this.

I went back to the Xerox machine and turned it on. I decided to make copies of the last five charts. When I finished the last copy, I folded them and slid them inside my shirt. Fatigue had overcome me. I hid the records again, and then beat a path to the exit.

Out in the hallway, the basement seemed somehow more deserted than when I had entered. It was an oppressive feeling, making my breath come in short bursts. I made for the stairs, ran up the treads, and walked as fast as I could toward the side exit.

I think some intuitive memory of what had happened to my Jeep stopped me for a moment and made me open the exit door slowly. I poked my head out and looked around at the empty parking lot, the bitterly cold windblown snow biting my skin. Looking down at the snow, I thought I saw a fresh set of footprints.

I must have sensed it coming. I ducked just enough to feel only the tear in my jacket. Something sharp pierced the fibers of my sleeve; a searing pain spread down my arm, quickly followed by a warm trickling sensation.

I spun to the left to see a man in a large overcoat with a ski mask covering his head, about to strike again. He groped for me. A glinting blade was raised. This time I dropped to the ground as he lunged, rolling at his feet. My chop block deserved at least a fifteen-yard penalty. He stumbled to the pavement. I was on my feet quickly, crashing my boot into his ribs. I heard him grunt, but I knew I'd checked him only temporarily.

Clearly, I wasn't enough of a fighter to take this thug on. My only possible escape was by car. I ran to the side of the rent-a-wreck and jumped into the passenger seat as the overcoat rose into view through the windshield from the side of the front fender. I cursed as I fumbled for the keys to the ignition.

My fingers found the key at the same time as the assailant's hand reached for the passenger door handle. I suddenly wished I hadn't been so cheap. *Please, start*, I thought. It was cold out, and I didn't know if the old brute still had enough inside to crank against this kind of weather. Fortunately, the motor hadn't been sitting idle long enough to freeze. It kicked over just as the right door started to open. I could see the knife blade as I jammed the gearshift into reverse and slammed the accelerator down.

The passenger door swung wide open from the sudden movement, hurling the assassin back into the parking lot. The tinny sound of the four-cylinder engine echoed against the brick wall. As I popped the gear into drive the door closed and the car fishtailed wildly, nearly crashing into a cement barricade. My tires were spinning, but I eased my foot off the pedal and made for the exit. I crashed through the wooden gate and didn't bother to look back.

CHAPTER 15

I WAS SCARED NOW. I HADN'T BARGAINED FOR THIS type of action when I got involved with the case. Now I wanted out. Whoever was stalking me would have to be caught by someone else. Hitting the street, I stopped, reached for the door, slammed it shut, and aimed the car toward the expressway, praying I'd stay alive. At this moment, my precarious life seemed very precious to me. Then I reached inside my jacket to make sure the copies were still there. There was a sharp pain in my arm, but I chose to ignore it.

Right or wrong, I was now convinced that the brake line was no accident. Whoever was following me wanted me dead. I jammed my foot on the accelerator, and the car swerved down the entrance ramp of the expressway. My hands were shaking so badly I held the cold steering wheel in a death grip.

I had to get myself under control. *Stay cool and head west,* I decided. Cars and billboards passed by like a kaleidoscope. I saw none of them. My mind was a jumble of fear and anger.

I thought of calling Jordan, but I was afraid, afraid for myself and afraid of entangling her deeper into this mess. I plunged on into the snow, with no plan in sight.

After twenty minutes of checking in the rearview mirror and changing lanes, I finally pulled off the expressway and into an all-night truck stop. I parked my car under a light near the front entrance, walked into the café, and headed back toward the restroom. At that time of night there were still people milling around, mostly teamsters forced to get off the road and wait out the storm.

Shouldering my way past a few truckers, I went inside the men's room and looked around. Thank God it was empty.

In front of the mirror, I unzipped my jacket and took it off slowly. Surveying the damage, I shrugged in solitary bravado at the rip in my sleeve. Then I looked at my shirt. It was stained with blood. That's when I began to think of the pain in my arm.

I unbuttoned my shirt, peeled it off, and looked at the area above my elbow in the mirror. I saw a superficial wound that extended about three inches along my triceps. I flexed the muscle. There was no pain.

I was lucky. The cut looked a lot worse than it was. I washed off some of the congealed blood along the small laceration. Because I had ducked, the knife had only grazed the skin. Another inch toward the inside and the thrust would have severed the radial artery, a bloody prelude to my death.

I washed the dried blood off my arm and hands, then looked around for something to bandage the wound. There were only paper towels. Just as I reached for one, the door banged open. I dropped my jacket on the counter and waited expectantly, my hands raised slightly, ready for trouble. Instead a big man, bearded, with long black hair coiled in a ponytail, walked in.

He surveyed me curiously for a minute. "Relax, mister. I only want to use the john." His face was open and friendly.

Everyone was not my enemy. "Sorry, I cut myself. I guess I'm a little jumpy."

He came over and looked at my arm. "No big thing. I get those kinds of cuts on my rig all the time hauling steel. Here, let me put a couple of Band -Aids on it."

He reached inside his hip pack, pulled out a couple of plastic strips, and put them on the wound. "Not much of a deal, you know. How'd you do it?"

"Slipped and hit my arm against the door," I replied.

He looked at my torn jacket. "Lucky you were wearing that thing. The filler in those jackets is better than Kevlar."

Looking from my jacket to my arm, I felt relieved. "I knew there was a reason I spent all that money on it."

"Got to be careful in this kind of weather. Sometimes it's the unexpected that gets you," he said, as he finished bandaging me up.

"You can say that again," I said, thinking there might still be hope for mankind. "Thanks for the help." I walked out into the restaurant area. I didn't feel safe anywhere. I was supposed to call Jordan, but I couldn't bring her into harm's way. I thought of calling the police. But what would they find? I had left the scene. A lone man attacking someone in the middle of a snowstorm. Besides, with my history they'd laugh me out of the station.

It was close to midnight. I went over to the counter and ordered a cup of the house blend and a gooey Danish. I took the medical charts from my jacket and looked at them. I studied the red-stamped sheets again, "*Phillip Pennington/ SVH*" and concluded that was probably just some kind of office code, probably the transcriptionist's initials.

Was I spinning some kind of crazy yarn? Who the hell was I, a detective? I had nothing, only misplaced anger toward someone I hardly knew. I was getting mad at myself.

I had to quit getting carried away with this detective stuff and hearing aids and worry about staying alive. One thing was for sure: I wasn't fabricating the intent on my life. But why? Someone must have figured out I knew something and wanted me silenced. I knew there was nowhere a person could hide from someone like that. The attacker had to be found; the question was who would do it, and would I still be alive before this person was caught?

Of course, I was out of my element and no match for a determined killer. *Forget it, Mr. Hero. Remember, you are a doctor. The only thing to do is run. Run away from here as fast as you can.* Head west, toward Chicago. Maybe some small town where they would never find me. Who was I kidding? This killer was obsessed and would pursue me. I would never be free.

I put my head in my hands and leaned over my coffee cup, trying to clear my mind. I must have looked like the loneliest person in the world, because my truck driver friend from the john came over and sat on the stool next to me.

"Rough night, huh?" he asked.

"Yeah, kinda."

"Storm is starting to let up, but they're telling me another few inches by morning," he said, making conversation.

"You guys run in this kind of weather?" I asked.

"Not a chance. My company pays for delivery, not for accidents. I'm holing up at the motel behind the restaurant. It ain't much, but it's clean." He called the waitress over. "I'll have the same thing as my friend."

"I should try and get a room there," I said weakly.

"No luck, pal. They told me I got the last place." The waitress set his food down in front of him.

"Shit," I sighed. "This is going to be a night to remember."

"Try my rig," he offered. "You know, the sleeper behind the cab. I only use it in emergencies. It's clean and warm. We keep the motors running all night, especially in this weather."

I was about to say no. It was my usual response. I could fend for myself. But then I thought, *not even the person who was trying to kill me would ever think of looking for me in the sleeper cab of a tractor-trailer rig.* I accepted.

The trucker was correct: the sleeper compartment was clean and warm. I thanked him and offered to pay. He told me to forget it, and pass the good deed on.

After he left, I slipped off my jacket and shoes and hunkered down into the sleeping bag. Something about the security of my hiding place made me feel free, at least for a night. Through the small window of the sleeping compartment I could see the swirling snow outside the window of the cab and wondered when I would get my Jeep back. That was my last thought before I fell asleep.

My dreams must have been pretty wild that night, because when I awoke at five a.m., I was lying outside the sleeping bag. I remembered a few of them. Most were about knives. All kinds of knives, all lined up in a row, marching toward me. On top of each was a fleshless skull crowned with a black skullcap. No wonder I had tossed around.

I trudged back to the truck stop. Even at this hour there were people stirring. I picked up a few toilet articles and a sewing kit and made my way into the bathroom. A quick shave and I felt half-decent. At least I was still alive.

I went back to the counter, ordered two eggs up and hash browns, and sat there studying the tear in my jacket. After about thirty seconds of inspection, I tried to thread the needle from my sewing kit. Licking the thread and ineptly trying to guide it through the eye made me regret every time I'd been short with a surgical nurse for not keeping up with my call for sutures.

It took about ten running horizontal mattress sutures, but when I was finished the tear looked airtight. I'd worry about replacing the jacket later. By the time the repair was finished, my breakfast had come.

I ate in silence, wiping my plate down with the last piece of toast. When I was finished, I picked up my jacket and felt the medical charts still in the inside pocket. One last time? I spread them out and stared at the words. Something was missing. Some thread of commonality between the patients that was eluding me. I must have been engrossed in my thoughts, because I didn't notice my bearded friend as he sidled up next to me.

"Sleep good last night?" he asked, as he sat down.

"Like a baby," I replied, picking up the papers and putting them back in my pocket.

"Watch out, you might like the trucker's life. No one in an office to bug you. You're your own boss." He sat down and looked over the menu.

"Not hardly. I hate to drive." I could see myself handling that rig, calling out on the CB. What would my handle be? "The Dyin' Doc?"

"Well, driving is a prerequisite for the job. That and being willing to be away from your family. It ain't much for home life. I never get to see the people I love, only talk with them."

The words hit me like a thunderbolt. "Listen, I gotta run. Can I buy you breakfast?"

. When he told me no, I laid a ten spot for the waitress and made for the nearest pay phone. No matter what, I needed to talk to Jordan. I reached her on the second ring, she sounded sleepy.

"I thought you were going to call last night." I prepared myself for an angry lecture, something I probably deserved. Instead, there was an upbeat tone to her voice. "I take back everything I said about TV forensic shows. You are one hell of a detective."

"Why?"

"Sennett had your bullet slug examined, the one you took from Ralph Gernowski's house. It matched the one that killed Faye Donaldson." I was as shocked as Jordan.

"Great. Now all we need to do is get Gernowski."

"At least we have some idea of who killed her."

I was so excited I forgot to tell her about the attack on my life.

CHAPTER 16

I MET JORDAN AND SENNETT AT HIS OFFICE. I guess my cleanup job didn't look as good as I thought.

"Jesus, Doc, you look like hell. What happened to you?" Sennett asked.

I told them about going to the hospital to look at the charts and then the attack. There was a look of consternation on Jordan's face that seemed to disappear when I said I was sorry I had forgotten to mention it earlier.

"Are you the absent-minded professor?" she asked.

"No, just a dumbass who is in over his head," I replied.

Sennett concurred quickly. He picked up the phone and spoke with Knudsen. He was sending a unit out to the site to see if he could get any evidence, but he doubted they would find anything.

"This is serious stuff, Ben. You are in over your head. I think you had better retire now," Sennett said with the tone of a man who had seen no good come out of these situations. "This is police business. It's what we spend our lives doing. You want to get messed up, just keep investigating."

Sennett had one of those rubber balls on his desk, the kind you squeeze to build up your hands and relieve stress. He was working it over pretty good. Then he started guffawing almost uncontrollably. I thought he was going to have a seizure. "You know, Doc, I gotta remember that one. The next time my girlfriend gets mad at me, I'm heading for the truck stop."

I didn't know what to say. Did he think Jordan and I were an item, or was this just a casual joke? I decided to follow the advice of one of my professors, who quoted Wadsworth to me once when I screwed up on rounds: sometimes it was better to be quiet and be thought of as a fool than to open your mouth and remove all doubt. I waited until Sennett stopped laughing.

"I appreciate the humor, lieutenant, but someone tried to kill me last night and right now I'm pretty damn scared. What have you learned about Ralph Gernowski? I asked seriously.

"Sorry. You're right to ask and as of now we probably don't know much more than you did at his house. He was from Cincinnati. We spoke to one of his relatives. They say he was a pretty normal kid until Vietnam. A land mine exploded near him, knocked out his hearing. According to this cousin we spoke with, after that had happened, he could never get it together. Drifted around, always a loner. She hadn't heard from him in years."

Sennett went on to tell us Gernowski had been arrested a couple of times on vagrancy charges, nothing else. Until this shooting Ralph Gernowski had never appeared on the radar.

"The only thing we can connect him to is the list of the five patients who had identical records," I said.

"So?"

"In medicine, there's a saying: "common things happen commonly." There has to be an association."

"What does that mean?" Jordan asked.

I explained that there was something that made these patients alike. We just had to find out what it was. "Did Knudsen find out any more about these five people?"

"You're not going to quit, are you?" Sennett asked with a look of frustration.

When I didn't answer, he took a sheaf of papers from the clutter on his desk and spread it out in front of him. He began describing each of the other four patients. Frank Strickland came from the Upper Peninsula where he worked at a copper mining facility. According to the Social Service records, he applied for disability in 1988 following an explosion at the plant he was working at. Apparently, he had lost his hearing. The claim was rejected because of a workers' compensation dispute. Numerous attempts were made to contact him, but according to the case worker, he had been depressed and angry that no one was helping him. He started drinking and was arrested for drug use a few times. The last contact he had with his worker was in 1995, when he came in looking for money. He was told that his workers' compensation claim had expired, and he didn't qualify for federal assistance. During the next decade he moved to Detroit and lived in a number of homeless shelters. The last note in the chart was his death notice in a hit and run accident in Detroit last year. There was no mention of his surgery.

Walter Trudeau had a similar story; the only difference was that his hearing loss came from meningitis. He had developed senile dementia and was living in an Alzheimer's unit when he died of natural causes.

Jack Hazeltine was currently residing in the Grand West Nursing Home. He was found wandering along the Cass Corridor in Downtown Detroit, yelling and screaming incoherently. Social Services traced down some records on him and found that he had dropped out of high school in Detroit after losing his hearing in a motor vehicle accident. Apparently, he had been an A student until then, but there was little or no family support. When he was taken in, he was non-communicative. According to the nursing home, he sat in a wheelchair all day mumbling, mostly about baseball.

Albert Henderson was a different story. He had been a computer analyst for Ford Motor Company until the mid-nineties when he was given antibiotics after a knee surgery. The medications caused a sudden hearing loss in both ears from which he never recovered. He stayed on at Ford for a few more years, working as a clerical staff assistant, but eventually, with the downsizing of the car industry, he was laid off. His became penniless after his wife divorced him. The only money he had left was a few bucks from his pension. Apparently, that's what he used for his room and board.

I listened intently as Sennett spoke, writing down everything on a yellow legal pad. When he was done, I arranged the things the men all had in common in columns. I could see that they were all around the same age, all were deaf, all were indigent, and they each had some type of hearing aid implant.

"Lieutenant, we need to talk with Phillip Pennington and see if he has any recollection of these patients."

"You know, Doc, I'm not keen on it, but I'm going to do it for two reasons. One is that you found that bullet. The second is that I'm worried about you. You've got yourself into something here that doesn't look right. I suppose we could look at the attack on you as a random incident, but I'm not taking any chances. Let me get Knudsen."

While we waited for the sergeant to come down the hall, I listened to Sennett tell us about the golf trip he was planning to Florida. Apparently, he was addicted to the game. He asked me if I played, and I told him playing golf for me was like getting my anus boil lanced without anesthesia.

"C'mon, Doc, you must have some sport you like."

"If I had any money, which I don't, I'd be sailing in the Caribbean or skiing in Colorado."

"Expensive tastes," Jordan said.

"No, just a good imagination." I was about to tell her that the thought was the mother of the deed, when Knudsen walked in. Sennett told him to call Pennington and arrange a meeting. Knudsen turned smartly on his heel and walked out.

"He's a good soldier, Knudsen. When you tell him something, he's like a dog on a bone. We'll get to Pennington and ask him about these people. In the meantime, I've got some boys out looking for Gernowski. A guy like that might be hard to find.

"What about some kind of protection for Ben?" Jordan asked.

Sennett shook his head. "I'd have a hard time convincing the chief to pop for that. I can tell you exactly what he would say: 'George, if we tried to protect every citizen in Detroit that was threatened, either verbally or physically, everyone would be employed by the police department.'"

"So what does he do?" Jordan asked. "Just wait until the next attack?"

"Hopefully there won't be one," Sennett said in a tone that let me know he was worried. "I want you to lay low, Ben, until we can find something out. We don't need full-time surveillance at this point, but make sure you vary your routine and be suspicious of everything. Also, I'd appreciate it if you would check in with me regularly. Here's my cell phone number."

He wrote down the number and handed it to me. As he finished, he got another call that he said would take a while. Jordan looked at her watch. Then, saying she had another appointment, we left his office and walked back to the elevators. Walking down the hall, Jordan slipped her arm through mine. I looked over at her and she smiled. When we reached the entrance, she pulled me aside.

"You're going to stay at my house, Ben. No discussion."

I knew it was going to happen; I just didn't know how to say no to her.

"What about the fact that there is someone out there who is trying to kill me? Do you honestly think, in spite of how much I want to stay with you, that I would bring that kind of danger to your home?"

As she spoke, she fiddled with the straps of her purse. I could see that, even for someone who was used to being under control, this obviously meant a lot to her. She tried to persuade me that she already had twenty-four-hour surveillance, and that she was used to this kind of threat. She wouldn't listen to my protests. I had the distinct feeling she was trying to protect me.

Instead of saying no, I told her I wanted to see what my boat was like first. I thought that would give me some wiggle room. All I did was make her angry.

"Stubbornness is not a good quality, Ben. I think you're being too macho. I can help you."

"Believe me, I have nothing to be macho about, and there isn't anything I would do to hurt you." Then I stared at her for a moment and thought carefully about what I was going to say. "I've been out in the cold and hanging on the edge for a long time. You might be the best thing that has ever happened to me. I don't know if that's true, but I want to find out. But first you are going to have to trust me on this one. I am not going to put you in danger."

I think she knew there was no hope of arguing, so she wrapped her arms around me and stood for a minute squeezing me close to her. When she let go, I could see tears running down her cheek. I felt like a heel, but I knew I was right. She didn't say anything more and strode out of the building. As I watched her leave, I had the distinct feeling that there was more to her tears than just having me stay with her. I needed to find out what it was, but I wasn't going to put her in jeopardy to do it.

I left police headquarters, questioning my decision to not involve Jordan. As I drove, I looked in the rearview mirror. It wasn't my usual casual glance. I was paranoid now. Every car was a potential threat; every side street carried a risk. I decided then and there that I was doing the right thing. I couldn't bring this kind of tension into Jordan's life.

The only place left was my boat. If Easy had it restored to some semblance of usability, I would gut it out until I found my way through this mess. When I got to the marina, there were a few cars around, which surprised me. Usually there's not much doing in the boat business during the winter, except maintenance and dreams of big sales. I parked my car by a shed near the water and walked over to the marina office. No need to knock. The secretaries never came in during the winter.

I pushed the door open, walked inside, and spotted Easy at his corner desk.

"What's all the commotion outside, Easy? Having a two-for-one sale?" I asked.

Easy and his stomach were folded into a slatted, swivel desk chair behind a gray metal desk cluttered with greasy engine parts. He was staring out of a clouded window at the slush covering the marina parking lot. figured he must have been daydreaming about dollar bills falling from the warm skies of summer, because he looked startled when he saw me.

"Doc, where the hell you been?" he asked.

"Around. Why?"

"I tried everywhere to find you last night."

"You sound like you lost your best friend," I observed.

"Not that, it's your boat," he said solemnly.

"What about it?" My stomach suddenly fluttered with fear. After last night's fiasco . . .

Easy turned his right thumb downward.

"It sunk last night."

My voice somehow sounded calm. "How? I thought things were under control."

"Fire. Must have been some old wiring in the shore power cord. We tried to save her, but she went down too fast. Like a brick."

"Shit. Let me see it." I knew the electrical system hadn't been in great shape, but it hadn't been bad enough to burn. And I had recently had Easy work on it. Hell, I'd even had an alarm installed. Why hadn't it worked? Then I thought about my brake line. Maybe Terry Scotten was making good on his threat.

With the bubbler off, the ice was already starting to close in on the burnt-out wreckage of the *Judy D*. The *Judy D*, named after my ex, was now poised in the water with its bow submerged, ass-end mooning me. A fitting end to the last remnant of my marriage. "What happens now?" I asked.

"We wait until the ice thaws and haul it out. Trust me, Doc. There ain't much left of that boat worth salvaging. If I were you, I'd get on the phone with the insurance company. You got a payout?" he asked hopefully.

"Yeah, sure, but what they insured this tub for is a fraction of what another one would cost me," I said miserably.

I shuffled along toward Easy's truck, my head focused on the ground. Something glistening in the snow caught my eye. I bent down, picked it up, and looked at it. It was one of those drink stirrers. I looked at it closely. The inscription read "Plain View." My pulse quickened, and I started to sweat in spite of the cold. Terry Scotten was at it again.

Easy must have seen my reaction. "You okay, Doc?"

"Yeah, no big deal."

"No place to stay, huh?" he asked.

"Yeah, well, I'm all right for now."

"Listen, I got a room in the back. Use it when the old lady kicks me out of the house. Why don't you move in for a while 'til you get yourself back together?"

Frankly, I wasn't used to that kind of kindness from a guy who built in a twenty percent carrying charge on all of his bills. But under the circumstances it would have to do. "What about rent? I'm kind of short."

"Don't worry about that right now, okay?" He paused for a moment. "I kind of like the idea of having a doctor in my office."

Some doctor. Living like a vagrant with no home, working for peanuts for the government. I was pissed. I wanted to say no, I was okay, but I couldn't. Then I thought a moment about what Jordan had said. Stubbornness was a family trait with the Daileys. That's when Easy handed me the key.

CHAPTER 17

I CHECKED IN WITH SENNETT like he had asked. He seemed happy to hear from me. When I told him about finding the cocktail stirrer at the site of my burnt-out boat, his voice became excited.

"I don't know what it is about you, Doc, but you've got a nose for the news. You also have a way of attracting trouble. Jordan might be right. Maybe you should have police protection."

"Not yet, but I would like to check out Terry Scotten. It's just too much coincidence, with my car and now my boat. He said he was going to ruin me and he's certainly trying to keep his promise."

Sennett told me he was going to send some of his guys to the marina and then call Scotten. He said that maybe the two of us should take a road trip over to the Plain View and make a house call. That's when I told him he might be in the wrong profession. He laughed and said blood gave him the creeps.

After I hung up, I called the Farmington Brake Shop. My car was ready. I couldn't wait to get back in the comfort of my beast. When I got there, I paid the man with my credit card, hoping I would get money from Sanderson before it was due, and drove away.

On the way over I had decided to check out the two deaf men who were still alive. As soon as I left the garage, I headed back on the expressway to the Grand West Nursing home to see Jack Hazeltine. The facility was at the Grand River exit just before the site of the old Olympia Stadium. I used to go to the old barn and watch the Red Wings when I was a kid: Howe, Lindsay, Sawchuk. Ghosts from the past, following me. Then I remembered what Sennett had said about being vigilant.

The thought frightened me. I decided to see if there was anyone following me, so I stopped the car and watched the passing traffic. A car stopped about a hundred feet from me. I stared at it intently as it made a U-turn, circled into a KFC across the street, and stopped in the drive-thru to place an order.

Watching the car stand in line, I realized how annoyed I was getting with myself. This detective business was making me jumpy. I shook my head. *Forget it.*

I drove the Jeep for another half mile and stopped in front of a dilapidated two-story cement and brick building. The sign in front announced that I had arrived at the Grand West Nursing Home. As I climbed the steps, I noticed papers and beer cans littering the front of the building. The front door was rusted and creaked as I pulled it open and walked inside.

At the entranceway I stamped my shoes on the dirty brown and white tile floor that probably hadn't been cleaned in years. Then I looked up at the sign directing me to the reception desk. Below it was a flowery wooden plaque, proclaiming that the Grand West Nursing Home was a place of warmth and dignity. I wondered how long ago that sign had been placed on the wall.

I strode up to the reception desk. Behind it was a large African American woman in a scrub suit topped with a floral print cotton jacket.

"Nice touch," I said to the clerk behind the counter.

"What's a nice touch?" the woman asked, taking her glasses off and letting them dangle in front of her on a long gold chain.

"The sign over there," I replied, pointing behind me.

"Oh, that. It was the owner's idea. Got it from a Good Housekeeping article. He thought it would look nice up in front." She looked at me closely. "Now, what can I help you with?"

"I'm looking for Jack Hazeltine. Do you know where I could find him?" I asked.

"Last I saw him he was in the main dining area." She pointed down the hall to a large room filled with two dozen elderly people making a dinner out of Salisbury steak, canned peas and mashed potatoes.

I thanked her and made my way to the entrance. A muscular, dark youth with a close-shaven head stood near the door. His blue and white nametag identified him as William Stokes, Attendant. I figured him to be eighteen.

He eyed me carefully as I extended my hand. "I'm Dr. Dailey, Mr. Stokes. I'm here to see Mr. Hazeltine."

The youth pointed to a wizened African American man with receding gray hair sitting at the dining table.

"Won't get much out of him, doc. All he does is sit in his chair, rub the back of his head, and mumble things." William scratched his own massive, triple-ripple neck as he surveyed the room.

"What things?" I asked.

"Can't make it out. Like "Wing Gad" or something like that."

He laughed as if it was the biggest joke he had ever heard. Just then the man he had pointed at dropped his coffee cup. It rattled against the cement floor and broke.

The episode jolted Stokes into action. He went up to the old man and grabbed him by the collar. "You see what you gone and done, Mr. Hazeltine? You made a mess, and now I got to clean it up. That makes me mad, you understand my drift, Mr. Hazeltine?"

The venerable man knit his brows, terrified and silent, as he looked down at his plate. He seemed to know what was going to happen. Stokes reached under the wheelchair and brought out a leather strap.

"Now you know, Mr. Hazeltine, I don't want to go and strap you down, but rules are rules." With that he bound the unfortunate man's arms and legs and wheeled him out of the room, to sit down the hall.

Stokes returned to where I was standing. "Got to teach these folks the right manners, otherwise they take advantage of you, make you their slave."

I looked at the youth for a moment. The Grand West Nursing Center didn't look so grand anymore. "Did you ever consider that it was an accident?" I asked.

"Look, man, I put up with these old people's shit all day long. I clean up after them and feed them. So don't be telling me what's right or wrong." His coal-black eyes glowed with the hot anger of youth.

"I'm just telling you to cool it. They may be old, but they're still human beings." Looking at the size of his biceps, I wondered what part of his body did the thinking for him. "William," I continued, a little more softly, "think of it this way. What if that was you sitting in the wheelchair? Is that the way you'd like to be treated?"

"Don't be giving me that guilt trip shit, man," he blurted out.

"Tell you what, William, how about I call the authorities? Tell them you're abusing these poor old people. You lose a job and the problem is solved."

My simple logic got through to him. His weekly paycheck meant more to him than a clinical statement on the psychological treatment of nursing home patients. I could see him hesitate for a moment. Then he went over to the elderly man. Hazeltine seemed grateful as he was led back to the table and the straps were taken off.

William brought his food back and, like a grateful pet, Hazeltine looked up with a toothless smile. Even William seemed moved. The young attendant wasn't evil; nobody had ever taken the time to explain to him how to take care of a geriatric patient.

"Feels good, doing something nice, doesn't it?" I asked.

"Yeah, man, it did. It's just hard being the only one here and having to deal with everything by myself," he confessed.

"I understand, William. Tell you what. How about I make an anonymous complaint about understaffing here? No guarantee, but maybe it'll help. In the meantime, you hold down the fort. Deal?"

"Deal." He smiled when he said it.

"Say, William, you think Mr. Hazeltine would talk to me?" I asked.

"You can try, man. But I don't think he hears me all the time." I watched the old man as soup dribbled down his chin. From the calm expression on his face, he didn't seem to mind.

William and I walked over to Hazeltine. I looked around his head for hearing aid wires. There was nothing there.

"William, you got a chart on this man?" I asked. Hazeltine turned his head and looked up at me, smiling, as if he liked the attention.

"Sure, doc." He went to the front desk and brought back the black loose-leaf book that chronicled Jack Hazeltine's stay at Grand West Nursing Home. It seemed that Hazeltine, like Walter Trudeau, was alone in the world.

"Does he ever have any visitors, William?" I asked, leafing through the book.

"None that I've seen. But you might ask Mrs. Raymond at the desk. Maybe she knows something."

I thanked him and walked up to the desk. Before I could say anything to the clerk, she spoke. "I watched what happened in there. That was a nice thing you did for Mr. Hazeltine and for William. Nobody ever teaches us nothing. Just throws us in with the patients and expects us to act like trained caregivers. It's not fair."

"Maybe we'll do something about it." I waited a moment and then began again. "Say, you ever see any relatives of Mr. Hazeltine?"

"Not while I've been here. Leastwise not for several months. Last person to visit him was a nice young man from the state. Showed me some papers. Said they wanted to take him out for a while, do some hearing tests. He had a paper with all the right credentials, so we let him go. Mr. Hazeltine was gone for a short while and came back. He wasn't much different than when he left."

"What about his hearing aid? I didn't see it on him. Does he still have it?" I asked.

"I never paid much attention, to tell you the truth. The only possessions he had are locked up. Only Mrs. Richardson has access to it, and she's not here today. But I tell you, when he came here his hearing wasn't very important. He didn't talk anyway."

When I asked Mrs. Raymond how I could get a hold of the nurse, she said she was off for a couple of days. I thanked her and then turned toward the door. As I did, I looked back at Hazeltine sitting in his wheelchair. I knew it was time to call it quits on this investigation.

As I walked out the door and back to my car, I slipped and nearly fell again getting into my car. It reminded me of my brake line problem, so I checked my boots again. There was nothing on them.

In spite of that, after I started the car, I carefully popped the gear into drive and tested the brakes. When I felt them hold, I wheeled out of the parking spot and back onto the main drag. The traffic light changed to green, and I started slowly toward the entrance of the expressway just ahead. I kept looking in the rearview mirror. This time the road was empty. I was right. This detective business was making me jumpy.

CHAPTER 18

I WAS FRUSTRATED BUT I KNEW MYSELF. I wasn't a quitter. That's why I went back to the motel on Livernois Avenue across from the Clark gas station and three blocks off the Lodge Freeway to see Albert Henderson. There were two cars in the street side parking, the rest of the spots were unoccupied.

In among the overflowing plastic garbage bins that cluttered the curb, I found unit 1A, its rusty number barely hanging from the door. Compared to this place, the Lazy Isles was a palace.

I knocked several times on the door but got no response. I was about to leave when I saw the reflection of a television program in the small, dirty front window. I peered in and tried to look around. I thought I saw someone sitting in a chair, so I raised my hand and waved. He didn't see me. I rapped my knuckles hard against the window. Again, he didn't move. There was a faint beeping sound coming through the window. Why couldn't he hear it? He had an aid.

I stared at him, sitting motionless on the chair. Something was wrong, really wrong. I looked around and found a rock on the ground. I smashed the window. There was a crashing sound, then the rush of a nauseating odor, similar to rotten eggs.

An African American man, probably Albert Henderson, lay slumped, unconscious and barely breathing. The television was on and an alarm was blaring. In the corner on the right was a battered couch and chair, the upholstery stained and ripped. To the left a small yellow plastic table sat in the dining alcove, an empty pizza box resting on top. Behind was the kitchenette area, with a filthy, grease-spattered stove and a six-pack of longnecks waiting to be taken in for the refund. The window was too small for me to climb through. I tried the front door. It was locked tight.

Looking around, I saw the manager's office and raced toward it. It seemed like an eternity until the scarred, green metal door opened to my pounding. This time when the disheveled manager stuck his Grateful Dead belly out, he looked stoned. "Sorry, no vacancy, Mack," he slurred.

I shoved my foot inside the door. "Wait. I don't want a room. It's the guy in Unit 1A. There's something wrong with him. I need to get inside."

"What are you, the police?" he asked.

"No. I'm his doctor, and I need to get inside. Quickly," I yelled.

"I'm busy right now. I haven't got time for—"

Grabbing him by the vest, I pulled him outside and into the cold air. "Look," I screamed. "You may be tied up, but if you don't open that unit for me now, you're going to be a helluva lot worse." He was a small man, and in his condition, it didn't take much for me to pin him against the wall.

"Okay, okay. Let me get my—my keys," he stammered.

I didn't wait for him outside but walked in to make sure he hurried. The place was filthy and smelled of pot. There on the couch was an unclad woman in a toked-out stupor, trying to pull some clothes around her. The effort was pointless, we were already out the door.

The rotten egg smell was evident from outside Henderson's unit now, even as the manager unlocked the door and pushed it open. The alarm grew louder. I raced to Henderson's side.

"Open the back door and keep the front door open. It's a gas leak. Check the stove," I yelled at the manager.

Putting my hand next to Henderson's face, I could feel the warmth of his breath against my skin. Desperately my eyes searched for the phone, finally finding it behind some empties in the corner. I reached for it, hands fumbling, and shakily dialed 911. By this time the manager was over at the stove and turning it off.

"Left the burner on," the manager said. "Gas is flowing out of the thing. There's a warning buzzer. Why didn't he turn it off?"

I asked myself the same question. "He couldn't hear it. He's deaf," I yelled back. By this time the emergency line had answered. It didn't take long to give them instructions.

Dropping the phone, I went back to Henderson. He had stopped breathing. "Help me pull him to the door. He needs fresh air," I shouted again. No response, so I turned around and saw Mr. Deadhead gazing aimlessly at the ceiling, useless.

I dragged the limp body by myself toward the open door. The air might be cold, but it was clean. By this time sirens were wailing in the distance. I went back inside, got an old wool blanket from the man's bed, wrapped him up, and started mouth-to-mouth. Between breaths, I felt for his pulse. Nothing.

The EMS guys drove up just as I began beating on his chest. Jumping out of the truck, they rushed to the door with an oxygen tank and mask. Within seconds they had clamped a mask on his mouth and began squeezing oxygen into his lungs. While they worked, I knelt beside them and felt his pulse. It had started back. I told them about the gas leak.

By now the technicians had an IV started and a blood pressure cuff attached. One of them was talking into a headset and getting instructions.

"Pressure's low, but a pulse is present," he said to his partner. "Let's get him to St. Vincent's."

Something told me no. Maybe it was my distaste for the hospital that had betrayed me, or maybe it was only a subliminal reluctance to run into one of my ex-colleagues. Whatever it was, I shook my head.

"Take him to Samaritan," I ordered.

"Can't. Our instructions are to take him to the nearest hospital," the tech replied. He had pulled out the man's wallet and identified him as Albert Henderson.

"You're halfway between Samaritan and St. Vincent's. Take him to Samaritan," I said firmly.

The tech was a burly man who didn't appear to be used to taking orders from anyone, especially not a civilian. "Got to have a doctor's authority to do that. So unless you're an M.D., we're going to St. Vincent's."

"I'm a doctor." I pulled out my card.

The tech scrutinized it carefully. "This card is expired," the tech said quickly. "I haven't got time to screw around."

I stood in front of him, blocking his way. "I didn't replace it with the new one. Now unless you want a lawsuit, get moving to Samaritan."

He looked at me for a moment and then turned to his co-driver.

"Do what the man says. We're going to Samaritan." They had already lifted Henderson onto the stretcher and were getting ready to move him into the van. I waited until he was inside and the door had closed. Then I got back in my car to follow them. As I left, I noticed another car moving out of the parking lot. I couldn't wait to see who it was.

It took ten minutes in the snow to get to Samaritan. Luckily the storm had kept people off the streets. I was right behind them at the emergency room entrance as they jumped out and brought the stretcher in.

The mechanical doors cranked open as they wheeled the man into the emergency room. A smaller, private hospital, Samaritan had a good reputation. Size wasn't everything. Looking around, I could see that everyone was ready.

I was about to go back into the emergency unit with the techs when a nurse stopped me.

"You can't go back there," she ordered. I was getting sick of people telling me what to do.

"I'm this man's doctor, Benjamin Dailey. I was making a house call when I found him overcome by a gas leak. Now let me by to follow up on him," I said commandingly.

There was something magical in mentioning the word physician to medical personnel. She let me pass without another word.

When I got to the inside of the emergency center, they already had a pulse oximeter hooked up and the EKG leads on. But I didn't need electronic devices to tell me Henderson was still in trouble. One glance at his ashen color and shallowly rising chest told me he still wasn't breathing well. The ER physician standing at the bedside must have made the same deduction.

"Give me a six tube with a stylet," he shouted. He looked to be in his early thirties, and a little bit scared. I read the name "Nate Sheldon" on his ID badge as it dangled over Henderson's head.

The nurse complied, and the doctor pried open the man's mouth with his fingers. "Damn, he's anterior. I can't see anything."

I watched the EKG monitor above the bed. Henderson was beginning to exhibit erratic heartbeats, a bad sign in an oxygen-deprived individual.

I could see the sweat building up on the doctor's forehead as Henderson's pressure began dropping. Sheldon took another look with the intubation blade, coming back with the tube in his hand and no airway.

The nurse turned to him. "Dr. Sheldon, he's in bigeminy."

"Give him twenty milligrams of lidocaine IV, now," he shouted again.

I couldn't stand by any longer. "He needs his neck extended and his head flexed," I shouted.

Sheldon and the rest of his crew looked up, as if a king were being chastised by a commoner.

"Who are you?" he inquired, putting the mask back on Henderson's face in an effort to get more oxygen into him.

"Ben Dailey. I'm a head and neck surgeon and this man's doctor. Would you like me to make a pass?" I asked quickly.

Sheldon looked at the EKG and then down at the patient. He knew my way was the last chance. "What about the legal ramifications? You're not on the staff here."

"Let him die or worry about the legalities. That's your decision," I said plainly.

Sheldon stared once more at the patient, then at the EKG, and handed me the laryngoscope. I took off my jacket, quickly put on a pair of gloves, and stood at Henderson's head.

"Give me an IV bag to put under his neck," I said.

The nurse complied, and I flexed his head and extended his neck as I had described. "Put a straight blade on the laryngoscope and give me a six tube with a stylet," I directed, holding out my hand.

The nurse handed me the stainless-steel scope, and I bent it at right angles until the light engaged. "Now give me some pressure on the mid-portion of his neck." I pointed to just below the Adam's apple and Sheldon complied.

With the patient positioned, I opened his mouth with my fingers and then pointed the lighted blade of the laryngoscope down his throat. All I could see was mucous and blood from the previous attempts at intubation.

"Suction," I commanded.

The nurse gave me a plastic Yankauer suction to clear the airway. As I did, a noise clacked behind me. My eyes went quickly to the EKG. Henderson was now officially in supraventricular tachycardia.

"What's his pulse oximeter read?" I asked as I pried open his mouth again.

"Seventy-five percent saturation and going down," the nurse replied.

Shit. It was now or never. I had one last pass.

I picked up the laryngoscope again. This time I could see the tip of the epiglottis, the topmost portion of the voice box, coming into view.

"Give me a little more pressure, Dr. Sheldon," I said, trying to remain calm.

He pressed down harder. I still couldn't see anything. I was going to have to make a blind pass. I pushed the tube down past the epiglottis, felt a slight resistance, and then felt it go into the trachea.

"Hook him up to the vent now!" I commanded.

Sheldon attached him to the mechanical ventilator and pushed down on the metal lever. Henderson's chest immediately started to rise and fall, as Sheldon regularly forced high-pressure air through the tube. Soon I could see the supraventricular tachycardia easing. Within minutes Henderson's eyes fluttered open and he started moving his head.

The nurse stroked his forehead. "It's all right, Mr. Henderson, you're going to be all right."

"He can't hear you," I said gently. "He's deaf. Let him wake up a little more, and we'll write him a note."

By now he was responding to finger commands. His cardiogram had returned to sinus rhythm and his blood oxygen saturation was back to normal. He was also struggling to get the tube out of his throat.

There wasn't much more for me to do, so I got up to leave. I told the nurse that I would be back later. I walked past Sheldon. He was at the desk on the phone. When he saw me he smiled, and gave me the thumbs up sign.

I went down to the cafeteria and decided to wait. I knew what had happened wasn't about me, it was about saving a man's life. But regardless, I had an intense feeling of elation, of pride. I could still do it; I could still be a doctor. I knew I would never let that feeling leave me again.

CHAPTER 19

A COUPLE OF HOURS PASSED before Henderson was fully awake and extubated. While I waited, I called Sennett and told him what had happened. He had Knudsen pull up the EMS information. He told me to call him back in a few minutes. When I did, he told me he had reviewed the incident report. The fire department called it an accident and nothing else. When I said it looked suspicious, he said he'd look into it, but he sounded annoyed, like I should be concentrating on trying to stay alive and not meddling in his business. I was never a good listener.

I hung the phone up and went back into the room. Henderson was awake now, watching the nurse fuss with his IV. I sat down next to him and picked up a yellow legal pad. He couldn't hear, so I wrote a note asking him what had become of his hearing aid.

He looked distressed and scribbled quickly that he couldn't find the control. I didn't know what he meant. There was nothing on his ear or in his ear canal that even resembled a hearing aid. He went on to explain that his hearing aid was deep inside his ear.

"He's been writing me since he woke up, wondering if someone could look in his ear and see if the hearing aid was still there," the nurse said.

I told her I would be glad to examine his ear and asked her if she had an otoscope. She looked at me a little funny, but I showed her my badge. When she saw it was from Great Lakes, she hesitated for a moment, deciding what to do, and then left the room. She returned with a Welch Allyn scope in a black case and a look of consternation on her face.

"Make sure you drop it off at the desk when you're done. My supervisor watches this equipment like a hawk," she said with a little edge to her voice.

I reassured her that I would return it, then took the scope out. It was a standard instrument with a magnifying lens and a light source. On the end was a small plastic tip to insert into the ear. I placed the tip into Henderson's ear, looked down the ear canal, and saw a small object. It was something I had never seen before. White mesh surrounded a small, circular device. I wrote Henderson what I found and he smiled. Then he wrote back that it was the one Dr. Pennington had put in. He said that without the control to adjust the sound it was useless.

The only hearing aids I had seen were relatively large, either behind the ear or in the ear canal. I had never seen a hearing aid like this one before. One thing was certain: it was not a cochlear implant. This was a completely different instrument.

I asked Henderson if he knew where I could find out more about it. He wrote down the word "computer." I excused myself and went out to the nurse's station to ask where I could log on.

The clerk suggested I go to the hospital library and directed me to the first floor of the hospital. When I got there, I told the librarian what I was looking for. "I'll need some key words," she said. We decided on the words "canal," "tympanic membrane," and "hearing aid." She worked over her computer for ten minutes and came back with three color reprints of articles from the internet on a new hearing aid called The Sonic.

According to the studies, these aids produced a whole new level of amplification, far better than conventional hearing aids. The amplification unit was placed directly into the ear canal, about four millimeters from the ear drum. If you could believe the reports, these hearing aids were a step up in terms of delivering sound to the ear.

I spent some time looking at the photographs of the aid. It was a small disc, red for the right ear and blue for the left. Around each aid was white mesh. I remembered looking at Henderson's aid. There was something distinctly different about it.

I took the articles with me and went back to Henderson's room. He was sitting up in his bed eating lunch. As far as I could tell, he was showing no ill effects from his near-death experience.

I picked up the otoscope and pointed to his ear for his permission to look. He put his fork down and nodded. This time when I looked down the canal, I studied the small disc in the ear more carefully. When I was done, I picked up the colored article. Henderson's aid was different, and I saw why: it was green.

Could it have been a mistake? I doubted it—Pennington was too much of a perfectionist for that. Why was it a different color? I decided I needed to look at it outside of the ear. I reached for the case that held the otoscope and found what I needed inside, a small alligator forcep. I took it out, put the otoscope back in Henderson's ear, and carefully reached in. I placed the jaws of the forceps on the white cloth-like material, and pulled gently. Slowly, the entire apparatus slid out of the canal.

I placed it on the table next to Henderson's bed and looked at it closely. There was something etched on the surface, but I couldn't make it out. I picked up the otoscope and took off the magnifying lens.

Looking through it closely, I could read the letters "SVH." It took me a moment to remember before I recognized it as the same letters that I had seen on Pennington's charts at Great Lakes.

I looked at Henderson, who studied the small metal object carefully. He reached over to the yellow pad, picked up his pen, and asked me what I thought. I showed him the reprints and pointed to the two different colors. He quickly noticed that there was also a difference in the shape. The red and blue versions were round, while the green one was oval. Albert Henderson was nobody's fool.

I asked him if I could take the aid with me so I could look it over more carefully. He wondered what I was looking for, and I told him I wanted a friend to check out how it worked.

He mulled it over for a few moments then nodded. *Promise you'll bring it back*, he wrote. I told him I would as long as he stayed out of trouble. He smiled, and we shook hands. I wrapped the aid in a napkin and put it in my jacket. When I got to the first floor, I stopped at a pay phone and dialed a number. I got Frank Scotten on the second ring.

Chapter 20

I THINK FRANK WAS SURPRISED TO HEAR FROM ME, based on our last meeting. I have to admit I was surprised I called him, but when it comes to acoustical engineers, my network is small. Besides, I figured that he had started me on this bullshit, he might as well finish it.

I decided to meet him at the Pipeline, on my turf and on my terms. I told Charlie there was a guy coming over to see me and said there might be some trouble. Charlie, a former Navy Seal, told me he had a couple of thumb screws behind the counter and not to worry. Somehow it didn't make me feel any better.

Frank Scotten showed up around nine o'clock. I was sitting at a corner table looking at the entrance. Like Wild Bill Hickock, I had decided to never turn my back on the door.

Scotten was wearing a sheepskin jacket pulled up at the collar and a navy blue watch cap. He came over to the table and sat down. We didn't shake hands. He took off his jacket and cap and looked around.

"A lot different than the Plain View," he commented casually.

"Not really. They've got entertainment here just like you do and . . . see that guy behind the bar?

Scotten looked over at Charlie.

"Unlike your father's boys, Charlie spent a tour in Kuwait during the Gulf War. He was with the Navy Seals. When they wanted something done, they called in Charlie. You know what I mean?"

Scotten looked both contrite and a little paler than I remembered him from the bar. "Listen, I had no idea my old man was going to be there. He was supposed to be at some fund raiser for the airport supervisor."

"Yeah, well if it's brown and soft and smells like shit, it must be shit, Frank, so cut the crap and tell me the truth, because, honestly, I don't have time for your academic runaround on high voltage electric energy and brain damage."

Frank stared ahead, looking like a kid caught in the cookie jar. By this time, Charlie had come over to the table and set a Labatt Blue in front of me. As he did, he glanced at Frank with his huge arms folded in front of him, showing off his "*Kill or Be Killed*" tattoo. "Anything for your friend?" he growled. Frank shook his head.

"Mr. Scotten and I are just going to have a little conversation, Charlie. Thanks."

I took a pull at the bottle and waited a moment. Then I explained about my car and boat. I told him if he had anything to do with this, I would follow him to his grave. Big talk from a guy with nothing, but I figured it might flush him out. Then I added, "Whatever your father thinks of me and whatever he thinks I did to your brother, you can tell him that hate and revenge are useless emotions. In the long run, no one cares."

"I tried to tell him a hundred times but it's no use. He can't let it go."

"Well, I don't want any part of it. Whatever the courts decided and however the hospital responded, it's done. I've moved on. Just tell him it's going to take more than a couple of punks to take care of me." I figured sounding tough was better than the truth.

"I'm sorry. Hate has a way of destroying someone. He can't tell the difference between his own anger and the loss of Jimmy. He has displaced everything on you."

"Well, that gives me a warm and fuzzy feeling, if you know what I mean." I explained my near-death experience on the expressway and the knife attack. Then I mentioned the fire that destroyed my boat and finding the drink stirrer in the snow.

"I just can't believe that he would do something like that."

"Who else would have a reason?"

Sid had just sat down with the boys and was playing "Take the A-train," Billy Strahorn's composition on a ride to Harlem. I wondered how Duke would have felt about his song being played by a trio instead of a big band. I thought it sounded great.

He shook his head. "I know my father. He would never do something like that."

I ignored his comment and told him about Albert Henderson and his hearing aid. The moment I mentioned it, his attention seemed to become sharper. He started asking me questions about the size of the aid and how it performed. When I told him the patient said it was like a miracle he edged closer to the table. When I told him I had the aid, I thought his eyes were going to pop out of his head.

"You do?" he asked excitedly.

That's when I extracted Henderson's aid from my pocket and handed it to him. He opened up the paper napkin and studied the device carefully, like a jeweler examining a diamond.

After a moment, I asked him if he had any idea what "SVH" stood for. He shook his head distractedly.

"Do you mind if I take this and test it in my lab in Ann Arbor?" he asked. "I might be able to tell you more about it. You know, circuitry, construction, that kind of thing."

"I don't want to sound ignorant, but we doctors don't really study how these things work."

"Don't feel stupid. Most doctors aren't into electronics. In theory, the hearing aid is really quite simple. It collects sound and delivers it close to the ear. Remember the old ear trumpets?" he asked. I nodded. "It's the same idea. The hearing aid captures sound waves and delivers them directly to the eardrum. In a modern hearing aid, there are three basic parts: the receiver that brings the sound in, the amplifier that boosts the decibels, or loudness, and the microphone that produces a sound to the ear."

I stared at Albert Henderson's aid. "Pretty small to do all that."

He smiled and went on to say that everything was miniature, with microchips and pre-wiring. "There are three different principles to an aid: the gain, the decibel slope, and the output. The gain is the part that magnifies the sound's presence. The slope filters out certain frequencies and lets some pitches through while keeping others out. The output is what eventually reaches the ear."

"It seems to me you would want to make the gain and the output as high as possible," I said.

"In theory, yes, but in reality it doesn't work that way," he explained. "The best that current aids can get is seventy-three decibels. Beyond that, the sound made the bone in the skull vibrate, which was something the average person couldn't tolerate. If someone could get the gain between eighty and eight-five decibels without doing that, he would make a major advancement and have a huge leg up on the competition. With patents, he could be in the driver's seat for years. Think of it this way: an aid like that would revolutionize the hearing aid business. Imagine being able to bring that much sound directly to the ear."

I told him that five patients might have had this hearing aid. I asked if he could somehow test it and see if it produced something different than a normal aid. His eyes lit up like a kid who was told he could go to Disney World. "Could I? For sure! Meet me in my lab in Ann Arbor tomorrow afternoon around five o'clock. Then we'll see what this baby can do."

CHAPTER 21

AFTER SCOTTEN LEFT, I CALLED JORDAN to tell her I was okay. She didn't press me about staying at her place, and I didn't offer any more information. She sounded irritated with me.

From the Pipeline I went back to Easy's place and bunked down for the night. The mattress was hard and the room was cold, but for some reason I slept like a log. I think the fact that no one knew where I was made me less anxious.

The next morning, I showered and shaved in Easy's marina. Because it was winter, I had the place to myself. By the time I was done, I looked in the mirror and somehow felt half presentable.

I drove to the diner down the street and had the two-dollar breakfast special. When I stepped outside, I could feel the wind blowing from the northeast, usually a sign of bad weather. About five minutes later, a light snow began falling. I stopped at a gas station and refueled my beast, then made for the payphone inside. George Sennett answered on the second ring. I told him I had spoken with Frank Scotten and wanted to visit his lab. He suggested that we meet in an hour. I looked in the rearview mirror. No one was following me.

By the time I reached police headquarters, the snow was coming down heavily. Sennett was in his office, looking over some papers and munching on a package of peanuts. With his reading glasses on, he looked like a college professor that specialized in football.

It took me a few minutes to explain what had happened the night before. It seemed like another thirty seconds before Sennett responded. "I don't know, Doc, you're making me nervous. Every time you dig up something it has trouble written all over it. I've seen it before."

"Yeah, where, on television?"

"Nah, I don't watch that stuff. It makes me nervous, like it's going to happen to me. By the way, a couple of the boys went over to Henderson's place after the EMS left. I thought you might be interested in the report."

He reached for some papers on his desk and handed it to me. I read it over carefully. It indicated that Albert Henderson lived like a vagrant. There were beer bottles and pizza boxes along with some old newspapers. On the stove was a pot with some beans in it. They were burnt and caked inside. Sennett said the crime scene guys felt the pot, and it was still warm.

"Looks like your man just left the stove on too long," he said.

I thought for a moment. "Kind of like the knife attack at the hospital. Something happens and nobody knows why."

"Kinda. We never found any evidence at the crime scene. No leads, no witnesses. Right now it's a dead end." As he finished speaking, he popped a few more peanuts in his mouth. The muscles in his jaws stood out as he pulverized them.

"Peanuts?"

"Huh?"

"You're eating peanuts."

"You bet. One of the five main food groups. It's high in protein."

"Funny, the way you're grinding on them I'd think there was another purpose."

He laughed for a second as he put Henderson's papers away. "Yeah, it's good stress relief." His face turned serious. "What made you go to Henderson's place?"

"I just felt there was something wrong with these five cases that I looked up at Great Lakes. After finding that bullet at Ralph Gernowski's house, I had a hunch there might be a pattern."

"You've just passed Police 101. Follow the evidence and listen to your feelings. I'm thinking you might have a talent for this."

"I suppose it's not much different than being a doctor. Keep digging 'til you find something." I suddenly realized that there was something ironic to that fact, and it was a little unsettling. Then I looked at Sennett's badge, the commendations on his wall, and the shoulder holster lying on his desk. It didn't take much self-convincing to realize I was out of my league.

Yet I wasn't dumb, and I didn't lack motivation. What did Sennett say, follow the evidence? That's when I explained about the hearing aid, and the meeting at Frank Scotten's lab.

Just as I finished, Sennett's cell phone buzzed. He answered it, listened, and then frowned; his heavy eyebrows tensed in furrows above his eyes. He flipped his cell phone closed, popped some more nuts in his mouth, and began chewing, this time a little more vigorously, enough so that the muscle of his jaw seemed to ripple under the skin of his face. "They found Ralph Gernowski down at the old Great Lakes Steel plant. He was dead. The crime scene guys are down there."

I was about to say something when there was a knock on the door and a "do you mind if I come in" sound from a feminine voice. I turned and there was Jordan. I felt a little sheepish, but there was no hint of anger on her face. "George told me I should come down. He said you wanted to go visit Frank Scotten."

I explained what had happened with Henderson and the hearing aid I found. Then I opened my big mouth and finished by telling her I didn't think it was a good idea for her to come, that I was exposing her to danger. As soon as I spoke, I realized I had said the wrong thing.

"Someday, Ben, you're going to realize that you cannot protect everyone. That includes me. In case you didn't understand, this is my job."

I looked over at Sennett for help. He shrugged his shoulders, as if to say, "She's right, bro."

"I stand corrected," I said. "We're going up to Ann Arbor to visit Frank Scotten at his lab." I went on to explain what I knew about the hearing aid.

"After what you told me it seems strange that you and Scotten are working together," Jordan said.

"Let's just say Frank and I had a heart to heart," I replied, pulling the keys out of my pocket. "We better get cracking, because this is going to be a hell of a trip."

Looking back, I should have said you would have to be out of your mind to travel on a day like that. By the time we left Sennett's office and stepped outside, the snow was already over our ankles. Snow trucks were on the streets, but it was clear that so far they were fighting a losing battle.

We piled into my Grand Wagoneer, with Jordan in the front and Sennett in the back. I fired up the heater, put the defroster on full, and pulled into the street and toward the expressway. I didn't check the rearview mirror. There was no way anyone in their right mind would be out tonight.

If there was one saving grace about driving in Detroit, it was that the economy had cut down the traffic. Instead of a convoy of slowly moving cars, there were only a few brave souls and a bunch of trucks moving down I-94 to Ann Arbor. I pulled behind one of the trucks, staying about a hundred feet behind to avoid the steady stream of snow coming off his tires. In spite of the convoy in front of my Jeep, I could feel my tires bouncing off ruts of deep snow. About halfway to Ann Arbor, ice started building up on my windshield, and I began to question my decision making. I stopped a couple of times to scrape the windshield off. By the time I got back in the car, my hands were frozen.

If all of this bothered Sennett or Jordan, they didn't show it. I heard Sennett crunching on his second bag of peanuts in the back seat. Jordan, for her part, kept texting on her cell phone.

The normal forty-five minute drive took us two hours. At about the time I swung onto the US-23 exit it was already getting dark. I made my way down Stadium and onto Washtenaw, moving slowly toward the main campus. It was close to eight o'clock by the time we made it to the Engineering School.

I parked in a campus parking space, figuring no one would be out. Besides, I was with the police. We had no sooner pushed our way out of the car that the snow, which was now blowing horizontal to ground, started to sting us in the face. I pulled the collar up on my jacket and looked over at Jordan. She had her scarf wrapped over her mouth and nose. Her body was bent against the wind as she trudged toward the building. Sennett, for his part, looked miserable. I guess when you live in the South all your life, you never get used to this kind of weather.

We made it to the front door, pulled it open, and stepped inside the modern steel and brick building. The lobby was empty. I got the feeling that only a fool would be out on a night like this. Sennett stamped his boots on the marble floor, trying to shake the cold out of his feet. He looked over at me as if we were both crazy. Maybe we were.

The directory said Scotten's lab was on the third floor. We went to the elevator and stood around, waiting for it to come. While we waited, I heard the entrance door slam behind us. In the shadow of the outside light I saw the hulk of a large man in a great coat walk in behind us. I couldn't see his face, but his presence made me uneasy.

I didn't say anything to Sennett or Jordan, but I placed myself between them and the man. When I glanced at him from the corner of my eye, I saw that he had opened his coat. I stood mesmerized as he started to pull out what looked like a round piece of pipe.

That was it. I turned and tackled Sennett and Jordan to the floor. As I did, a shot ricocheted off the cement wall, exploding shards of concrete. I heard Sennett grunt as I rolled to the right just as the next round hit the floor. The door to the elevator opened, and I shoved Jordan inside. There was a fire alarm in the elevator. I pulled it down to stop the elevator and rolled back into the lobby.

As I did, I heard Sennett yelling something. I looked over at him. Blood was running down his forehead. By this time he had his gun out and fired two shots that exploded the front entrance window, the man in the coat had already left.

I CHECKED ON JORDAN—SHE WAS ON HER FEET and looking for help. Then I looked at Sennett. The blood that was dripping down his face came from a small cut on his forehead. He was bitching like hell, but he seemed all right. I heard the shriek of fire engines in the distance.

As soon as I saw they were all right, I rushed out of the entrance hall and up the stairs, taking the steps two at a time. I was seriously out of breath by the time I got to the third floor. I raced down the corridor and found the light in Frank Scotten's lab shining through the door window. I looked in and saw him standing in front of a work bench, apparently oblivious to everything that had just happened. In front of him were a number of electronic instruments.

I jerked the door open and rushed toward him. When he heard the noise, he turned around, appearing startled at the sound. In two seconds, I was on him. I grabbed him by his lab coat and slammed him against the wall. He grunted, and I could hear the air rush out of him.

"Okay," I yelled, "tell me why you set us up and tell me now!"

He just shook his head as if he didn't understand. "I didn't do anything. What happened?" he gasped.

"Don't give me that bullshit, Frankie, or I'll beat it out of you."

I was about to give him my best roundhouse, when I heard Jordan shouting. "Ben, don't hit him!"

I tried stopping in mid-swing, but the momentum carried my fist a few inches from Frank's nose. There was no mistaking the fear in his eyes.

I looked at Jordan. She was standing in the doorway. A firefighter was with her. He peeked in and, when he saw there was no problem for him, continued to walk down the hallway.

"What happened to George?" I asked, still raging inside.

"He's seems all right," Jordan said, her voice still a little shaky. "They said there was a small laceration on the scalp."

"You know this was a set up, Jordan." I pointed my finger at Scotten. "We almost got killed because of his old man."

"Wait a minute. What happened?" Scotten asked. Jordan explained the shooting, and Frank looked genuinely shocked. He claimed he neither knew nor heard anything. Then he asked me why he would set me up while he was in the lab trying to find out what was inside the hearing aid. I didn't have a good answer. When Jordan agreed, I backed off.

As I began to cool down, Scotten seemed to relax. Oddly, he seemed unconcerned about my accusations. Instead of pursuing the conversation about what had happened, he began to talk excitedly about Albert Henderson's hearing aid. He said he had some equipment in his lab that he was using for research on acoustic emissions in outer space. He had taken Henderson's aid and hooked it up to a large, green, oblong-shaped instrument with the name Madsen on the outside. "I wanted to check the results against the specs of other hearing aids. There's nothing like this aid in the world."

When I asked him how he proved it, he said he used a Real Energy Analyzer. He called it a Madsen HT 200 with a 2 cc coupler, a device that measures the pure tone and white noise levels of the aid, covering frequencies between 20 and 20,000 hertz. That's about everything the human ear can handle.

"Unbelievable!" he said. "I've never seen such a gain come out of a hearing aid." But he cautioned that there was a big jump from a lab experiment to producing a usable hearing device.

"There was something else," he said, fiddling with Henderson's aid, which was sitting on the worktable. "I noticed on the screen some peculiarities that you'd have to get rid of."

"Like what?" I asked.

"You'd have to get some kind of filter in the system."

"Why's that? I thought sound was sound."

"There was a peculiar surge in the high frequencies when I was testing the aid at 20,000 hertz and over. I'm sure it has to do with the crude way we hooked it up." Frank pulled out a piece of paper from his pocket and showed me the graphs he had traced from his readings.

"What effect would such a surge have?"

"Probably nothing. The human ear can't perceive it, so I suspect it's of academic interest only. It certainly wouldn't be a major stumbling block to developing the product." He handed the graphs to me.

"What do you make of all this?" I asked.

"I think Jimmy was on to something. I don't know what, but he was."

By this time the police had come into the building and made their way up to Frank's lab. We spent a half-hour talking to them, then we went downstairs. Sennett was sitting on a chair, holding a pad against his forehead. He was arguing with the firefighters, telling them he didn't have to go to the hospital. Thankfully, they didn't listen to him. Instead, they put him in an ambulance, and Jordan and I followed them to the hospital. By the time we parked the car and reached the emergency room, Sennett was on a gurney.

"How many stitches?" I asked, as the emergency room doc finished putting the last 5-O nylon into the jagged cut in the hairline.

"Enough to close it," he said nonchalantly.

"I was hoping for a little change, like maybe Jamie Foxx or Samuel L. Jackson," Sennett said under the drapes.

I suggested Freddie Kreuger, but he didn't laugh. As I spoke, I looked outside into the blizzard through the doors of the emergency room. The snow was coming down in waves.

"I hope you're not planning on going anywhere," Sennett said.

"Yeah, we're going find a hotel. You want to come, lieutenant?" Jordan said.

"I can't. The cops are waiting to talk with me, and the doctor here wants me to have an x-ray. I could be here for a couple of hours. Are you sure you want to take your car out in this blizzard?"

"That's for ordinary cars. I've got a four-wheel beast that eats snow for dinner. We can make it back easily."

Sennett almost jumped out of the gurney. "Are you crazy? I wouldn't care what kind of car you got. A night like this is death. It's zero visibility. I heard the state police have already closed the expressway from Ann Arbor to Detroit." I looked at Jordan and shrugged. I could think of worse things than to be trapped there with her.

"Any suggestions?" I said.

Sennett thought for a moment, then answered. "There's a Marriott Courtyard up the street. It's your best bet. The ones along the expressway are filled with stranded motorists. But I wouldn't waste any time." If he was thinking anything about the two of us spending the night together, he didn't show it.

I decided to change the subject. "Lieutenant, when we were in the building and the shots rang out, I heard you yelling something. Who were you yelling at?"

"Myself. I was complaining."

"About what?"

He smiled ruefully. "They say that God lets the people who complain the most live the longest."

"I didn't know you were a religious man."

"I am when my safety locks and someone is trying to kill me." He said it with the nervous laugh of a survivor.

I looked at Jordan, feeling protective and scared at the same time. If she was upset, her business-as-usual face didn't show it. She started putting on her coat just as Sennett put his huge paw on my shoulder.

He stared intently at me, as if what he had to say was important. "By the way, doc, I owe you." It was a simple statement of appreciation, but the way he spoke the words seemed ominous, like he might actually pay me back. He didn't say anything else, as the orderly pushed the gurney down to x-ray. I had the feeling he didn't say those words very often.

JORDAN AND I STOOD AT THE DOOR for a moment, then she grabbed my arm and led me out of the emergency room. We high-stepped through the snow to the car and got in. I started the engine and then looked over at her. Before I could say anything, she reached across the console held my face in her hands and kissed me on the cheek. "Thanks, I owe you too."

I could feel my face turning red. "I'm just thankful that Sennett didn't show his appreciation the same way." She laughed.

"Is the Marriott okay?" I asked.

She nodded, accepting the fact that driving back to Detroit was out of the question. It took us an hour, but somehow we made it to the motel. I figured the place would be empty. Instead they had only one room left, with one queen-sized bed. What was I going to do?

Don't get me wrong. I would love to go to bed with Jordan. I just didn't want it to be some forced, awkward deal like this. But who was I kidding? It had been so long since I had been with someone that I cared for, I couldn't remember the feeling. I think I was just nervous.

Jordan merely laughed. I think she enjoyed my discomfort.

"It's all right, Ben," she said standing at the counter. "It's a place to hole up for the night."

Jordan paid the sixty-seven fifty for the room. Another expense to tack onto the taxpayer's tab. When I saw the room, I figured no one would accuse us of living high off the hog at the government's expense. It was plastic heaven, but, compared to the Lazy Isles, the room was a palace. Even the towels matched.

We were trapped by the weather. Nothing to do but make the best of it. She suggested we get something to eat and said she would put it on her expense account.

It was eight o'clock by the time we walked over to the adjacent restaurant, no small feat in view of the weather. A foot of new snow lay on the ground and more was falling.

The place was called the Blue Man's Inn, a piano bar dedicated to my local football team and their favorite colors, Maize and Blue. I had been there many times as a student. The restaurant was campus-chic with photos of present and past players and coaches and tables carved with the names of the thousands of visitors that had been there. If you looked closely, you could have even seen my face in one of the team pictures. We sat down at a booth near a window festooned with a banner that displayed the words, "Champions of the West" in bright yellow against a blue background.

Once seated, I looked around. Surprisingly, there were still people sitting in the room. Most of them were near the bar, staring at the Weather Channel. Jordan spent a couple of minutes searching through the laminated menu without making up her mind.

By this time the waitress came over. She was tall and lean, with a face wrinkled by too many cigarettes and dulled by too many one-night stands.

"If you're looking for health food here, forget it. Everyone has to get the Champion Burger once in their life," she said mechanically.

I nodded in agreement. "Jordan, I know this will sound odd coming from a doctor, but I have this theory."

"What's that?" she asked.

"When it comes to food, no sugar, no fat, no taste."

She laughed and ordered the burger along with curly fries and a chocolate malt. I said make it two. The waitress smiled crookedly as she walked away, seemingly satisfied with the knowledge that she had converted someone else to the dark side.

"Now that takes me back to college," Jordan said.

As it turned out, the food was great but eating was a side issue. Jordan wanted to talk, and I didn't mind listening.

"You know, I had been engaged at one time."

"What happened?"

"His name was Matt Forester. He was a special agent with the FBI. I convinced him to take me with him on a stakeout on the Miami waterfront, going after a bunch of Cuban drug runners. I got caught in a crossfire, and he came back to get me. That's when they shot him. He died in my arms before EMS could get there." Her face was still, almost plastic. The only trace of emotion was the tear at the corner of her eye.

"You still miss him, don't you?"

She nodded. "It's the memory. The way he died. The things I never got to say to him." Then she stopped for a moment. "Matt tried to protect me, the same way you did tonight. If you hadn't, I'd be dead, just like Matt."

I didn't know what to say, so I said nothing. The conversation slowed, as if it were my turn to open up. I looked around for a moment to gauge what to say next. I cursed myself for my cowardice and asked her if she wanted a nightcap. She seemed to like the idea.

The bar was getting more crowded, probably on the theory that if you couldn't leave you might as well drink. We went in, sat down at a table near the entrance, and ordered a couple of Black Russians. In the corner, Jordan noticed a small piano that no one was playing.

"Why don't you play, Ben?" she encouraged me. "I'm sure no one would mind."

I was feeling uncomfortable sitting there, and the piano would be a perfect excuse not to talk about myself. "I'm not an exhibitionist. Maybe these folks don't want to hear."

"The hell with them," she said with a laugh. "Good jazz plays anywhere."

What did I have to lose? Play for a few minutes, and avoid delving into my past. I went over to the chipped, black Yamaha. A few scornful glances from the people in the bar revealed their assessment of this unscheduled amateur night. I sat down and played anyway.

For whatever reason, that night I was in the zone. Oscar Peterson, Brubeck, Horace Silver, and a little rock and roll. It was all there. And as I played, the crowd grew too. Word must have spread through the motel that there was something more than snow falling outside. After an hour there were over a hundred people crowded into the little room. And the drinks were flowing.

I didn't notice. I wasn't the filler man anymore. I was the main act, and it felt good. People clapping, handing me drinks from the bar. By the time two o'clock came around I had a big time Black Russian/three martini buzz and the fading glow of an endorphin rush. That's when the bartender told me they had to close.

Swinging my legs from under the piano, I thought I was feeling good. That was until I stood up and felt the room swaying. As I started slowly toward the door, I saw Jordan in the corner, smiling.

"Not bad," she said, coming up to me and slipping her arm through mine. "You had the place hopping."

"Yeah, well they were a sympathetic crowd," I said, slurring my words slightly. "Listen, I'm beat. If you want me to stay down here in the lobby, it's all right, I'll just . . ."

"It's the new millennium, Ben, remember. Sharing the same room, it's no big deal." I nodded solemnly, as if I understood what the hell she meant. I didn't have to wait long for my confusion to catch up.

I guessed she saw I wasn't steady on my feet, because she guided me to the front of the restaurant with her chest pressed close to me. We walked out the door and back to the motel. My mind was whirling, intoxicated by the booze and by the beautiful woman next to me. Even in my state, I said to myself, *Old fool, making like a stud walking up to a motel room with a hot chick like this. Who are you kidding?*

But like a lot of things that had happened to me, it was too late—my real brain was in charge.

We reached the second floor. The elevator door opened, and it seemed like forever until we negotiated our way to the room. A balding man in corduroys and hush puppies walked past us with an ice bucket and a leering gaze. Strangely, the look made me feel proud.

I fumbled for the key, opened the door, and walked inside. There was an awkward moment. What would a real lady like Jordan want with an older guy? She touched my sleeve and paused. I was helpless. I reached out and suddenly her mouth was on mine exploring, probing. I felt like a player in a distant drama, drunkenness, fatigue, and excitement intermingled.

My hand trembled as it slid under her sweater, touching her breasts and feeling her firm nipples. I tried to one-hand her bra hook, while she pressed herself close against me. Fuck. It wouldn't open.

Jordan laughed. "You need more work on your hand-eye coordination." As she said it, she reached behind her and quickly undid the clasp.

I could feel my face redden.

"No, I . . . I just didn't want you to get the wrong impression," I stammered, feeling weak and strong at the same time.

"I think I have the right impression." As she said it, she impishly rubbed her hand against me. My little head nodded its approval.

She slipped out of her sweater and then took off her dress, throwing it on the chair next to the bed, and stood in front of me wearing only a red thong. The vision of her naked body with uplifted breasts pointing directly at my face drifted in and out of my consciousness. I couldn't be sure if it was the alcohol or her presence that had intoxicated me.

She loosened my belt and unzipped my pants. I heard the belt buckle ring off the bedpost contrapuntal to the rapid beating of my heart. Putting my arms around her, I pressed her to me, and we fell across the bed. I remember gazing up at the ceiling, the alcohol, the piano playing, and Jordan, all whirling around dizzily in my mind. A kind of manmade torture, a dream of reality. I closed my eyes for just a second, a futile attempt to get organized.

The next thing I knew, I was slowly becoming aware of lights in my eyes. I had a vague memory of a naked body undulating against me, a soothing hand against my chest, and then a warm kiss on my lips. I blinked again.

The lights were on, and Jordan was already dressed. That's when I realized it. I'd had the most gorgeous woman in the city alone in a motel room, and I'd passed out. I could hear Sid and Charlie howling now: *"Ain't that the doc? Loose as a goose . . . damn, bro, lock up your women!"*

I got up from the chair. My head was pounding. "Did I make a fool out of myself last night?" I croaked groggily.

"Not really," she replied. "Everyone really liked the Jerry Lee Lewis routine. You even have his kind of voice. When you took your shoes off and started playing with your feet, that really got them going."

"Oh, shit," I said, feeling my face get red. "Anything else?"

"A little snoring, and you kept mumbling Judy D, or something like that." As she spoke, she brushed her hair in front of the mirror.

"My boat. The one that sank. No, I mean was there anything else?"

"You mean, like, did we get it on?"

I nodded sheepishly.

"Well, I have a smile on my face. Does that mean something?"

"It depends on what you're smiling at," I said with a trace of anxiety.

"Don't worry about your masculinity, Ben. You were fantastic." As she said it, she playfully poked me in the ribs.

"That's a relief. You wouldn't want to reenact the encounter, would you? Then I could find the real me." She laughed, but not enough to say yes.

"It's still snowing, and I need to get back to Detroit." By now she looked perfect, nothing out of place, hair brushed back and lipstick flawless. How did women do that? When I was dressed, she came over to me.

I finished tucking my shirt into my pants. She moved over from the mirror and stood in front of me, putting her arms around my neck and kissing me long and softly. I think she felt me getting excited again, because she backed off just enough so that I couldn't feel her.

"Not now, Ben. Maybe another time." Maybe another time? Who was she kidding? I didn't want "maybe another time." I wanted tonight, Saturday afternoon, Sunday evening. In the car, on her couch, in her bed. But I was too proud to beg, so I changed the subject. "Do you think the library would be open?" I asked, picking my coat up from the corner chair.

"The library? I doubt it, not on a day like today." Then she looked at me for second. "Don't you want to eat first?"

"Why? Do I look that hung over?"

"Only your eyes, the color of your skin, the . . ."

"Okay, I get the idea. Maybe you're right."

I went to the john, gargled with the house mouthwash, washed my face, and brushed back my hair with some water. Gazing at myself in the mirror, I realized that I looked as bad as I felt. If I ever ran into a Black Russian again, I'd kick his ass.

CHAPTER 22

I OPENED THE DOOR, AND WE BOTH stepped into the corridor. Waiting for us was a uniformed officer stationed by the elevator, courtesy of George Sennett. He was a big man with a tight-fitting blue shirt and an array of guns, tasers, cuffs, and a baton attached to his waist. He told us he would be around as long as we were in Ann Arbor. After chatting with him for a couple of minutes, we made for the elevator.

The officer didn't appear again until we were in the restaurant. He declined our invitation to eat with us, so we got a table, and immediately walked up to the buffet and circled it. Scrambled eggs, bacon, cereal. Jordan loaded her plate. I opted for coffee, dry toast, and orange juice.

I asked her how long we were going to have police protection and she merely shrugged, as if to say you can stay with me and enjoy it or do it the lieutenant's way. Then she changed the subject. "What do you expect to find at the library?" Jordan asked as we sat down.

"I remembered something in the newspaper they found with Faye Donaldson. I want to check it out."

"I can't believe any public building would be open today," she said between bites.

"You don't know the University. The libraries never close, especially when it's this close to final exams."

"Just in case, why don't you call?"

I went to the phone near the entrance of the restaurant. A quick call and I found out I was right. The campus had struggled through the night but had managed to keep its buildings open. Even Jordan was surprised. I hung up the phone, went back to the table, and told Jordan that they were open.

"We need to hit the stacks."

"For what?" she asked.

"Electromagnetics," I replied. Jordan looked at me as if I were crazy.

We made our way to the medical library. Our police shadow was close behind. It didn't take long to find the book I was looking for. I fumbled my way through it until I located electromagnetic radiation. I might as well have picked a topic like science, or industry, or auto mechanics. The subject was overwhelming. Electromagnetics in atom structure, electromagnetics in sound production, electromagnetics in light.

The student sitting across the table from us must have been watching. I guess it's not every day that someone comes to the library with a policeman in attendance. "Having trouble finding something?" he asked quietly.

"Yeah, it has to do with taking my ancient medical school knowledge and translating it into modern scientific terms," I admitted.

"What do you need?" he asked with a humorous look in his eyes.

"I need a simplified explanation of electromagnetic radiation."

"Are you kidding? That would take six volumes of scientific textbooks. Can you be more specific?"

"I would, if I could." I appealed to his good nature.

"Try the reference on biophysics on the basic science shelf. It's on the second row labeled biomechanics. There's a primer there called the *Concise Columbia Encyclopedia*. Use that as a starting point."

"Thanks," I whispered.

As he predicted, there was the book. I opened it up to electromagnetic radiation and soon discovered why it was such a general designation. Electromagnetic radiation was any form of wave caused by an electric field interacting with a magnetic field. In simple terms, any time a charged particle was set in motion, it gave off some kind of energy. This ranged all the way from low frequency radiation, like radio waves, to the ultra high frequency energy seen in x-rays. A narrower focus, that's what I needed.

We went to the librarian and asked for help, giving her the topic of electromagnetic radiation and effects on the brain, along with the *American Journal of Epidemiology*. She lightly tapped the keys of her computer, and in few moments pulled up two articles.

I read over the two studies and then the attached bibliographies. There were five additional articles of interest. Another ten minutes and I had them all. I was turning into a library pro.

We went back to our table with our coats and spread them out in front of us. Jordan sat next to me as I read the material, taking each article and looking through it when I was finished.

The first article I perused was "The distribution of induced currents in magnetic stimulation of the nervous system," in *Physiologic Medical Biology*. In the article the author described how magnetic stimulation could be used to activate certain centers of the brain. It was a direct replacement for electrical current stimulation. I got lost in the formulas, but the basic concept was clear: create direct initiation of a nervous system response with electromagnetic coils. I handed it over to Jordan and picked up the next one.

"How am I supposed to understand this stuff?" she asked in her best whispery library voice.

"Just read the summary at the top of the article," I whispered back. "The rest of the stuff is a bunch of Latin mumbo-jumbo and doctor-speak."

I became increasingly fascinated as I read on through the list the computer had provided. There was an article in *Acupuncture and Electro-therapeutic Research*, claiming that color TV, microwaves, and personal computers could cause some types of abnormal brain physiology. Electromagnetic waves were causing brain damage. If household items could do this, then why couldn't a hearing aid? It was a logical deduction.

Next was "Glioblastoma Multiforme and the Cellular Telephone Scare" in the *Journal of Neurosurgery*. It was a disclaimer article, trying to calm unreasonable fears about hand-held phones and brain tumors. Reading it after seeing the first article was like having the judge tell the jury to disregard those awful things that were said in a courtroom. It smelled of scientific cover-up to me.

The fourth article was a little more disconcerting. "Generalized seizures induced by transcranial magnetic stimulation of motor cortex" in *The Lancet*. According to the authors, electrical stimuli used to study the brain had caused a seizure in a patient. Each time I passed an article over to Jordan, she seemed more intent on reading the whole thing.

Finally, at eleven o'clock, I finished the last article and looked at my watch. "I've seen enough," I said, turning to Jordan. "Whatever Faye Donaldson was studying in the *Times* was no accident. Whether there is definitely a connection between electromagnetic radiation and brain damage is moot, but it was certainly a real possibility to her."

"Where do you go from here?" she asked, reaching for her coat.

"I think that Phillip Pennington had put a new type of device in Albert Henderson. And that's not to say it's bad. The problem is we don't know enough about it."

When Jordan suggested that we talk with Pennington directly, I told her that I had learned a lot from my time spent with lawyers: never ask a question you don't know the answer to.

We walked into the foyer of the library entrance. When we reached the door, Jordan turned to me. "Faye Donaldson knew something, and, if she did, then maybe Ralph Gernowski did too. Your two problems are thus: How does her knowledge relate to the hearing aid, and how do you go about connecting the two of them?"

"You heard what Frank Scotten said about the amplifier. When he hooked it up to the implant, he noted a weird emission."

"Electromagnetic radiation?"

I nodded, not knowing what the hell it meant.

THE OFFICER FOLLOWED US TO THE HOSPITAL where we picked up Sennett. He looked grumpy. His suit was rumpled from an all-night stay on the gurney in the ER, and he had the beginnings of a five o'clock shadow that made his dark skin look angry. When he flashed us a smile and gave us a thumbs up, I knew it was all an act. He opened the rear door of the Jeep and found his place in the back.

There wasn't a police escort this time. Sennett told me he was good enough for the ride back, but I should expect the police around for a while. I told him I didn't want to seem ungrateful, but having a policeman around me was unsettling. He just laughed and said I'd get used to it. I wasn't so sure.

The ride back to Jordan's office in the daytime didn't seem quite as harrowing as the trip the night before, but it was still slow going. Sennett made the time go by, regaling us with a couple of stories, including an anecdote about a guy who came into the ER the night before with a light bulb shoved up his rear. He said he heard one of the doctors laughingly referring to it as the light at the end of the tunnel.

I dropped Sennett off at police headquarters and then drove Jordan back to her Toyota Camry. I stopped behind it and studied the vehicle for a moment. "You're not actually going to drive this roller skate home, are you?" I asked, appalled.

"Sure. Front wheel drive, anti-lock brakes, and an air bag. What else do you need?" she said, opening her purse and reaching for her keys.

"Four-wheel drive, a V-8 engine, and 5000 pounds of traction," I replied.

"I'm sure I'll be all right. I've gotten used to winter in the Midwest. Besides, I've got to go to Chicago tomorrow, so all I have to do is get home," she said, getting out of my car.

"Chicago? In this weather?" I asked, surprised anyone was planning to fly in this storm.

"Drug case. I've been working on it for months. It's a no-big-deal commuter flight. I'll take a cab to the airport. They always seem to move, no matter what the weather," she said, getting behind the wheel of her car.

I waited until her engine started. There was no problem.

"I was wondering, if you were going to put a new device in someone, what would you have to do to comply with the law?"

"What do you mean?" she asked.

"If Phillip Pennington was trying out a new hearing aid, he must have had to pass some kind of governmental testing."

"A good question. There's an admin in the office that works with the FDA. I'll ask her." She hesitated for moment and then smiled. "See, I told you it would be all right." She reached out and held my bare hand for a moment. "You know, aside from the weather and our little incident at the lab, I had a great time." It wasn't only the cold that made me shiver.

"Thanks," I managed to answer. "Listen, there is something serious and dangerous going on here. We can't ignore it. I've got to keep my distance until we find out what's going on."

She focused her eyes intently on me. "What happened last night doesn't happen very often with me. I lost Matt. I'm *not* going to lose you," she added quickly. "Don't fight Sennett on the protection. Take it." Her voice was stern. Stern enough that I wasn't sure I wanted to get into a debate with her. Instead, I bent down and kissed her. It was the kind of kiss that said we weren't done just yet.

CHAPTER 23

After I dropped Jordan off, I sat in my jeep and called Sennett. Arguing with Jordan was not an option, but I knew I couldn't live with a policeman tailing me. Instinctively, I knew I was on to something. If Sennett and Jordan sensed there was trouble, I sensed something else. Whatever was going on involved me in a deeper way than I could understand. I needed to flush out whoever was after me, and I couldn't do it with a police tail.

When I told Sennett what I thought, he spent ten minutes explaining why I was crazy. At the end of the conversation I agreed that I was, in fact, unbalanced, and he agreed to call off his watch dogs. We both agreed not to say anything to Jordan just yet.

From there I went to visit Albert Henderson. It was mid-morning when I entered his room. He was sitting up in bed, reading the latest issue of *Good Housekeeping*, a tray of half-eaten breakfast in front of him. His eyes were focused on a picture of a buffet table full of delicacies.

I wrote him a note on the yellow legal pad on his bed, asking what he was doing reading the magazine. He pointed at the watery eggs and cold toast sitting on his tray. I got the idea.

I began questioning him about what had happened in his room. After several minutes of writing back and forth, I found out that he had made some beans on the stove and turned on the TV. He said that since he could hear, he spent most of his time watching television. He fell asleep and the next thing he knew he was in the emergency room. He claimed he had never heard the alarm, and now that his aid was gone, he couldn't hear anything. He said it made him frightened and nervous.

I tried to reassure him, telling him that the police had the aid and were examining it. He seemed frantic at the news and unimpressed that the police were involved. Then he looked at me and started writing fast, faster than he had before. He noticed he had been acting strangely over the past few months, doing irrational things he couldn't understand. It was like he was back on drugs except he had been clean for five years.

He stopped writing and sat back for a while, just staring at the wall and then looking at me. I asked him how he lost his hearing. He wrote: *He was working in a mobile hospital unit in Nam when the rocket hit.* When I asked him if he liked hanging around doctors, he smiled ruefully as if to say: *Are you kidding?"*

That's when I got the idea. "Why did you see a doc about your hearing if you dislike them so much?"

The Beacon Street Clinic sent me a letter saying they might be able to help my hearing.

The fact that he was at the clinic intrigued me. He said he had been a patient there for years. Then he added that the clinic was a Godsend for him. He loved the people there, so when they suggested that he see a doctor regarding his hearing, he immediately responded.

"Is that how you got to see Dr. Pennington?" He nodded.

As I moved to leave the room, Henderson tapped me on the shoulder and wrote me another note, asking me when I could get his aid back. I told him we would try and get it back to him as soon as possible. I could have told him we might never get it back, but I didn't have the heart.

He scribbled, "Thanks for saving my life. Not everyone would do that for a bum like me." I smiled back and wrote, "You're not a bum, Al. You got a bum deal."

I told Henderson that I had to run, but when he got out of the hospital, he should go to Beacon Street for a follow-up. I waved goodbye and made it to the elevators just in time to see a repairman put up an out-of-service sign. Typical for hospitals, I never saw all the elevators working at one time.

I headed warily for the stairs, taking them slowly to make sure no one was following me. But the stairwell was filled with other climbers and descenders, and I made it to the main floor without incident. This whole business was making me paranoid.

I left the front entrance and went back to my car. This time I was much more careful, circling the car a couple of times before I got in. I started the Jeep and drove off, wondering if I'd ever feel safe again.

After an angry hour of jockeying around stalled cars and snowdrifts, I finally made it to the Beacon Street Clinic. The place looked almost like a Norman Rockwell painting in its heavy covering of snow. Even the crack houses and the beer and wine stores looked less menacing. It was as if, with one swoop of the paintbrush, nature had cured the city of its ills.

As I entered, I spotted Vijay Patel, a hard-working, industrious, and honest family practice doc. He was one of those foreign graduates the medical administrators thought they could con into being their coolie, working them long hours at a private hospital like St. Vincent's for the privilege of getting an American license. But doctors like Vijay Patel didn't earn degrees by being stupid. They wanted the same things every other doctor wanted: security, prestige, and a sense of accomplishment. So instead of going out to the fancy suburbs, they were willing to work in the city where their skill was desperately needed. There was never a shortage of patients for Vijay Patel. I had helped get him his clinic job six years ago.

Most of the nursing staff had called in, on account of the weather, except for Phyllis Carter. As I walked up to the desk, I saw her waiting to call patients in, looking and sounding like a drill sergeant, with her short, cropped hair and commanding voice. When she recognized me, she didn't look happy.

"You're not here to do filing, are you?" she asked.

"No, I wanted to see Dr. Patel."

"He's busy seeing patients. Is it important?"

"Urgent," I said firmly. Phyllis looked at me for a moment, sizing me up, then she relented.

"Wait here. I'll get him," she replied condescendingly.

It didn't take long before a short, balding doctor of Indian descent appeared. "Ben, nice to see you. It's been so long," he said with a slight accent.

As I shook his hand, I told him I knew he would be here in spite of the weather. He shrugged, claiming it was his duty. Vijay Patel lived by the book of rules.

I told him I needed to look at some charts. He glanced at me quizzically for a moment, then took out a small pamphlet from his coat pocket and studied it. After a couple of moments, he shrugged his shoulders and told the nurse to help. I looked at the book as he put it back in his pocket. It said, "hospital regulations." I guessed that it hadn't covered this kind of contingency.

"You know I can't divulge their medical histories without a release form." He was right and I did know it.

"No problem. I just need to see if they've been here." I looked around the mechanized office. It was quite high tech for an inner city clinic.

"Beacon Street recently moved into St. Vincent's computer system and purged a lot of records. To tell you the truth, I can give you the number of patients with the codes you need, but that's about all."

"That would be a start," I said encouragingly.

We went over to the front desk, and he quickly punched in the information. I watched him sign in with his password. I was surprised at the complexity of the computer system. We hadn't had one when we started the clinic. He explained that when Great Lakes took over the clinic, they integrated Beacon Street into their system. I didn't know that the medical school had taken over St. Vincent's, but he explained that it was just the residency programs.

"How do they segregate the diseases on the computer?" I asked.

"It's all done by ICD coding numbers. What's the disease you're looking up?"

"Sensorineural hearing loss," I replied.

"There's a search button here. Let's see if it can direct us to the proper code." He typed sensorineural hearing loss and clicked the mouse on the diagnosis. A number came up, *38912*. "That's your number."

"It's interesting, but I'm too computer illiterate to deal with it. Here, type in these names and see if they register with your friend here."

Patel typed them in. Before long, names began flashing on the screen. One after another they appeared: Gernowski, Strickland, Hazeltine, Trudeau, and Henderson. They had all been patients at Beacon Street, and now all of them were dead except Hazeltine and Henderson. Of the two, only Henderson could possibly help me.

A woman was at the front desk. She had a threadbare woolen coat, with a dirty red scarf wrapped around her head to protect her from the cold. Her eyes were bloodshot and her hand trembled as she signed the intake sheet. Phyllis knew trouble when she saw it and came over and gave Patel an impatient, keep-it-moving look.

"Got to run, Ben. Too many patients, too little time," he said apologetically.

"I understand," I said, shaking hands with him. As I walked out of the clinic, I felt perplexed and confused. My hunch had proven correct, but where did it lead me? Once again, I was staring at a dead end.

I was halfway to my car when I suddenly turned around. I needed more advice from an expert. When I returned to the clinic, Phyllis was still guarding the front desk. She seemed half-expectant to see me.

"Back already?"

"I wonder if you could print up those patients for me."

She smiled, punched a couple of keys, and out spat the paper from the computer. I scanned one of the pieces of paper and looked at the heading. It read "The Beacon Street Clinic—One of the SVH Medical Service Centers."

I felt like I had seen a ghost. I remembered the registration form and the red stamp with Phillip Pennington/SVH. What was he doing at St. Vincent's?

CHAPTER 24

I CALLED KNUDSEN AT HIS DESK. HE said Jordan's secretary had faxed a bunch of regulations from the FDA. When I told him I would be there in a few minutes, he said he would wait. There was a sound of obedience in his voice. In actuality it took me thirty minutes to plow through endless snowdrifts until I arrived at police headquarters. I was stiff from sitting in the car, so I took the stairs to Sennett's office.

Knudsen was at his desk waiting for me. I looked at him, sitting upright in his chair, desk devoid of papers, starched blue uniform shirt neatly pressed, and shoes polished to a high gleam. This was a military man in every way. I assumed he was going to stand and come to attention if I called him by his rank.

Instead, I said, "What's up?" As soon as I said it, he seemed to relax. I asked him if he had the papers from Jordan, and he handed them to me in a neat manila folder. I sat down in the chair next to his desk and started thumbing through them.

Eventually, I found a summary of the rules and regulations for the submission of a new device. According to the document, a new external device required detailed electronic specifications. These included working drawings and the actual functioning of the device as examined by the testing services of the FDA. After completing the actual bench testing of the aid, a clinical trial was necessary. In the case of this type of device, six patient cases, along with pre-approval of the electronic design, and confirmation of pre and post insertion audiograms were required. When I finished, I put the papers back on his desk. Knudsen quickly scooped them up and placed them neatly in a file next to the desk.

"Does Lieutenant Sennett have the papers taken from Faye Donaldson's computer?"

"Yes, sir," he replied smartly. "The lieutenant took them with him."

I asked Knudsen if Sennett was around. When he said he was out on a call, I asked him to have Sennett meet me at The Pipeline. Knudsen said that if he couldn't be there, he would leave a message on my cell.

He answered me so smartly, I almost had the notion to ask him if the floors had been polished and the latrines cleaned, but I resisted. Instead, I thanked him and made it back to my car. It had started snowing again, a blustering flurry of snow that lasted five minutes and then blew itself out. By the time I had reached the Pipeline it was dark.

I pulled up my Jeep and parked it in the side lot. William, Sid's car attendant, was asleep inside his little heated booth along the street. It was early, and I didn't feel like waking him up.

When I walked in Sennett was already waiting for me at a side table. He looked a little worn. There was a small Band-Aid over his right brow and the remnants of yellowing bruise around his eye. As soon as he flashed me his wide grin, I knew everything was all right.

"You don't look much worse for the wear."

"Looks can be deceiving."

By this time, Charlie had ambled over with three longnecks and sat down with us. The place was empty and the Jazz Crusaders were playing on the overhead speakers. A snowstorm in Detroit spelled recession for the jazz business.

"Doc, what do you think?" Charlie asked me to arbitrate.

"About what?"

"The lieutenant and I are having a little debate about fighting and hockey."

That set off a fifteen minute deliberation about the sport that eventually ended with a discussion of Detroit's greatest sports icon, Gordie Howe, perhaps the toughest fighter in the history of the game. They discussed his one-punch knockout of Lou Fontinato of the Rangers. It was interesting, but my heart wasn't in the conversation. I wanted to see the folder in front of Sennett. He must have understood, because he shoved it across the table.

Charlie took the cue and walked back to the bar as I started thumbing through the papers. Faye Donaldson had done a certification of a new hearing aid for a company called Panatone. There was a picture of the unit in the papers. It was identical to the one I had taken from Albert Henderson.

I looked at the engineering inspection report. The results seemed good enough. Then I took the papers from Frank Scotten and spread them out on the table. I compared the graphs from the two tests. They were identical. The gain was impressive. The only difference was that the report from Faye Donaldson didn't show the high tone gain that Frank noted.

Sennett and I chatted for a little while, mostly about the incident in Ann Arbor. The police hadn't found the shooter, but they had cleared Frank Scotten.

Charlie came over and asked us if we wanted another beer. I shook my head. It was getting late.

Charlie was fascinated with how Sennett had survived a near-death experience. We talked about it for a few more minutes, mostly about what to do when someone is shooting at you.

"Nobody had a good answer," Sennett said, pointing his finger at me. "I wouldn't have been here tonight if he hadn't knocked me down." I told him it was just dumb luck.

Charlie started shaking his head in disagreement. He said when he was with the Seals in Kuwait, he was sent to protect one of the local mullahs on a trip to Kuwait City. They were driving through the desert when the cleric said he had to take a leak. They stopped at the side of the road and Charlie got out of his vehicle and waited. While he was standing there, the light from his Jeep shone across the road. "That's when I saw a wire running in front of me. I ordered everyone out of the Jeep just in time to see an improvised explosive device go off."

When we asked him how he knew to look at the road, he said sometimes you just had to listen to your inner self.

When Charlie left, Sennett pulled out a paper from his inside coat pocket and spread it on the table.

"I thought you'd be interested in this."

I stared at the paper. It was a bunch of notations regarding a fingerprint. "What's this about?"

"We're still trying to hunt down whoever torched your boat. This the forensics report on that cocktail stirrer we found at the marina. There were a set of prints on it. We'll need to check yours."

"Anyone else?"

"I think we're going to make a trip to see your friend, Mr. Scotten."

IT WAS MY FIRST TIME IN A POLICE CRUISER. Not that it was any big deal, but the radio, the gun sitting next to Sennett, and the revolving light on the back seat infused me with a feeling of power. We were driving out to the airport again to visit the owner of the Plain View. This time it would be on my terms.

It was after midnight when Sennett pulled up to the front of the club and parked next to the valet stand. When the attendant stepped out to tell him to move his car, Sennett glared at him and shoved his badge in his face. The kid moved out of the way quickly, and we walked inside. The same Christmas music was coming out of the speakers.

Inside the club it was as if the scene hadn't changed, only there were fewer people. It was weird. Loud rock and roll music, flashing lights, and topless girls lounging against the bar, looking bored, as if they were waiting for a bus.

Sennett stopped at the bar and asked where he could find Terry Scotten. The bartender pointed to an office at the end of a dimly lit hallway. When we got to the office, we saw two men in suits guarding the door. I recognized them as the two thugs I had run into the other night. In the faint light they didn't recognize me.

Sennett showed them his badge. The way he stood in front of them, I thought he was begging them to start something. They didn't, just sullenly opened the door. We walked into the office, a small room with prefab knotty pine paneling, a couple of fake leather chairs, and a metal desk heaped with papers. Behind it sat Terry Scotten.

He looked surprised. The surprise quickly turned to anger. "Who the fuck are you, and what are you doing with this prick?" he said, pointing at me.

"Lieutenant George Sennett," he said slowly as he pulled out his badge again. "I'm here with Dr. Dailey, and if you don't cooperate with me, I'm going to drag your sorry ass down to the station."

Scotten must have been around the track a few times with the police, because he told Sennett that unless he had a search warrant, he didn't have to tell him squat. Then he looked at me with a sneer and told me to get the fuck out too.

I was surprised when Sennett nodded, grabbed me by the elbow, and led me to the door.

"And don't come back," Scotten yelled as we walked out into the hall.

Sennett ignored Scotten's thugs and walked about ten feet past them to a closed door. But instead of continuing down the hall he grabbed the knob and slammed his shoulder against the door.

Before the two men could react, we bolted into a darkly lit room. Sennett flipped on the light switch. There on a bed was a naked man. On top of him were two women, one with her crotch hovering over his face and the other with his erection in her mouth. When they saw us, everyone started shouting.

Scotten's men rushed into the room. By this time Sennett had his gun in one hand and his badge in the other.

"Police. Stop where you are, or there will be trouble!"

There was a sudden silence as the girls looked for something to cover themselves and the man reached for his pants. By this time Scotten was inside the room.

"You can't do this!" he yelled.

"Why don't you come down to the station and tell that to the captain? In the meantime, we'll shut your club down for prostitution."

Scotten raised his hands in surrender. "What do you want with me?"

Sennett led him back to his office and started grilling him about his whereabouts the night before. It wasn't pretty, and I have to admit I enjoyed seeing

Scotten squirm. However, after thirty minutes it was clear, even to me, that Scotten wasn't going to give us anything.

That's when Sennett pulled out a small box and set it on Scotten's desk. He opened the container and set out a stamp pad and a card with squares imprinted on it on the desktop.

"What the fuck," Scotten exclaimed. "You're not going to print me."

"I need your prints to identify an object we have at the station."

"For what? You got nothing on me."

"It's about something we found at a marina where a boat was set on fire." Sennett smiled just enough so Scotten could see his teeth. "You know arson is a serious crime."

"You got shit, that's what you got," Scotten shouted.

"It's like I said, Jocko, you can do it the easy way, or you can do it hard. It's your choice." Sennett's voice was cool as he fixed his eyes on Scotten, like a cat that had cornered his prey. "You know resisting arrest is a significant matter. If you choose the hard way, I can assure you I'm going to mess you up."

Scotten first looked at Sennett's face, and then I saw him glance down at the lieutenant's huge hands. I thought of Gordie Howe's one punch knockout—the fight was over.

Sennett opened the stamp pad and slowly pressed each of Scotten's fingers in the ink and then rolled them on the card. When he was finished, he closed the pad and put the card in the box.

He didn't bother to give Scotten anything to wipe his hands. Instead, he got up and towered over him. "Okay, asshole, don't leave town. We know where to find you."

With that, we both walked out of the office and back into the club. A couple of girls near the entrance, naked except for their small thongs, were smoking cigarettes. I recognized one of them. She was the redhead I had seen when I was there with Frank Scotten. But there was something else. It was only when I looked a second time that I realized she was also the girl who had been with Chip Thornton at the basketball game.

I told Sennett I'd be right with him. Then I stopped to talk to the girl. She didn't look the same. Sure, she was half-naked, but this time a dull purple bruise half covered with makeup extended down the side of her jaw. When I approached her, she raised her head slowly, her eyes filled with the dullness of either boredom or drugs. "You want something nice?" she asked dutifully.

"Not what you're thinking. I want some information."

She looked at me quizzically. "What kind of information?"

"You were with a guy at the basketball game the other night at the Palace." I felt uncomfortable having a serious conversation with a three-quarters naked woman at a strip joint, but it was what it was.

"Yeah, that was me. I was with that asshole, Chip."

"I take it you and Chip aren't getting along."

"Getting along? That prick hit me. You see this mark?" She went on to explain that he always got rough with her. When she started talking about the anal sex thing, I put my hands up.

"Listen, I'm not interested in your sex life. How did you come to be with him?"

"Be with him, are you kidding? He's down here all the time. He's been with half the girls down here. You'd think he owned the place, and me."

She went on to explain that he and Terry Scotten were friends. Scotten had introduced them. They went out a few times, then he became possessive. She didn't like it, and that's when the trouble began. I was going to tell her that any guy would be upset if his girlfriend was flashing her naked body for money, but I didn't feel like defending Thornton. She looked at me a little closer and then asked me again if I wanted anything. For the second time, I told her I wasn't interested. Looking at her, I don't think she would have remembered even if I told her again.

I walked outside and Sennett was waiting by the cruiser. He gave me that "I-know-what-you-were-doing" look as he turned the key.

"What's so funny?"

"Did you know that girl in there? The way you stared at her, I thought you might have seen her once or twice."

"She's not my type. I like girls with bigger boobs and a tighter ass," I said jokingly.

He changed the subject. "Did you see the look on Scotten's face? I thought he was going to shit his pants."

"Forget that. How did you know that guy was going to be in that room with those women?"

"The same way you know a patient has cancer by listening to his voice. Experience, doc, experience."

CHAPTER 25

ON THE WAY BACK TO THE PIPELINE, Sennett told me he was deeply worried about me.

"There's something bad going on here, doc. I can feel it. You are in a mess, and it's going to be tough to get out. I want you to reconsider having protection until we figure out where this is going."

I took what he said seriously. This man wasn't given to idle chitchat. But I had another view. His protection was my prison. I wanted my independence. I'd take my chances that I could take care of myself.

"Jordan must have gotten your ear."

"That girl cares about you, doc. Don't take it lightly."

"Believe me, lieutenant, I don't. I just have a few things to take care of."

I think he saw that arguing with me would be useless. So he changed the subject. He told me he was going to send the vice guys over to the Plain View, but he figured Scotten would already have the place fixed up. He said most of the people that ran these joints were like stockbrokers; they managed risk. He figured Scotten would lay low with his girls for a while.

When he dropped me off at my jeep, he reminded me to check in with him regularly. I thanked him and watched him drive away. It was like watching the boat sail away from the deserted island without me.

By the time I got to the marina, it was two in the morning. It didn't take me long to fall asleep, but it was fitful. Something Sennett said must have come to me in my sleep, because the next morning I woke up thinking about stockbrokers. That's when Herb Albright's name came to me. Herb was a stockbroker who used to pester me incessantly to invest with him. That was when I had money. He was persistent enough that I actually dropped a few thousand with him in my IRA.

During that time period, he somehow had also kept me ahead of inflation. I'd thought he'd done a pretty decent job, and, for that matter, so had my ex-wife's attorney. I remember his smile when he saw the amount. By the time she got hers and he got his, there wasn't much left. But that wasn't Herb's fault. Anyway, he seemed like a walking encyclopedia of the stock market, and that was just what I needed.

When I called, he sounded a little surprised to hear from me. After all, I hadn't been in the investing mode recently.

"You're a voice from the past. How have you been, Ben?" he asked cheerfully.

"Just regaining my voice," I replied.

"I've got a good tip for you."

He never stopped. Even though I told him I wasn't looking right now, it didn't seem to faze him, and for the next ten minutes I had to listen to him extol Friendship Labs, an environmental company. He told me the stock was cheap, and I could control a hundred thousand shares for around a thousand dollars.

At least he knew what kind of league I was playing in. "I'm not in great financial shape right now, Herb."

"We got terms, Ben. Give me a try," he pleaded. Great, I was calling for information and it was going to cost me a thousand dollars that I didn't have. Then he gave me the famous last words from a stockbroker: "Trust me." I decided to ignore it.

"Listen, Herb, there's something else I want you to look into."

"What's up?" he said seriously.

"I want you to find anything you can about the Panatone Corporation. You know, what it does, who owns it, and what their financial status is."

"You know something?" he asked.

"Yeah, but not anything that would help you, Herb. How long do you think it would take to find out?"

"No time. Just a couple of taps on my computer and it'll give us the latest information."

I heard the keyboard again. Then silence. "You picked a winner, buddy boy," he said.

"How so?" I asked.

"Seems as though Panatone has had a little uptick over the past year. It's a ten dollar stock that's gone up two points in the past six months. Let's see if there's any news on the wire."

Again, the keyboard and silence.

"It says here that a Dr. Phillip Pennington has been working on a new implantable hearing aid that is going to revolutionize the hearing aid business. This might really be something, Ben. Are you interested in investing in it?" he asked.

"Not right now," I replied cautiously.

"I'll tell you what," Herb said. "I'm going to request their annual report. When I get the paper, I'll send it to you. Where can I reach you?"

I gave him Coastal Life's number and told him to leave a message for me with Bruce Sanderson's secretary.

My next call was to Jordan. I got her on the second ring.

I had a moral dilemma as to whether I should tell her about the previous night. I decided to 'fess up, figuring it would help convince her we shouldn't be together for right now. What I didn't figure was her response.

"Dammit, Ben, I'm so angry with you. You've got to stop playing the detective game."

I looked outside and saw the snow flurries, whipping around so hard it reminded me of a swarm of birds flying back and forth without rhyme or reason. Someone once told me there was a pattern to chaos, we just had to understand it.

"I'd like to promise you that, but I don't want to lie to you. I'm in this for the long haul. Someone is out to get me, and I can either run or figure out what the hell is going on. If I run, I'll never be safe. I'm not trying to be anything I'm not. I'm just trying to stay alive."

There was a moment of silence that I took to mean she had given up. Then I told her I would see her when she got back.

From the way she said goodbye, I knew I was on a short leash.

CHAPTER 26

I WAS IN A DILEMMA. I WAS being watched. Whoever was after me knew what my habits were. I couldn't stay hidden at the marina. I needed to move around, but not in my car. My only hope was Easy. I asked him if he had a vehicle I could use for a couple of days. The only thing he had was his beat-up red F-150. He agreed to trade the truck for my Wagoneer for a couple of weeks.

His truck was a mess: parts from an old pump on the passenger seat, candy wrappers on the floor, and the smell of engine oil permeating the cab. It wasn't great, but under the circumstances it would do.

I pulled out of the marina and headed back to the city along Jefferson Avenue. As I drove, I kept checking out the rearview mirror while mulling over what was happening. If this whole business was involved somehow with the hearing aids, something was going to happen soon. There were six cases needed before a product could go to market. Only five had been implanted. If I was going to make any progress, I had to find out in whom the last one was going to be implanted.

And this wasn't just any old, everyday hearing aid implant. This was a potentially dangerous business. Ralph Gernowski had worn it, and they found bullets that were a match. Albert Henderson had worn one and almost died from a gas leak that might or might not have been an accident. Frank Strickland had worn one and had died in an auto accident. The other two patients were incoherent.

There was no proof as to whether this was a coincidence or not. But I did know one thing: Whoever was going to be the next recipient had to be warned. That sounded like good advice, but coming from an excommunicated doctor, my credibility wasn't great. What the hell, it even sounded like idle chatter to

me. My mind was buzzing with thoughts. *Lay low and take Jordan's advice,*
that's the best way. No risk and I'm out of here.

Then there was the question of Phillip Pennington. He must know that the
hearing aid was giving good results. Did he know what had happened to Ralph
Gernowski, and did he know about the high-tone surge in the aid? If he knew,
why was he continuing to implant the aids? It couldn't be for money. He had a
big-time job and a world-class reputation. He might be an academic asshole,
but he couldn't be that stupid.

After a couple of miles of driving, I eased back in the seat. I was getting a feel
for the truck now. It wasn't like driving my Wagoneer. Too much gas and the
rear end would fishtail, so I had to be careful. I'd almost made it to downtown
Detroit when my stomach started rumbling. I decided to head down to Gus's
place. If all else failed, I knew he would have some smart word. Fortunately, he
was open.

I parked in the back lot and plunged through a couple of snowbanks on my
way into the diner. When I walked in, the place was empty, and he was getting
ready to shut down. Looking up from the grill, he smiled. "Say, Doc," he said.
"You know how to make a guy's day. I was almost going to have to admit that I
was shut down for the first time in twenty years."

"Don't say I never did anything for anybody." I took off my coat and sat
down at the counter. "Chicken gyro, smothered in onions, and a small Greek
salad, Gus."

"Comin' right up." He turned around, put some chicken on the grill, then
pulled out a wrapped salad from his refrigerator.

"Gus, tell me something. You got a problem. Somebody is doing something
wrong and maybe they don't know it. Somebody powerful. Somebody who
doesn't like being wrong. If you stick your nose in it, you might get yourself into
deep trouble. Who do you turn to?" I asked.

He looked surprised. "Me? I call my cousin Freddie. He has this friend on
the police force and . . ."

"No, not that way. The police aren't interested. No proof, bureaucracy, that
kind of thing."

Gus nodded as he put the chicken in the pita bread and spread on his yo-
gurt sauce. "I get it. I had that happen to me when I first opened up the shop
here. Kids came along, started harassing me, painting the side of my building,
like that. I asked myself, why me? I went to the police and they laughed at me.
Dumb Greek guy, what do you expect, doing business in the city? I figured I
had to take care of this myself. So I waited outside one night and caught one of
those little bastards just as he was about to spray paint my store. He was about
fifteen years old. I scared the crap out of him. He told me everything. A guy a
few blocks away owns a sub shop. He's worried about the competition. So he

sends these kids over and pays them ten bucks a piece to harass me. You know what I do?"

"What?" I grabbed the sandwich and took a bite.

"I wait until the sub shop is ready to close. The owner is walking out to his car. I take this baseball bat, and, as he's about to get into the car, I walk up to him real quiet." Gus took hold of a wooden spoon to show me how he did it. "Little guy. So frightened he pissed his pants. I tell him, if he sends one more kid to my place, it'll be the last time he ever opens the door to his shop, if you know what I mean."

"What happened then?"

"Never heard from the guy again. Eventually he went out of business. Food wasn't any good anyway." Gus laughed as he told the story, but his eyes were dead serious.

"You did the right thing, Gus," I washed the sandwich down with coffee.

"I did more than the right thing, Doc. I learned a big lesson about America," he said, as he began to put things away.

"What's that?"

"You wanna get something done, don't depend on nobody but yourself. Guy's doing something wrong, you got to stand up and take care of it. Otherwise, you'll never be able to live with yourself. A little piece of you dies, you know what I mean?"

A shiver went down my spine again. Yeah, I knew what he meant. I pushed my food away. Gus must have noticed.

"What's the matter, Doc, you not feeling good?"

"Just the weather, Gus." I got up to leave. "Thanks for the advice." I laid some money down on the counter and headed for the door.

"Say, Doc, don't forget what I said, huh?"

"I won't, Gus, I won't."

My fate was sealed, and I knew it. There was no longer any choice. I got back into the truck and headed into the inner city. There was one more aid that was going to be implanted, and I had to find out about it. I couldn't rush in and tell Pennington to stop the operation. He'd laugh me out of the hospital. I'd have to have proof. I had to find out who that person was and stop Pennington from putting it in. And that answer was at the Beacon Street Clinic.

I reached the clinic shortly after closing time. Fortunately, when I drove into the parking lot, there was a van parked by the door. I pulled up by it, got out, and walked through the open door.

"Anyone here?" I yelled.

I walked in a little closer and suddenly a huge African American man appeared, holding a mop and carrying out a trash can. He looked startled when he saw me.

"Sorry, didn't mean to scare you. I'm Dr. Dailey. I needed to get something, and I saw the door was open, so I walked in."

"Man, you frightened the crap out of me. I thought I had locked the door. Must have left it open to go to the dumpster." He wiped his forehead with the back of his sleeve.

I nodded. "I'll stay out of your way. I only need something from the desk."

"I'm almost done, anyway. Go ahead." He walked toward a large container, picked it up as if it were a paper bag, and walked to the door.

I made my way to the front desk and stared at the computer. What the hell, if Patel could use it, why couldn't I learn? I pushed the computer "ON" button and the Microsoft screen appeared in front of me. The sign in code appeared. Shit, what was I going to use? At first I tried Patel's sign-in username, but that got me nowhere. I tried "PENNINGTON.SV." Nothing happened. Then I remembered what Patel had said about an eight-character sign-on key. So I tried "PENNGTSV." Again, nothing happened.

It occurred to me that, if Pennington was going to be able to use this computer system, there had to be another sign-on code for his hospital. I tried it again. This time I pecked at the keys and typed in "PENNGTGL" for Great Lakes. Suddenly the screen lit up and Pennington's office address came up on the screen. With it came the edit button. I couldn't believe it, but I was in and working with a computer. It was actually exciting.

I remembered Dr. Patel using the computer. When he wanted to look for something, he hit the "search" screen. I found the "search" icon at the bottom of the screen and touched it with the mouse arrow. When it came up, I typed in "sensorineural hearing loss." About a hundred names suddenly appeared on the screen, all of them patients of Phillip Pennington. It was impossible to write all the names down. It was all the cases of sensorineural hearing loss he had seen in the past year. This was ridiculous. I could never wade through all that material.

I went back to the search screen and typed in "sensorineural hearing loss-Beacon Street" under the "search" column. I touched the screen and twenty-three names appeared. This would be easier.

I copied on paper the names of each of the patients. After spending half an hour on the phone, I had reached only twelve.

I was about to make another call to a patient when I heard a voice from the back hall.

"Gonna close up, boss. Check you later."

Before I could reply, the door slammed shut. There was a little beeping sound and then nothing. Locked in. I'd deal with that later.

Picking up the phone, I dialed St. Vincent's. It was where all the other implants had been done and my best chance of finding the prospective patient.

Once I got the operator, I asked for the night clerk in admissions, identifying myself as one of Pennington's residents.

"Sorry to bother you so late, but I'm checking my surgery schedule, and I wondered if you could review your computer screen to see what Dr. Pennington has on for the next two weeks?"

"No problem. But there's probably going to be some changes," she offered.

"Why's that?" I asked.

"You know, the storm and everything. Messes things up big time. There are going to be some angry surgeons for the next couple of days." There was a sound of pleasure in her voice, as if she was going to be happy to call them up and tell them their surgery had been canceled. "Here's your list now."

I heard the printer running and then she read off the names. I scanned my list. My heart jumped. There was the name. Bernard Frasker, ear implant, tomorrow afternoon at three.

I put the phone down for a moment and quickly looked over my files. Paydirt. Bernard Frasker, sixty-six, unmarried. Lived alone at a rooming house on the west side. Totally deaf since an episode of meningitis twenty years ago. It was Pennington's ideal "veterinary experiment." I looked at my watch. It was already eight p.m. But I had to be sure.

"Listen, since I've got you on the phone, is there any chance you could plug into Great Lakes and check my schedule there?" I asked, trying make sure I left no stone unturned.

"You're a resident, aren't you?" she inquired.

"Yeah, why?"

"Just checking. We're not supposed to give out that information." More key tapping and printer rolling and then she read the list. "Nothing matches," she announced. "The only thing he has on the schedule is some tube insertions. By the way, if I were you I'd leave some extra time for the drive," she added.

That was it. Tomorrow would be the end. I'd call Pennington's office and talk with him. Warn him about the implant. I'd make him believe me.

I picked up my coat and walked to the back door. Then I saw the red light flashing. Shit. Not only was I locked in, but they had the burglar alarm on. One step outside and they'd have every cop in Detroit on me.

I looked at my watch. Nine o'clock. I was dead tired. *The hell with it, I'm bedding down here for the night.* I found an examining room with a padded table. Rummaging around in the closet, I pulled out a blanket, ignoring its moth-ball smell. Once I had my bed made, I took off my shoes and laid down.

A last thought slashed across my mind before I drifted off. I was really scared.

CHAPTER 27

I WAS WAKENED THE NEXT MORNING BY the sound of the telephone in the outer corridor. I shook my head. It took me a few moments to realize where I was. Then I looked at my watch. Six o'clock. The clerical help would be coming soon.

I jumped off the examining table and put the blanket away. In the mirror over the sink, I examined the stubble growing on my face. I found a razor set in the cabinet. It was meant for shaving the scalp around a laceration, giving less than a smooth-as-silk look. Beggars couldn't be choosers. I opened it up, made a lather out of soap, and shaved. It wasn't the greatest, a few nicks here and there, but when I finished, I looked halfway presentable.

As I'd predicted, the clerks arrived at six-thirty. I stood near the door; after they entered, I slid out the door and into my truck. I had to wait another half hour until the operating rooms opened.

The snow had stopped but there was still a frozen coating on the windshield. I scraped off my car and let the motor run for a while. It gave me a chance to think. I saw the office manager, Phyllis Peterson, drive up. She gave me a "what are you doing here" look, got out of her car, and walked inside. She was the one person to whom I didn't want to make any explanations.

I drove away for a quick breakfast at the local McDonald's and then made a couple of phone calls. My mind was in full gear, trying to decide how to approach Pennington. In the light of day, I wasn't so cocksure of myself. I had a few more moments of indecision. Then I remembered Gus's comment from last night. That's when I finally made up my mind.

Faye Donaldson had handled the certification of Pennington's hearing aid and had conveniently left off the high frequency discharge from the specifications. Did she have some contact with Phillip Pennington? I couldn't bring myself to believe that. For his part, Pennington was aggressive, brilliant, and, yes, maybe even ruthless. But I didn't see him as a killer. I wondered if he knew what happened to Ralph Gernowski and his hearing aid. I'd have to explain it to him, make him understand.

There was a phone near the entrance. I went over to it and dialed Pennington's office. His secretary answered.

"This is Dr. Benjamin Dailey. I was in the other day on an interview," I said in a businesslike tone.

"Oh yes, Dr. Dailey. As of yet, Dr. Pennington hasn't made any decision on the position," she replied in a monotone.

"It's not that. There's a matter of great importance that I must talk to him about." I didn't want her to think I was nuts, so I kept the level of my voice low.

"I'm sure I can transfer the message," she responded, trying to put me off.

"I would prefer to talk with him personally," I insisted, realizing I would never get past this telephone barricade.

"He's not in," she replied stiffly. "According to his schedule, he is due at St. Vincent's Hospital this morning," she said.

"I'm going to try and get hold of him there. In case I don't, would you please give him this message?" I asked.

"If you wish, I'll try to pass it on. Dr. Pennington doesn't always check in for messages. I can't promise anything, but if he calls, I'll tell him."

"Tell him to delay performing his implant surgery, at least until I get hold of him." I tried not to sound too dramatic.

"Is there a reason I can give?" she said worriedly.

"No, just tell him this. It's serious."

She told me she would try to get the message to him. Personally, I wasn't betting on it. She sounded too self-important to be passing on messages from the likes of me. I looked at my watch. Still plenty of time to get to St. Vincent's and take care of it myself.

When I arrived, I stopped to survey the 600-bed hospital I had practiced at for so many years. This was it, my triumphant return to St. Vincent's. Some return. What the hell was I going to do when I got to Pennington anyway, prevent him from doing the surgery? Too late for debates. I had to stop the operation.

Unlike Great Lakes, I knew St. Vincent's well. Parking in a side lot, I pinned on my Great Lakes badge, slammed out of the truck, and hurdled over some snowdrifts toward the side entrance, the one they keep locked only at night.

I stepped into the warmth of the stairwell and out into the corridor. It was bustling with doctors in white coats, patients, orderlies. And then there was me. Dressed in a torn Patagonia jacket, disheveled, and sporting a phony ID badge.

Not wanting to meet someone I knew, I looked down at the floor as I made my way to the operating room and took the rear stairs to avoid the main entrance to the surgical suite. I was still indecisive. Should I barge right in or sneak in with scrubs and a mask on? I looked at my watch. It was 8:45 at night.

I came around the corner and stood at the desk at the entrance to the operating rooms. This was my old haunt. The place I had spent endless hours working. The place where I had done so much good. I was nervous standing there, but no one recognized me. People change, faces change, no one is irreplaceable, not even the doctors.

I went up to the desk, trying not to show my emotion, and waited for the secretary. It seemed like forever.

"May I help you?" she asked.

"Yes, I'm Dr. Dailey, and I was wondering if Dr. Pennington has begun surgery on a Mr. Bernard Frasker."

She glanced down at her list. "Oh, Mr. Frasker. That case has been canceled, along with all the morning surgery."

"It can't be," I said a little too loudly. "I called last night and they said everything was a go. Nine o'clock."

"The snow caused a ventilator problem. They're up there fixing it now, but the anesthesia department won't start unless the hospital can assure them that the gas scavenger system is working."

I wasn't about to take no for an answer. "Is there somewhere else that the case was taken? Did they say anything else when it was canceled?" No one knew.

It was clear my return to St. Vincent's was fruitless, so I made for the front entrance. *Sit down, get control of yourself, and think.* There had to be an answer. I folded onto one of the waiting chairs in the lobby and stared at the salt-stained carpeting. Not at all like the St. Vincent's I once worked at. What a dump the hospital had become. If they keep this up it would change into one of those second-rate healthcare facilities that people complain about.

Quit worrying about St. Vincent's, dummy. I had to figure out where Pennington was. My first choice was to call back to his office.

I went to the payphone and got Pennington's secretary back on the line. This time she wasn't so polite.

"Dr. Dailey, I passed your message to the chief resident. Beyond that there is nothing I can do for you," she replied flatly.

"I realize that. I'm just wondering if I could speak to Dr. Pennington personally."

"He's a very busy man. I'm sure today would be a bad day to try to make contact, but as I said, I'll leave a message," she replied coldly.

"Maybe you could tell me where he is, and I could wait for him," I pleaded.

"He hasn't checked in with me, so I haven't a clue. Now if you'll excuse me, I must be going, there's another phone ringing." The phone went dead.

I suspected that Phillip Pennington wasn't going to give up so easily. He needed to get the sixth case completed for the FDA, otherwise his implant was useless. My guess was that he wanted to get it done quickly. To do that, it must be boarded to get space in the operating room. That left only one option: another hospital in the Detroit area.

I picked up the phone again and dialed the Oakdale County Medical Society. Pennington was chief at Great Lakes and St. Vincent's. There wouldn't be any need for him to be on the staff anywhere else, but it was worth a shot. I hadn't kept up my membership, so I didn't know where this notion might lead.

The receptionist answered. "Oakdale County Medical Society."

"Yes, I want to make an appointment with Dr. Phillip Pennington, but before I do, I wanted to check where he practices at. I was wondering if you could look that information up for me?" I asked.

"Certainly, I'll have that information for you in a moment," she replied politely. There was a moment's pause. "The records show that Dr. Pennington is listed at Great Lakes Medical Center, St. Vincent's and Flushing Community Hospital. Is that all you need?"

"Yes, thank you." Flushing was a small, exclusive private hospital in the suburbs. He probably retained privileges at it to do an occasional case on some wealthy suburbanite. It was worth a try. I went over to the pay phone and dialed the number. It wasn't hard to get into the operating room suite.

"This is Dr. Dailey, calling from Great Lakes. I was supposed to scrub with Dr. Pennington on Bernard Frasker's case. I was wondering whether it had started yet." I asked nervously.

"You're a little late," the voice at the other answered. "Dr. Pennington is already in the operating room getting ready to start Mr. Frasker's case."

My heart sank. "Maybe you could tell me how long the case was boarded for?"

"Four hours. He should be done by two o'clock."

Shit, I wish Jordan were here. What was I going to do, barge into the operating room and stop him from doing the procedure? I picked up the phone again and dialed Jordan's office. Answering machine, voicemail. I needed a real person.

In desperation, I decided to call Sheila Pryzbycki, at Coastal Life. She was the only live body I could halfway depend on. I didn't have anything to lose, so I dialed the number.

"Coastal Life," the voice whined.

"Sheila, this is Ben Dailey." Silence for a moment. I couldn't tell if I was getting her usual response, but it was the best I could do.

I got the usual. "Sorry, Ben. Mr. Sanderson doesn't have anything today."

I could feel she was getting ready to hang up. "Wait, Sheila. This hasn't anything to do with Sanderson. I need you to call someone for me. It's important."

"In case you didn't notice, I've already got a boss." So much for my reclaimed respect.

"It's all right, Sheila, Mr. Sanderson told me to have you make the call." She could put me off all she wanted, but the threat of bucking her boss was more than she was ready to tackle, even if it was a lie.

"Are you sure?" she asked.

"Trust me, Sheila," I said, feeling exasperated and ready to explode.

"If you're sure he said it was okay, I'll do it," she relented. "By the way," she added, "a Mr. Herb Albright, a stockbroker, dropped off something for you at the office."

I knew I couldn't make it over to Bruce's office, so on the promise that I had a Christmas present for her and would deliver it personally, she said she would take the package to Jordan's office on her way home. Then she hung up. I could only hope she would get it to her.

The thought of Herb made me stop by the phone for a moment and quickly dial his number. I owed it to him. It took a moment for him to come to the line.

"Herb, this is Ben Dailey. I understand you left something for me," I said.

"Nothing big, just the information on the corporate setup of Panatone. Interesting little company." Herb spent a few precious minutes describing the corporate background of the company.

"Listen, Herb, I'd like to talk longer with you, but I'm in a hurry. But if you want some inside advice, I'll give it to you."

"Sure. What do you know?"

"Tell your clients to sell Panatone short. Do it now," I said quickly then hung up.

That was it. Except I wasn't quite ready to leave St. Vincent's. I went back to the stairwell and two-stepped down the stairs. This time I wasn't about to go to the surgery suite. Instead, I went to the orderlies' room and walked in. There were a couple of people lounging around, but dressed in my torn jacket, I went unnoticed. I took out a pair of extra-large scrubs and changed my clothes in the corner of the locker room.

There was a plastic bag in the corner left over from some drug company. I stuffed my clothes in it and walked out. I could have passed for anyone at the hospital. With my clothes in hand I walked back to the stairs and out into the cold.

Two o'clock and it would be all over, unless I stopped Phillip Pennington. I got into the truck and started the engine. I heard a noise behind me and turned around. Before I could move there was a sharp pain in the back of my head and then nothing.

CHAPTER 28

I REGAINED CONSCIOUSNESS SLOWLY on the bare floor of a cold, damp room. After a few moments I remembered the car. My eyes started to focus. Gray cement walls, machinery running, and the pungent aroma of engine oil. *Got to get up, call for help.* I moved my arm, but nothing happened. I struggled again and realized that I was bound with tape.

Wildly, I shook my head, trying to release myself. It was no use. Whoever had immobilized me knew what he was doing. I turned my head to the right, looking for some escape. Instead, all I saw were pipes and huge, rusted machines. A basement, the mechanical room most likely. There was water on the floor and the sound of a pump.

I turned the other way and saw my arm strapped to what looked like a metal stanchion. My legs were also bound in tape.

Shit. What was I doing in this swamp pit anyway? I struggled again to free myself. I was certain this scene was the prelim to my death, and whoever had me there was going to perform the execution shortly.

Looking around again, I could see that I was wedged into a corner of the basement, next to a running generator and some large pumps. No one would hear me yell over the sound of the equipment.

There had to be an object I could free myself with, or use to cut the tape. The edge of the generator caught my eye, and I struggled to get near it, thrusting my body to the left. After a couple of minutes all I had to show for my efforts was a cramp in the deep muscles of my back.

I looked over to the left again and studied the machine more carefully. The first thing that struck me was the painted red letters on the dark green casing that read "sump pump." From the sound of its motor running there must have been plenty of water to be removed, just like in my boat. Must have the same kind of parts too: intake pipe, electric motor, and discharge pipe.

My hand was a few inches from the discharge pipe. I carefully inched toward it. When my skin touched the black, metal tubing, I could feel the water coursing out. No question, it was operating full tilt. I looked at the pipe again. There were two short, thick wires that went back under the housing that covered the electric pump motor. The sump on my boat had one like this, a discharge wire that regulated the outflow. Looking at the red, insulated wire, I realized it was my only hope. *Black to ground, red to hot*, the electronic guru's words echoed in my ears. Then I remembered how I always screwed up the first time.

My right hand grasped the wire, and I tried to roll over to disconnect it. A slight budge, then nothing. I rolled again, this time a little harder, and, suddenly, it was free. Now I was really scared, holding a live 110 line, lying on a wet floor, a black and red wire sticking out from my hand. Touch the wrong end to metal and I was a goner.

Too late, I heard a sound of metal scraping against the concrete floor that penetrated above the din of the equipment. I hid the wire next to me and waited.

The sound came closer, and, suddenly, I was looking at the face of a large man with a brush cut. It took me a moment of disbelief to realize I had seen him before. It was Willard Donaldson, Faye Donaldson's husband.

"Have a nice sleep, asshole?" he asked contemptuously, as he wheeled a handcart near my feet. I looked up at the stretcher and saw a body bag on top of it. I knew it was for me.

"What are you doing here?" I gurgled.

"I work here. Remember, I told you my job is to tear down old buildings? Well, welcome to "E" building at the old Ford Rouge Plant." His viscous smile contorted his face.

"What the hell is this about?"

"What this is about is you. This is what you get for nosing around in other people's business."

"I hardly know you. What could I possibly have done?"

"I heard from one of Faye's co-workers that you've been snooping around, checking out her computer, asking questions. You were going to screw everything up."

"Screw what up?"

"Don't play dumb with me, jerkoff. Double the money, that's what."

"You mean the life insurance money from the government?"

"Yeah, the real money. More money than her Coastal policy would ever pay."

I looked at him incredulously. His eyes were dancing crazily from side to side.

"I've got to get rid of you. You know too much. You said it yourself. You were going to the police and help find out who did this. Tell everything to the insurance company. They would cancel the payout on the policy. I've waited too long for this."

"You'll never get away with this, Donaldson. We know all about the hearing aid and Pennington." I glared upside down at his face. He looked like a large, grotesque, moveable puppet, staring at me with a quizzical look.

"I don't give a shit about fucking hearing aids or anything else. I want my money, and I'm not going to let you stand in the way. I tried to get rid of you at the hospital, but you got lucky. This time I'm not going to fail."

"So *you* were the person that did all that. You told Gernowski that Faye was to blame for his condition. Why didn't you just kill me the way Gernowski killed your wife?"

"You liked that, huh? Wasn't that the perfect crime, using someone else to do it? Killing you will be a little more complicated."

"What do you mean?" I could tell he wanted to brag about what had happened. I wanted him to talk.

"How do you think he found out about Faye? She told me she had this hearing aid approval she was working on for the FDA. That it was something big, but she always said that about everything. Then she showed me the angry letters that this guy kept sending her about his hearing. She said he was crazy, that he blamed his hearing aid for making him lose control. That he was going to get the bastard that did this to him. That's when I got the idea. I called him and told him Faye was responsible. Then I met with him and gave him her number and address. He told me he was going to take care of her. It was a simple thing to get him angry. I knew he would." Donaldson smiled as he spoke.

"Murder by proxy by a deranged man with wild accusations, so you get the insurance, no one knows, no money changes hands, no one can connect you."

"Exactly. For a working stiff, it was a pretty cool deal, huh? He got rid of her. Then I killed him. A perfect crime." Willard Donaldson may have been a factory worker, but he was no dummy. It was a perfect crime.

"What about torching my boat and the shooting in Ann Arbor?"

His face went blank. "I don't know anything about your fucking boat or the shooting, but I'm sorry someone else didn't take you out and save me the trouble. Now let's get this done."

He had a small black bag next to him. I stared as he started rummaging through it. He pulled out a wire from the bag and attached it to two wooden handles at each end. I didn't need to be a rocket scientist to figure out what he was going to do.

"I'm going to enjoy this. It'll make up for all the aggravation you've given me."

"No good deed goes unpunished, right?" I asked, thinking about how misguided I had been in trying to help this evil bastard.

"Right. It was going perfectly until you came along and started snooping around for the insurance company. You got in my way, and now I need you out. I worked thirty years in the plants, and all of a sudden they were going to screw me out of my pension and benefits. I planned to get the policy years ago. It just took the right time to do it."

And now I was going to die, all because Bruce Sanderson was trying to give me some work. I struggled against the tape. He shrugged his massive shoulders. "No use fighting. You'll never break that tape."

"Do you ever look at yourself in the mirror and see what a fucking animal you are, what you will have to live with?"

"Won't make much difference to you what I am, pal. After I cut your throat, I put you on the cart in the body bag and that's that."

"How are you going to explain my death?" I countered.

"They'll never find you," he said matter-of-factly. "That's what they have steel mills for."

"The police will find you. I have contacts," I shouted.

"Why don't you start calling them now," he said, sneering.

I fought against the tape, but it was futile. "You didn't do this by yourself, Donaldson. Who helped you? Was it that bimbo next to the Harley?"

His face turned almost purple and the rage flamed in his eyes. He reached down, grabbed my jacket, and shook me like I was a rag doll. "Okay, that's enough, mother fucker. That's my girlfriend you're talking about. I'm sick of your bullshit."

With that he slammed me back on the floor, knocking the breath out of me. I watched as he picked up the wire and stretched it out, ready to curl it around my neck. I tried to roll away, but all I succeeded in doing was stretching the wire in my hand as I shifted myself closer to the metal pole. Donaldson saw it and instinctively reached for the steel pole. My chance.

I waited until his hand was firmly around the metal stanchion and, then, holding onto the insulated portion, I brought the live wire up to the base, praying to the god of electricity. Donaldson must have seen my hand move, but his reaction was a fraction of a second too late. There was a bright flash; a scream tore from his lips. His hand seemed glued to the pole as his body jerked and convulsed, only inches from me, for twenty or thirty seconds. I watched his eyes, wild and furious. His 250 pounds collapsed to the ground next to me.

"God, I love electronics!" I yelled.

No time for exultation. I had to get out of there. Reaching into Donaldson's pocket, I pulled out a pair of the cutters. Two minutes of cutting and I was free.

My body ached as I pushed Donaldson away from me and struggled dizzily to my feet. I looked first at my hands, red and swollen in the dim light of the basement, and rubbed them to restore the circulation. Then I warily bent down next to Donaldson's motionless body. I didn't bother checking for a pulse to see if he was really dead. Instead, I pulled the keys to the truck out of his pocket.

Looking at him motionless on the floor, I had a strange and sick feeling. Somehow I didn't feel like a conqueror. More like a survivor. I had had patients die before, but that was in a vain attempt to save their lives. This was different; I had never killed anyone.

I panicked. It was cold and damp in the basement. I had to get out of there.

CHAPTER 29

I CLIMBED A FLIGHT OF RUSTED METAL STAIRS, searching for sunlight. At the top of the stairs I walked into large warehouse with broken windows. Rusted chains hung from the metal ceiling, and remnants of useless machinery lay scattered on the cement floor. If this building was being used for anything, it wasn't obvious.

The howling wind was swirling through the cracked windows, blowing flurries of dust in my face as I staggered toward a subdued light near the front of the building. In my scrub suit I was starting to shiver uncontrollably. The thought of surviving a sinking boat again flashed through my mind.

I looked for an exit from the building. There appeared to be an opening to my right back toward the stairs I had climbed. I walked toward it, trying to avoid the metal debris on the floor. To my surprise there was a door just to the left of the stairs. I tried the handle, and it budged slightly. I thought I could open it, so I started pushing against the entranceway with my shoulder. On the third try I had just started to feel the wooden frame move, when I was suddenly hit from behind and pushed into the door jamb. The wind rushed out of my chest from the blow.

I fell to the cement floor, scraping my elbow. I looked up in shock and saw the crazed face of Willard Donaldson above me. There was a burn on his face and his jacket sleeve looked charred.

"You motherfucker! Now I am really going to kill you!" he yelled.

He picked up a pipe from the floor and brought it above his head. As he swung it down, I rolled to the side. Then I leg-whipped him. He grunted and toppled over, the pipe clattering to the floor. I sensed he was hurting from the way he staggered back to his feet.

Instinctively, I reached for the pipe on the floor and swung it at his leg. I must have aimed it at the right spot, because he yelled in pain and grabbed at his knee. As he did, he fell on top of me. His huge hands reached for my neck. All I could think of was Sennett's comment about Joey and the boys. I reached for his balls and squeezed for all I could. There was another shriek and he let go, rolling onto his side.

This time, I didn't take any chances. I pulled his woolen coat over his head, so that the sleeves immobilized his arms. With his knee damaged and his arms controlled, there wasn't much he could do. I reached down and took the belt off his pants and tied his arms behind his back.

I saw a piece of steel wire on the floor. My hands were frozen, but I managed to get the metal around his legs. Using the pipe, I twisted the wire down around his legs tightly. He screamed at the pain as the metal tightened. I tore at his shirt, ripped off a strip of flannel cloth, and stuffed it into his mouth.

"I'm glad you didn't die downstairs, Donaldson," I said standing over him. "It wouldn't have been real justice." With that I went back to the door. The force of his push had jarred the door loose. I pushed it again and walked outside.

I looked to the right. This building stood out among a bunch of other unused facilities. There was no one around. I walked to the corner of the building and saw Easy's truck. Running to it, I got inside and started the engine. It didn't take me long to make it to the service road on the huge auto plant grounds. I followed it until I came to a gate. There was a security guard standing watch. I stopped the truck.

"There's a guy in Building E on the floor. He's not feeling too good. You need to call 911."

The guy was speechless. I drove off before he had time to reply. I had seen enough of the Rouge Plant. Now I had to sort out what had just happened to me. Something told me no one was going to listen, no matter what I said.

Driving back, the facts of what had just happened to me started to sink in. I was pretty shaken. Having a street fight with a killer and surviving was not my usual routine. Even worse were the unanswered questions. I had solved the murder of Faye Donaldson, but what about my boat and the shooting in Ann Arbor? Donaldson said he knew nothing about it, and, as crazy as he was, I believed him. I wondered what Sennett would have to say.

It took me fifteen minutes to negotiate the road back to the Shore Garden Marina. I parked the truck outside, took the bag with my clothes, and went to the bathroom. I looked in the mirror. No wonder the guard looked shocked. I had blood on my face and my scrub suit was a mess.

I dumped my clothes out of the bag. As they fell on the floor, I saw a bunch of surgical sponges in promotion packages. I opened one of the packages and saw the familiar gauze pad with the blue strip in the center. I had used them hundreds of times in the operating room. In spite of my other problems, I stared at the cotton pad. It appeared strange to me.

I wondered why. *I must be hallucinating, some kind of post-traumatic stress reaction.* Isn't that what the shrinks would have called it? How could I be worrying about a sponge after what had just happened to me? After a few moments, I gave up and went back to getting cleaned up. A minute later it suddenly came to me.

I wrapped a towel around my neck and went back to my room to find my duffel. When I got there, I pulled out the black folder, the one filled with photographs and legal documents, things I had poured over dozens of times, trying to find an answer as to how I had screwed up. I found the document I was looking for, the trial testimony of Allan Davis, the pathologist who testified against me in my malpractice case. I found the page I was looking for and as I read it, I remembered him holding a piece of gauze just like the sample ones in front of the jury. I found the page and read the deposition.

"Dr. Davis," the attorney asked, "where was this sponge taken from?"

"From the patient's wound," he replied.

"And who put it there?"

"Why, Dr. Dailey, I'm sure."

I remembered the words as if it were yesterday. They were spoken with the arrogance of someone who knew everything and questioned nothing. I had sat there, helpless, loathing his response but unable to find any defense.

I had the same anger now, but somehow it was different. I reached back into the folder and pulled out Chip Thornton's operative report. But this time, I didn't do it out of depression. I sensed there was something I had missed in these documents. I read the dictation of the operation, and, again, it seemed clean. I read through the anesthesiologist's records, again nothing. Another dead end, another futile effort. I felt like I was going mad. Then I looked at the nurses' notes. This time I studied an innocent notation I had passed over many times without thinking. There was a break in the case while a new nurse had scrubbed in. At first glance, there was nothing unusual about it; scrub nurses changed all the time. Did it mean anything to this case?

Frustrated, I shoved the document back in the duffel and angrily zipped it shut. How could I possibly resurrect facts from five years ago? I went back to the bathroom and finished cleaning up my face. Wetting another sponge in the sink, I dabbed at the cuts on my face. They were all abrasions, nothing that required surgery. I stared at the sponge once again, almost wishing it could somehow tell me what I searching for. When I finished, I changed out of my scrubs and back into my street clothes.

I went back to my room, gathered my things, and called Sennett. While I did, I flipped on the television in the corner. I reached Knudsen on the first ring. He said the lieutenant was investigating something that had happened out at the Rouge Plant. I was about to tell him that it was my doing when I looked over at the TV and saw Easy's truck on the screen.

I should have known there would have been a television camera at the gate. I told Knudsen I'd call him back. Then I listened to the reporter describe a vicious assault on an employee of the Ford Motor Company at their Rouge Plant. That was followed by a grainy picture of my face on the screen with an announcement that the police were looking for me as a person of interest. Great.

My plans had suddenly changed. I had gone from being a victim of a murder plot to a suspect in a vicious assault. I needed to talk to Sennett, but now it had to be on my terms.

I knew someone had Easy's license, and they would be at the marina soon. I snatched up my bag of clothes and all of the papers I had and raced out to the Jeep. I pulled out the spare keys from a metal lock box under the front wheel well. Slowly, I drove past Easy's office. Down the street I saw two squad cars racing down Jefferson Avenue with their sirens wailing. I'd have to settle up with Easy later.

I pulled out of the drive slowly behind the shelter of a large Waste Management truck. I was sure I hadn't been seen. As I proceeded down the street, I checked the rearview mirror. The squad cars were entering the marina.

CHAPTER 30

I FELT LIKE A JUGGLER with five balls in the air. With so many thoughts bouncing around in my head, I had trouble focusing on anything. Slowly, I began to feel the worst dread of all. I realized that I was afraid—afraid of the legal system. The thought of facing a judge and jury had paralyzed me into inaction.

I was sure part of my confusion was a natural response to someone like Willard Donaldson trying to kill me. But in spite of what other people might have said about me, I wasn't a nutcase. In my life as a doctor, I had been in plenty of tight situations. My hands never shook. Sure, I had plenty of reason to feel anxious, but I instinctively I knew there was something else that caused it. I kept thinking about the nurses' note from the operation. That's when I decided to see Allan Davis.

Davis could be an irritating person, and, in fact, he was on most days. Maybe it came with his job as a pathologist and medical examiner, stuck in a lab. Muddling around dead tissue could do that to a person. But I always thought there was more to it.

Allan Davis was right by definition. To question his diagnoses was to challenge his very being. Not infrequently the word intellectual snob had been affixed to him. Maybe it was a little perverse on my part, but on occasion I enjoyed pushing his buttons over some clinical issue just to see his face get red and his bottom lip quiver with anger.

But like most people, he wasn't all bad. In fact, he had an encyclopedic knowledge of music. When we weren't talking medicine, I would frequently pick his brain about various composers. That was before the trial. I had never forgiven him for throwing me under the bus.

I knew his habits. It was my bet that Alan Davis would never miss a day of work, even with bad weather. When he came to the phone, I was relieved until I heard the tone of his voice.

"What can I do for you, doctor?" He always used the title when he was irritated.

"I need a favor, Al."

"I've got three autopsies yet to do and only one helper. If anyone needs help, it's me."

"I believe you, and I'm sorry to call. But you're the only one who can help me."

There was a moment of hesitation. "You know, Ben, ever since we met, I've known you and I were going to lock horns. What is it you need?" There was a patronizing sound to his voice.

It took me about five minutes of explanation for him to agree to meet me and another thirty minutes on the expressway to make it to the Detroit City Morgue. The building was located near the medical center. On a cold, dreary December day in Detroit, nothing looked gloomier.

I walked inside. Davis was waiting for me in the lobby. I strode up to him quickly and extended my hand. The hand that was returned was soft and clammy. I looked at Davis standing there, tall and gawky with a balding head, sallow complexion, and wire-rimmed glasses perched on the beak of his large nose. Ichabod Crane came to mind, a perfect fit for a medical examiner.

"This'd better be good, Ben," he said, adjusting his arm around several large files he was carrying next to his chest, "or you and I are going to have some serious words."

"If it isn't right, Al, I promise I'll never bother you again." No need to. I'd be out of town for good.

"We'll worry about that later. I'm more interested in putting my involvement with your legal troubles to rest, once and for all. Now let's get down to the office and get this over."

With that we made our way down the stairwell to the basement offices of the pathology department. We were both wearing badges. Davis strode past the clerks unnoticed and took me back to a room labeled "Surgical specimens— Litigation." As we passed them, he turned to me and snickered. "Sometimes you just have to give it up and admit you did something wrong." I didn't say anything in return. Instead I followed him inside. It was a ghoulish place, full of green metal shelves lined with jars of organs preserved in formaldehyde. He set his files down on a table and moved toward the racks.

"We have a policy to save all specimens associated with lawsuits," he continued, not bothering to look back and see if anyone was following us. "The specimen from your case should still be here." As he spoke, he reached into a shelf and started sliding jars around. His bony finger seemed to know exactly where to find what he wanted.

"Scotten, James," he said. "Here it is. I'll show you what I found in the jar."

He pulled the small container down, set it on a Formica counter, and then spread out some paper towels. From a box in the corner he fished out a pair of rubber gloves, unscrewed the cap, and reached in for the specimen. I never understood how pathologists could be so blasé about dead tissue. The smell of formaldehyde and the thought of what he was doing were making me sick.

"Here it is, Ben. See, just like I said it was." He pulled out the cotton gauze sponge that was retrieved from Jimmy Scotten's neck. "What else do you need to be convinced you made a fatal error?"

I stared at the specimen on the table. It was then that I noticed what years of pouring over legal documents had eluded me.

"Open the sponge up, Al, will you?" I asked quickly.

Davis spread the four-by-eight sponge completely open on the table. "Still don't believe me, do you? Looks like a pretty average sponge to me," he said indignantly.

"It is," I replied. "There's only one problem."

"What's that?"

"Operating room sponges have a blue marking thread in them, so they'll show up on an x-ray. If someone had taken an x-ray of Jimmy Scotten's neck, this sponge never would have shown up," I said slowly.

"So? A sponge is a sponge."

"Not in the operating room. They don't use this kind of sponge there. If you were a surgeon, you'd know that. They only use the ones with the x-ray marker, so in case one is missing they can find it on an x-ray." I could feel rage building inside me.

"That's true," he admitted, shocked. "Then where did this sponge come from?" he added quickly.

"I'm about to find out, Al. I'm about to find out." I answered through clenched teeth.

Davis's face had turned ashen when he realized that he might have leaped too quickly to judgment. "Ben, I swear to you, all I did was report my findings. I had nothing to do with the conclusions reached," he said defensively.

"Don't worry, Al. It's not your fault. You couldn't have known." What I wanted to say was, "You were too big a jerk to question anything." But I had bigger fish to fry than Allan Davis, so I remained silent while my mind spun wildly in thought. Could I have been framed?

I didn't bother shaking his hand. Instead, I turned on my heel and walked out of his storage room and down the long hallway to the entrance. There was a payphone at the front door. I called the number Jordan said she would be at, and she picked up on the second ring.

CHAPTER 31

I QUICKLY TOLD HER EVERYTHING that had happened. She listened in silence, almost as if she knew that something like this was going to take place. "Ben, you need to call Sennett up and arrange to surrender to the police."

"I'm sorry, Jordan, but I'm not going to do that. I don't trust anyone, except you. There is something strange that has taken place." I told her about the sponge and Allan Davis.

"Are you saying someone planted the evidence?"

"Maybe. This case runs deeper than Faye Donaldson's death. I believe that it is connected to Phillip Pennington and those hearing aids." I told her that Knudsen had sent some things over to her office. I needed her to get them to me.

"Ben, if I do this, I am aiding and abetting a possible suspect in a crime."

"Trust me, I'm a doctor." It was the only thing I could think of to say.

I KNEW IT WOULD ONLY BE A MATTER OF TIME until the police would be searching for my car. I had to act quickly. Jordan said she would have her secretary leave the folder at the counter at the Greyhound Bus Terminal. She asked me for a name, and I told her Chet Baker. It was risky, but if I got over there immediately, I might get away with it.

The next thing I did was stop at a small hardware store. I picked up some blue masking tape and a small bag of rags. I pulled the Jeep into the rear of the parking lot with the back of the car facing toward the fence. Kneeling in the snow, I tore off strips of the dark blue masking tape and changed the letters and numbers on the license plate. Then I took out some rags, dropped them in the dirty slush of the parking lot, and washed the metal license plate. I stepped back and looked at my creation. From a distance it looked like any other dirty, illegible plate in the winter.

From there I drove to the bus terminal, staying on side streets and avoiding the downtown area. The bus station was a two-story gray, aluminum-sided building with large windows and a greyhound emblem at the top. It was just off the Lodge freeway, but like much of the city, the surrounding neighborhood was deserted. In the cold weather, like tonight, the place was usually frequented by homeless people looking for warmth and the occasional traveler looking for a cheap ride to Chicago, Cleveland, or Pittsburgh.

When I arrived, I parked on a side street, then got out and surveyed the location. From across the street the Jeep was partially obscured by a dumpster, to the point that I had a hard time seeing it myself. I walked around the back of the station looking for anything that might give me away. When I was satisfied it was clear, I trudged through the melting snow to the station entrance.

At the front door I hunched down into the collar of my jacket. For all intents and purposes, I wasn't a person of interest, I was just another lost soul looking for a way out of Detroit.

I walked inside with my head down, convinced they had television cameras in the place. When I reached the ticket desk, there was a family waiting in front of me, a baby in a stroller, a small boy, and their mother. I stood there for a moment. As soon as the baby saw me, she began crying and her brother pushed a pacifier back into her mouth. He looked up and smiled at me. I winked back at him and then turned my head back down to look at the floor. After a couple of minutes, I got to the counter and asked for a package from Ms. Dalkind. The ticket agent asked for a name, and I replied Chet Baker. With my luck the guy would be a jazz nut.

He didn't say anything until I reached the door. "Hey, mister, you got to come back." I wanted to bolt, but instead turned around and slowly headed back to the counter. "You forgot to sign for the package."

When I signed the sheet, he smiled. "I always wanted the autograph of a famous person," he laughed. I mumbled something about being the wrong person, turned around, and made it back to the front door and outside before he could say anything else.

When I reached the car, I slid into the driver's seat, turned on the engine, and started opening the package. A bunch of papers fell out. I looked at them carefully. There were bank receipts from Faye Donaldson, a report on Phillip Pennington, and the stock pages from Herb Albright. I decided to start with Pennington.

I started reading his profile again. Pennington actually grew up in Detroit. He said he was a poor kid, but he was obviously smart enough to get a scholarship to one of those fancy private schools in the suburbs. He went on to

Dartmouth on scholarship and then Hopkins Medical School, graduating number two in his class. A residency and fellowship at Stanford, a year at the Karolinska Institute in Sweden, and then he worked his way up the academic ladder in Boston. So far so good.

His position as chairman of the department in Detroit was his first. I wondered why he took it. Great Lakes Medical Center was a second-tier school, definitely not up to his pedigree.

There wasn't much else, just a summary of his papers and presentations and a current address with phone number. I was about to set the papers aside when I felt another paper stapled onto the back page. I stared at it for a moment. It was a copy of a brief police report, a misdemeanor dating back to the early seventies for disturbing the peace in Bloomfield Hills, a posh suburb north of Detroit.

It sounded like just a kid thing. I should know; I'd had a few scrapes myself. There was only one difference—the complaint was signed by a woman. I made out the name, Marni Slanell. I decided to check it out.

I got out of the car and walked back to the bus station. This time I ducked into an alcove where the pay phone was located. I picked up the phone and called information to see if there was still a Marni Slanell in the greater Detroit area. Believe it or not, there was.

I called the number. Someone answered on the third ring. It was Marni Slanell. We spoke for a moment. When I said this was about an incident in high school involving Phillip Pennington, she sounded surprised. When I asked to see her, she said I should come over.

I walked out of the bus station, turned the corner, and stopped. There, parked near my car, was a police cruiser. I stood paralyzed. What was I going to do? If I went to the car, I was a goner. If I didn't, I'd never get out of there.

I decided to take a chance. I walked down the street. The cop was getting out of the squad car.

"Hi," I said. "What did I do?"

"Parking in a loading zone."

Shit, I said to myself. "Sorry, I didn't see the sign."

"You're right on that one. The dumpster is blocking the sign. I wasn't going to give you a ticket, but I couldn't read your license plate from the street."

I told him I was sorry, that I was going to wash the car tomorrow. He must have known how stupid this was, because he smiled and said it was a Christmas present from the police department. I thanked him, wished him happy holidays, and got in behind the wheel. Life was getting complicated.

CHAPTER 32

MARNI SLANELL LIVED A CONDO in downtown Royal Oak, Detroit's answer to a party district. It was on the second floor of a four-story building that overlooked Main Street and the throng of young people that filled the sidewalks. It was around seven when I knocked on her door.

When it opened, the woman at the door who identified herself as Marni must have been in her mid-forties but looked older. She was an overweight five-eight with straight dyed reddish hair combed to hide the fleshiness of her face. I glanced at her body. She wore a v-neck cashmere sweater that showed a little too much cleavage and jeans that were a little too tight for the weight of her thighs. Dark circles under her eyes accentuated the puffiness of her face and belied the bright red lipstick that tried to liven up her appearance. I guessed at one time she might have been an attractive woman, but that was before she drank too many whiskey sours and smoked too many cigarettes.

She asked me into the living room, which was richly appointed with two leather couches facing each other with a long marble coffee table in between. There was a small fireplace at the end of the room with a carved wooden mantle. Above it was a modern painting with splashes of red and green and yellow arranged in a geometric pattern.

She must have seen me staring at the painting.

"That's a Vassarelly. My first husband loved that piece. It was part of the settlement." Marni Slanell must have divorced well. She motioned for me to sit on the couch, then sat across from me with her legs crossed. "What is this about Phillip Pennington?"

I explained that I was asked by an insurance company to look at a case involving a loss of life. Phillip Pennington's name came up because of the possibility that an instrument he devised might have been involved. She didn't seem to care about the insurance case, but she did want to talk about Pennington.

"I hated that boy."

When I asked why, she told me he was associated with those rich bastards who ruined her life.

"What did Pennington do?"

"He was a dweeb," she replied in a deep, husky voice, "a real geek. You know, greasy hair, pants that were too short, slide rule, that kind of thing. He even wore those tennis shoes from K-Mart."

"He was listed on a juvenile complaint. Your name was on it."

"What do you know about it?" Her voice sounded a little too defensive.

"That's what I wanted to ask you. There were seven or eight boys mentioned, and then you. It sounded a little strange. I'm wondering if you could tell me what happened."

"There's not much to tell. It was so long ago I guess it doesn't make much difference. We had just graduated. Ronnie Granmeier had a party over at his house. It got out of hand and the police came."

"In the complaint it said that you were found naked in the bedroom."

A shade of gray came across her face. Her eyes narrowed. "Yeah, that's what they always said about me. You want to find Marni, check the nearest bedroom."

"What exactly happened?"

"You want to know what happened? I'll tell you. They gang raped me, all those bastards."

"Including Phillip Pennington?"

"He was in the room," she replied in a halting voice.

"Did you tell what happened to the police?"

"Are you kidding? It was the seventies, and these were the richest kids in Detroit. Their fathers owned the judges. Their attorneys were from New York."

"So nothing came of it?"

"Oh, plenty came of it. One of the kids had a video of the whole thing. He bragged to me about it. When I told my father, he went to the parents and threatened to tell the cops."

"What happened then?"

"They gave my father a hundred thousand dollars to keep quiet." The color of her face became sallower and her cheeks seemed to droop with every word she spoke. Suddenly the makeup didn't hide the creases and wrinkles of her middle-age face.

"And what did you get?"

"Nothing, absolutely nothing. My father told me he needed the money for his business. That's all my self-respect was worth to him, a hundred thousand dollars." Tears streamed down her face. Black smudges of mascara dotted her cheeks.

"Did you ever see the tape?"

"No. My father took care of it."

"What happened to it?"

"Gone, burned. That's the way they handle everything. Destroy the evidence and get rid of people that are in their way."

I felt sorry for Marni Slanell. "Do you think that tape was really destroyed?" She shrugged, as if it didn't matter. I knew it did. "Who were the other boys that were involved?"

She listed the names of the boys. The last one was Chip Thornton.

CHAPTER 33

I LEFT MARNI'S PLACE AND WENT BACK TO MY JEEP. The car was in the open in the snow-covered parking lot now, a fact that made me wary. I kept looking from side to side to see if any one was following me. There was no one.

I got inside and sat for a minute. Then I made up my mind. I was going to see Phillip Pennington.

I found his address in the folder and quickly recognized it as one of those exclusive neighborhoods near the Cranbrook School. I suspected that, on his salary from the medical school, he could afford it.

My suspicion turned out to be true. He lived in a large Tudor house on a hill with a long driveway. There were spruce trees everywhere, obscuring the house from the road along with limestone entrance pylons with copper lions on the top, each of them with one paw in the air, mouth open. I thought it was a nice touch, simple but elegant.

A halogen light illuminated the front porch. I drove up the circular driveway and parked just past the door. Walking up the step, I saw the doorbell and pushed it twice. I heard a loud chiming, reminding me of a church.

I stood to the side of the door as it opened. When it did, I pushed it open.

Pennington was standing in the foyer wearing a black satin robe, red striped pajamas, black leather house slippers, and a surprised look on his face. When he saw it was me, he took a step backward. Then he glanced from side to side, as if he was looking for someone to help him.

"Don't worry, Dr. Pennington, I'm not here to hurt you. This may be my only chance to help you."

He looked at disdain. "Help me? How could someone like you help me?"

I went on to tell him about Ralph Gernowski and the possibility that the hearing aid he implanted could have produced enough electromagnetic radiation to cause brain abnormalities. Maybe even enough to change a normal man into a killer.

He looked at me incredulously. "Are you out of your mind? Those aids passed the scrutiny of the FDA. There is not a thing wrong with them. Now if that is what you are here for, I'm calling the police." He turned to go to the next room to get a telephone.

"Wait, I have proof."

Pennington turned and faced me. His face was red and his mustached upper lip quivered with rage.

"You've got nothing, Dailey. You are a washed-up doctor with a checkered past and no future. Now get out!"

There wasn't much more I could say. I wanted him to hear me out, listen to what I had to say about the high frequency gain. Ask him about Marni Slanell. It wasn't going to happen and I knew it. But it wasn't all bad. I had made him uncontrollably angry, and there was no telling what an irrational person would do. I intended to find out.

I walked back to my car, realizing that I had learned a lot from my brief meeting with Pennington. I didn't think he was lying about his hearing aid and seriously doubted that he knew anything about Ralph Gernowski or any other of his implant patients. To him, they were vagrants, insignificant poor people whom he had helped with his remarkable aid; for him, that was justification enough. He probably got a postoperative hearing exam on them to show the FDA they worked and then never saw them again.

But if he didn't know, somebody did. And that somebody was manipulating him for personal advantage. How could a smart guy like Pennington be that stupid? It didn't make sense.

Instinctively, I knew the answer to that question was the key to unlocking the mystery of what had happened to me. Now all I had to do was wait until Pennington did something stupid.

IT WAS LATE WHEN I LEFT PENNINGTON'S HOUSE. I had never been in trouble with the police. Now I was on the television and in the newspapers. It was unnerving to say the least.

I was beat and needed a place to hole up for the evening. I also needed something to eat. So I stopped at a Dunkin' Donuts shop for a chocolate covered donut with sprinkles and a cup of coffee and ate inside with my head down, watching the snowplows piling the white stuff in mountains twice as high as my car. When I was finished, I went to the pay phone, made a call, and then headed for the Pipeline.

It was one in the morning when I gave the car to William and asked him to park it somewhere that no one would find it. I took Jordan's folder with me and got out of the car. Before I walked in, I asked him if the lieutenant had been there. He said that he left about an hour ago.

Entering through the front door, I saw that the place was half full. Sid wasn't there but that didn't stop the boys. They were just finishing the Sonny Rollins classic, "St. Thomas." The few people there seemed to be enjoying it. I looked over to the bar and saw Charlie. He nodded and then pointed to a corner table. There was Frank Scotten, looking down at some papers and sipping at a beer.

I slid into the seat next to him. "Thanks for coming down," I said. He nodded. The boys started playing again. This time they picked "Killer Joe." Somehow it seemed fitting.

"From what I've seen on the TV, that's the least I can do." He sounded genuinely remorseful.

I explained what had happened to Ralph Gernowski and then told him I was at a dead end. The only common thread that connected this whole business was the implanted hearing aid. I told him there was something here I just couldn't fathom. That's when he decided to tell me the truth.

"I feel bad. I've dragged you into this mess."

"What do you mean?"

"I know Jimmy didn't commit suicide. Someone killed him. Someone he knew." Then he confessed. "That night at the lab in Ann Arbor. Those were Jimmy's experiments, not mine. He knew something. More than I could figure out. I told the police, but it was too much for them. They have too many murders and not enough people. I needed a medical person, and you were the only one who I figured would be motivated."

There it was—somehow my life was going to be forever involved in a death spiral with the Scotten family.

"You could have asked me." As I spoke, the three-note arpeggio of Quincy Jones's classic pulsated in the background. "Killer Joe." Maybe someone was trying to tell me something.

"Right, after what my family did to you? Not a chance."

"It's too late now, I'm in for the duration. Tell me, Frank, what does Chip Thornton have to do with your family's business?"

He explained that he thought Thornton had helped his father out with some money. Now he just hung around the place. When he told me he had a bad reputation, I wasn't surprised.

"I need to know if Jimmy told you anything else." He shook his head.

We talked about the hearing aid for a while longer, but nothing came out of it. I was about to get up when I thought of one other thing. "Can you think of anything in his room or on him personally that would make you think he didn't commit suicide?"

He thought a moment. "Nothing in particular, just some pencils and paper on the desk, a couple of books, and an electronics magazine." He stopped for a moment. "There was one thing I remember. There were some pieces of tape rolled up like small cylinders. I picked them up and took them back to my apartment. I still have them."

I took a paper napkin and tore off half of it, then started to roll it tightly. When I was finished, it looked like a small pointed plug, the kind you would use to stop a leak.

"That's it," Frank exclaimed. "What do you use that for?"

"I don't know," I said hesitantly. "Jimmy couldn't go without his tracheotomy tube, could he?"

"No, not since his surgery." I think he realized what he said and that I was responsible. His face reddened, then he said he was sorry.

So was I. Maybe this thing never would have happened if I hadn't screwed up. The boys played the last note of "Killer Joe," and I took it as my cue. I thanked him for coming down and told him I would be in touch. He wanted to talk more, but I got up from the table, shook his hand, and began to walk to the back of the bar.

Frank didn't say anything else, just put his coat back on and walked silently to the door. Watching him leave the Pipeline, his head down and his shoulders hunched, I couldn't help but feel bad for him. Whatever happened to his brother had, in its own way, affected him as much as me. We were both inmates, looking for a way out of our prison.

After he left, I went to the back of the bar to talk with Charlie. As I approached, he pointed to the back room and then came up behind me. When we reached the back hallway, he said, "On the lam, huh?" I should have known this would be all over town.

I told Charlie that I had done nothing wrong, but I had to stay out of sight until I could work my way out of the problem. He looked around for a moment. "Sid's gone home for the evening. Why don't you duck into his office and hole up there?" When I asked if he thought Sid would mind, Charlie brushed me off, telling me his boss already owed me more than he could ever repay.

Sid's office was down the hall from the bar and across from the restrooms with a simple sign saying "office" on the thick wooden door. I walked inside. It was anything but simple. The room was paneled in dark oak with a high gloss varnish. On almost every square inch of space there were framed photographs.

I spent a few minutes walking around and looking at them. Satchmo, Lester Young, Duke Ellington, John Coltrane, Miles Davis. They were all signed. It was like being at a jazz hall of fame.

There was a leather couch along the wall and an antique desk in the corner.

I dropped the folder on the desk and went over to the couch. I lay down for a moment, too tired to think.

The next thing I knew I was in a hotel room with Jordan. I could see, almost feel, the warmth of her naked body on top of me, her hands in my hair, her lips probing my mouth. She said she wanted me inside. I could feel myself grow hard. There was a murmur of delight in my ear as I slipped past her soft, silky entrance. And then I suddenly woke up, breathing heavily and looking down at an erection that hadn't found its home. The dream had been vivid, so real that I knew it had happened. True love so desperately close. Then I realized how far away it really was. My ardor was gone.

I looked at the clock on the wall sandwiched between photographs of Johnny Hodges and Coleman Hawkins. 5 a.m. I had to get up. Brushing something from around my face, I was surprised to find a tablecloth blanket draped over me, undoubtedly a gift from Charlie. I sat up and looked around at Sid's office, my gaze eventually focusing on the folder on the desk.

Reluctantly, I pushed myself off the couch and towards the restroom, got cleaned up, and then came back to the desk.

I sat down on the leather chair and turned on the brass reading light. A photograph caught my eye. It showed a young girl, I guessed ten or eleven, with her arms around Sid. Attached to it was one of those Crayon drawings kids make. It said, "I love you, Daddy." It was strange. I never even knew he was married.

I opened the folder and started scanning the pages. The first thing I looked at was Faye Donaldson's bank account. There were deposits and checks dating back for the last two years. I stared at her account balance. For a secretary working for the government, she had a pretty tidy sum in her savings. Willard Donaldson must have known what his wife had in the bank. To kill her was like hitting the lottery: insurance money plus her bank account.

I wondered where she would get this kind of money, so I looked at the photocopies of the checks that were deposited. Most of them came from Wellington Industries. The total came to around $150,000. I had no idea what Wellington Industries was, but I could bet it had something to do with Pennington's hearing aid.

I looked at my watch. It read 5:30. There was no longer any doubt as to what I was going to do. I had to get moving.

CHAPTER 34

I PICKED UP THE FOLDER FROM THE DESK, walked out of Sid's office, and went to the front entrance. As I opened the door to the club, I felt the cold sting of the north wind blowing from Lake St. Clair. It went through my jacket like I was wearing a thin t-shirt.

I got in my Jeep, set the folder next to me, started the engine, and made for the suburbs again. I wasn't done with Phillip Pennington.

On the way over I stopped at a Tim Horton's and picked up a coffee and bagel. It took me ten minutes to eat the bagel and finish the drink. It took me fifteen minutes to reach Pennington's house.

This time, instead of pulling into his driveway, I drove down the street and waited at the curb. While I did, I turned on the overhead light, opened up the folder again, and started surveying the rest of the material Jordan had left for me.

The glossy corporate report on Panatone that Herb Albright had sent was stuck in the back of the accordion file. It was replete with income statements and a letter from the Chief Financial Officer. I leafed through the pages quickly, realizing that there was nothing there that would help. I was about to throw it back on the seat, when I noticed a diagram of the corporate structure. It turned out that Panatone was a subsidiary of Wellington Industries.

I was going to study the other papers again when I saw the garage door open and Phillip Pennington pull out of his driveway. I waited for moment, and then edged my Jeep away from the curb. It was dark out, so following his car was a little difficult. I had to stay as close as I could.

Pennington swung out onto Woodward Avenue. I followed him through Birmingham, Royal Oak and Ferndale until we passed the underground

Reuther Expressway, often called the DMZ in Detroit. South of this expressway lay the no man's land of the inner city.

I hit the inside of the city limits, swerving in and out of traffic and narrowly missing two cars to make a changing traffic light and keep up with Pennington. I felt out of control, so I loosened my grip on the steering wheel and started taking regular deep breaths. Gradually, I slowed myself down. With it my tension eased, and I started thinking more clearly. I needed a plan, a careful plan.

I followed the taillights of his black Mercedes past Comerica Park and Symphony Hall, thinking he might be going to the medical center. Instead he continued toward downtown Detroit. We passed Campus Martius and Grand Circus Park. Up ahead was the giant Penobscot building. He turned left on Griswold and pulled up to the ornate First National Bank building. I drove past him and watched as he stopped at a small restaurant near the building.

I parked in a lot across the street and waited until he came out. While I waited, I pulled out the folder again and thumbed through the pages, hoping to find something. I picked up Marni Slanell's complaint and went over each page again.

I was about to go over the corporate report once more when I saw Pennington come out of the restaurant. He was dressed in a black wool coat with a white silk scarf and black fedora. Striding quickly across the street, his stylish appearance looked in keeping with the art deco building he was about to enter.

I stepped out of the Jeep and started walking, looking down at my folder. I was about to open it again when I bumped into someone. I looked up and saw the face of a uniformed cop. Just my luck.

I put my head down and mumbled something. He must have seen my face, because he shouted at me. "Hey, you, stop!"

I was not about to have a discussion with him, so I crooked the folder in my elbow like a football and started running. I wanted to make for the entrance of the building, but I knew I would be trapped. Instead I ran toward the restaurant across the street. I looked behind me and saw the policeman sprinting after me.

I burst through the front door of the diner and ran past several tables, glancing at the startled faces of businessmen ready to start their day. In the process I knocked over a couple of chairs. The cop must have been in the restaurant, because I heard someone yelling at me as I swiveled toward the kitchen. I didn't stop to make the Heisman pose.

Passing the busboy carrying a tray full of dishes, I pushed through the swinging door. The cook, who was flipping pancakes, gave me a startled look and missed his pan. I kept running toward the rear door, turned the handle, and stepped into the cold.

There was a dumpster in the alleyway. The side door was open. I looked inside and saw that the floor was strewn with garbage. Then I heard the door to the restaurant open. Out of desperation, I jumped inside the dumpster.

I pressed against the side of the cold metal container. There were more sounds now: two or three sets of footsteps and loud voices. I hoped they couldn't see where my feet had imprinted the snow. I just stood still. Then I heard another noise, this time inside the dumpster. I looked down at a rat climbing over my boots. It took all my willpower, but I managed to stand still until I heard the footsteps of the policemen disappearing. I peeked out of the dumpster, and seeing no one in the alley, I crept around to the edge of the restaurant and saw a gaggle of flashing police cars, most of them surrounding my Jeep. There was no way I was going to be able to get into the First National Building.

I circled down to the other end of the alley and exited onto the side street. I bent my head down and walked until I saw the delivery entrance. Quickly, I ran across the street and hid behind a UPS truck. There was a metal stairway leading into the delivery room.

I took the folder out of my jacket and held it in my hand. The man at the service entrance looked at me for a moment. I held up the folder.

"I'm supposed to deliver this. Where do I go?"

The guy gave me a queer look. I must have smelled or was carrying something on me that looked funny. Then I looked down on my boots. There was a leaf of lettuce trapped in my shoelaces.

I smiled at him. "There was a box of produce on the ground outside. I must have stepped in it." He didn't say anything, just pointed at the sign that said "Lobby."

I took the lettuce off my boots, walked through the door and into a brightly-lit lobby with mosaic tiled walls and a vaulted ceiling. It was one of architect Albert Kahn's masterpieces. I didn't have time to admire it.

Instead, I went over to the directory to see if I could find some reason why Phillip Pennington had just walked into the building. It took me until the W's until I found it—Wellington Industries. Pennington, Panatone, and Wellington Industries; it was a match made in heaven. I just needed to find out whom he was meeting with.

There were several upholstered couches in the lobby. I chose one facing away from the main entrance door. Then I spent some time writing a few notes to myself. When I finished, I got up and went to the reception desk. I asked the receptionist for a directory of Wellington Industries offices in the hope that I would recognize one of the photos of the officers. It didn't take me long to find who I was looking for.

Before going up to the offices, I went into a small store inside the building that sold stationery. Looking around I picked out a few things, including a pad of paper, a pen, and a small miniature tape recorder. When I finished purchasing the items, I walked back into the lobby and copied my notes on the yellow legal paper.

I pulled out my cell phone and quickly called Sennett's office. Knudsen answered on the second ring. He seemed surprised to hear from me. When I asked for Sennett, he said he wasn't there. That's when I told him it was urgent for the lieutenant to meet me at Wellington Industries offices. I didn't wait for a reply.

I took the elevator to the twenty-fifth floor and quickly stepped into a world of corporate opulence. Rich rosewood paneling, solid brass fixtures, original art, and a perfectly coifed and manicured receptionist at the desk.

"May I help you, sir?" she asked with perfectly crisp diction. I must not have looked too appealing, because there was a derisive look on her face, as if she had just smelled something bad.

"Terrance Scotten. I'm here to see your boss," I replied, shuffling nervously in front of her as she scanned a sheet of paper on her desk.

When she didn't see Scotten's name, she made a phone call and then replied, "Yes, right this way." I followed her tailored rear-end down a short hallway and into an outer waiting room of a corporate suite. Another secretary was waiting for me, a little older than the receptionist, but just as meticulous: heavy makeup, thick lipstick, manicured nails.

"Mr. Scotten?" she asked, eyeing my shabby clothes with a look of disdain.

I nodded without answering. She must have been used to the silent treatment, because she got up from her chair and led me into the office of the Chairman of the Board of Wellington Industries. It was what I would have expected of a highly paid, high-profile industrialist: thick, wool Berber rugs, one of those in-vogue, freeform marble coffee tables, and leather seating.

"Have a seat in the chair. He'll be right with you," she said politely, pointing to an overstuffed, high-backed leather chair next to his desk. "He had to step out for a moment."

I eased my bruised and sore body into the chair and looked out the floor-to-ceiling windows at the lightening Detroit skyline. I didn't mind the wait. It gave me a chance to get my head together, adjust my coat, and survey his digs.

Not bad. *So this is how the upper echelon of industry and power lives*. Ming vases in the corners, highly polished desk with gold pen set, and pictures of dignitaries on the wall. I even recognized two presidents. These industrialists got around, all right.

My thoughts were jolted when I heard the side door to a small conference room open. My back was to the door. I didn't turn around.

"Nice to see you, Terry. It's an unexpected pleasure," a deep voice called out from behind me.

"Not exactly, Chuck," I replied.

I stood up and faced Charles Thornton, the Chairman of the Board of Wellington Industries and St. Vincent's Hospital.

The arrogance that had consumed the elder Thornton's face was replaced by a strange look of amusement. It produced a crease in his forehead that gave his jowly, imperious face a tinge of clownlike humor. "Chip, bring Dr. Pennington in so he can see what the cat dragged in."

I could see the younger Thornton through the doorway, lounging in the chair, come to a lackadaisical upright position. He got up slowly and sauntered into his father's office. Behind him walked Pennington, looking angry and confused.

"Dailey, what the hell are you doing here?" the elder Thornton asked, trying to recover from his surprise at seeing me. "They told me someone else was here waiting for me."

"You mean your buddy, Scotten? Consider me a substitution."

"Yes, well, I really don't have time for your comedy routine," Thornton said, regaining his chilly composure.

"Father, I can call the guards to take Dailey out of here." Chip Thornton spoke in the authoritative voice of someone used to being protected by others. His father reached for his phone.

I moved over to Thornton's desk and put my hand on the receiver. As I did, I told them that they should listen to me now or read my statements in the police report and the paper tomorrow. From the side, I could see Pennington move closer to Charles Thornton, as if searching for protection. Thornton took his hand away.

'I'll give you two minutes," he muttered.

I slid to the front of the desk, keeping Pennington and Chip in full view. "What I've got to say goes deeper than the board of trustees of a minor operation like St. Vincent's. It has to do with control of a company called Panatone." I opened up my jacket and stood so I was facing Charles Thornton.

Thornton blinked, but seemed unfazed and reached again for the phone. "So far no good."

"Your aid won't work, Chuck." I knew he hated being called that.

Thornton sat down in his thickly padded leather chair and looked up at me. "What aid?" he asked. He was unable to conceal a sudden shake in his hand.

"The aid that Dr. Pennington implanted at Flushing Community Hospital."

"I don't know what you're talking about," he said, poker-faced.

"I think you do, Chuck. And so does your son. Why don't we ask Dr. Pennington? Do you think he can dispute the surgery he had performed?" Thornton must have recognized that I meant business. He smoothed back his thinning silver-gray hair and leaned back in his chair.

"What do you want, Dailey?"

"I need to tell you a little story," I began. I explained that this was about a crazy idea originating in the mind of a brilliant doctor who tinkered in his lab with hearing aids. The device he developed could produce more gain than any ordinary model on the market. Not a particularly new idea, except that he figured out a way to get the amplified sound more directly into the inner ear. He did it by building a different type of microcircuit directly into the implant.

I moved closer to the desk as I spoke. "This doctor was Phillip Pennington, and it was a fabulous concept. And you know what? It worked. The aid delivered more power to the inner ear than any other device ever developed."

By now Thornton had leaned back further in his leather chair, hands behind his head. Pennington paced nervously behind him, while Chip flopped insolently into the leather sofa next to the desk.

I moved closer to Thornton's desk, as I explained that Phillip Pennington was no ordinary lab rat, a queer duck, a nerd, a poor boy from the city growing up with trust fund kids: the only thing that separated him from everyone else was that he was smart. Smart enough to create a fabulous engineering marvel. His only drawback was his naiveté.

"Tell me, Phil, where was it that Thornton got in touch with you? At one of the meetings?" Pennington nodded silently.

I told him that as smart as he thought he was, Thornton was smarter. When I mentioned that the contact was made by Chip, he nodded.

"What did he do, pal around with you, renew an old friendship, get to be your friend, show interest in your invention? You always wanted to be accepted by these rich kids, didn't you?" He didn't answer.

"You invite him to your lab where you show him your invention, and Chip Thornton tells you his father owns Panatone and tries to convince you to let him try and sell the idea to the hearing aid company."

"Don't answer him, Phillip. He doesn't know anything," Thornton demanded from behind his desk.

Chip got out of his chair and started circling toward me. "You didn't want to do it, did you?" I continued. "You could see through cheap opportunists. You were an academic. You wouldn't sell out. Not you. Why did you do it, Phil?"

"That's enough, Dailey," Chip shouted.

As he spoke, he reached up and grabbed me by the collar. I ducked under his arm and came up with a forearm shiver to his jaw. He reeled backward and hit up against a Ming vase, cracking it into multiple shards, and then slumped onto the sofa. He sat there dazed, eyes glassy. Then he spat out two teeth onto the carpet.

"You broke my jaw," he gurgled.

"I'm afraid it's going to be worse than that for you, Chipper."

Charles Thornton reached for the phone again. I grabbed it out of his hand and pulled out the cord.

"It was the tape, wasn't it?" I yelled at Pennington. When I said it, I could see him sag. The haughty arrogance had fled from his face. His eyes drooped and his mustache seemed to hang at the corner of his mouth.

"Chip Thornton was there, wasn't he?"

"You don't know anything," Pennington said weakly.

"I don't? How about this arrest report with yours and Chip Thornton's name on it?" I took the paper out from the folder and held it up to Pennington's face. I thought his eyes would come out of their sockets.

"What did they tell you? They'd expose your past and ruin you? Bring in Marni Slanell to make a statement?"

His head was bobbing up and down. "I had no choice," he whimpered.

I explained that once they had, him they were home free. They had the right academic with impeccable credentials to ensure FDA approval. Not any ordinary professor; no, they had someone trying to move up in the academic world, who understood that owning research grants was the key to everything in academic medicine. I moved to the side of the desk, making sure I faced Thornton.

"That's why the hearing aid was so important. Hearing aids are big business. A big corporation like yours would make millions off a product like he developed. And for Dr. Pennington, no NIH grant rigmarole, no competition from medical schools, just millions of dollars, under Phillip Pennington's control. Something a big academic institution, much bigger than Great Lakes, would slobber over. Enough to make him chairman of a department much larger than Great Lakes. He wanted that more than anything in his life. It was the prestige he had never gotten. That's why it didn't take much to convince him."

I watched Thornton from behind his desk. So far he hadn't lost his cool. "You're talking in circles. What's your point?" Thornton hissed.

"'Talking in circles,'" I repeated carefully. "Not hardly, Chuck. With you as chairman of the board of directors of Panatone and chairman of the board of one of the biggest hospitals in the Midwest you could set up everything."

I looked over at Chip again; he was now bent over on the couch, holding a bloody handkerchief under his mouth and moaning. Still, I was worried about him. He was erratic and unpredictable. When I was satisfied that he wasn't going anywhere, I told Thornton that all he had to do now was to get FDA approval. Six cases and Pennington's reputation were all he needed to get his new aid off the ground. I was close to Thornton's desk as I spoke. Close enough to hear the sound of his breathing. "The only problem you had was the high frequency gain on the hearing aid."

"There is no problem with the aid," Pennington shouted. "That was only in animals."

I was a little surprised when he said it. Thornton for his part just smiled and played with a couple of paper clips on his desk, almost as if nothing was happening. I kept on talking.

"You knew you had some problems. First, the specifications for the FDA had to be right. You solved that problem with Faye Donaldson. Pay her a few bucks and get her to rewrite the specs to conform to FDA standards, no high frequency output. Second, you had to find patients that would not be traceable in case anything went wrong. Perfect, you had an indigent clinic with plenty of patient material. Third, you had to do the implants in secrecy where no one could question what you were doing. No problem, you owned St. Vincent's Hospital. All you had to do was get rid of the chief that was already there so you could do your trials in secrecy."

I explained that this was a little tricky. The people at the hospital liked the current chief; he'd done a lot of good things, he was respected. "But you knew you could get rid of Ben Dailey. Just to make sure, of course, you were distanced from his exit. That's where Jimmy Scotten came in."

"You're being paranoid, Ben," Thornton said. The tone of his voice became a little more strained.

"Am I? You had the perfect setup." I told him how Chip, as Chief of Surgery, could fix it up. He would have instant access to any patient in the hospital system. It would be easy for him to switch patients, even add a left- behind sponge. Then accept the blame from the hospital, settle quickly, and leave the doctor to be vilified by the press as incompetent and careless. Make a deal with the plaintiff, tell him how bad his doctor was, even help him get out of financial trouble. "It was perfect. Shit-can me, and put Pennington in as chief of service. He could do anything he wanted, and no one would question him. It must have seemed to you that God himself was on your side, you cocksucker."

"I promise you I don't know what you're talking about, Ben," Thornton protested stiffly, his face a frozen mask.

I ignored him. "You got rid of me, and Pennington commenced his work. Forget the patients! They were only worthless indigents, veterinary experiments. There was only one problem—Ralph Gernowski."

"Who?" Pennington suddenly asked, appearing to be mystified by the entire conversation.

"The patient you operated on, you arrogant ass," I said. "He meant nothing to you, but your hearing aid did him in. It gave off a high frequency electromagnetic discharge that made him do strange things. Such as kill other people." I described Gernowski's contacts with Faye Donaldson and her subsequent murder. Gernowski might have been indigent, but he wasn't stupid. He must have done some reading, looked at Pennington's research articles and wondered whether the hearing aid was doing something to him. He was looking for an answer. That's how he came to find out about Faye Donaldson. But by that time it was too late. He was already psychotic." I stared hard into Thornton's eyes as I spoke.

"I swear to you, I never knew anything about this," Pennington said in a whining, apologetic voice. "No one ever said a word to me."

"Why would they tell you? This was about money, not about medicine. All they needed was a postoperative hearing test showing that the aid worked and, poof, you never see the patient again."

"You can't prove anything," Thornton replied.

"Don't fuck around with me, Chuckie. I have Faye Donaldson's bank statement with the payment from Wellington Industries and the results of the hearing aid from one of your other lab experiments, a guy named Albert Henderson, showing the abnormal discharge. You paid her off to change the reports to the FDA." For the first time I saw Thornton blink. There was a trace of sweat on his forehead.

"You must believe me, I didn't know any of this, Ben." It was the first crack in Thornton's armor.

"I don't really believe that, Mr. Thornton. You see, you've had a major crisis with your Panatone stock. It had been dropping precipitously over the past five years." He blinked again. "It's true. Even peons like me can find out these things, just by asking a stockbroker. Competition, poor quality aids, and bad service. The public knows what to buy. Your company needed a shot in the arm, or you stood to lose millions. The new implant was your savior. There was nothing about this whole extended crime that you didn't know," I said harshly.

"You can talk all you want about your theories, but you won't be able to make anything stick with this Scotten affair. It's all a mistake. The courts will throw it out in a New York second," Thornton replied sullenly.

I stared at him, then looked over at Chip, who seemed to be coming out of his daze. "It might have actually worked," I went on. All you had to do was get back the aids, return to the lab, and filter out the high-frequency discharge. In the meantime, the stock would soar, and you would make out like a bandit.

"It worked," he pleaded. "The patients had fantastic results. Pennington showed me."

"You knew about the high frequency discharge, didn't you?"

Thornton looked down at his desk. "Not until the project was underway."

"So, now the businessman had to make a decision. Lose millions or admit the product was defective."

"We had it organized. Once we got approval, we would correct the problem. We couldn't afford to stop the project," Thornton was practically shouting.

"'Couldn't afford?' What about those people who had the aids? The one who killed Faye Donaldson, because it made him crazy?" I asked softly.

"They were only indigent people, Ben. People with no future. They're help-ing form the basis for a whole new era in hearing aids."

"Corporate fraud, blackmail, perjury. It's a sad legacy."

"I swear to you, Ben. Pennington made the aid. It was his fault."

At this point Pennington became enraged. "You conned me, Thornton. You told me it was all perfectly legal. I knew nothing about these patients or the fact that the aid may have caused a problem. I never heard about any of these problems."

Thornton stared over at him with an icy glare that put Pennington back in his seat. He gave me one of his corporate smiles. "We can salvage this debacle, Ben. I can restore you to a prominent position at St. Vincent's and put you on the payroll of Wellington Industries as a consultant, with a six-figure salary."

All the money I would ever need. Maybe even enough to get a new boat. Thornton really knew how to tempt a guy. I thought for a moment about what had happened to me over the past five years. I was tired. I wanted to put my life back together and enjoy what life I had with Jordan. I desperately wanted out of this mess.

I was not prepared for Thornton's offer. It almost paralyzed me. Money. The word gave me life and killed me at the same time. But as much as access to a fortune consumed me as a means to stay alive, it was worse for Charles Thornton, because he actually believed it was good. I looked at this despicable man, whose life was spent buying and selling people like commodities on the stock exchange, and decided I would never want to live knowing I would die like him. Whatever it would do for me would never erase what had happened.

I looked at him with contempt. "Indigent people used as lab experiments, cheating the public with fraudulent FDA testing. Blackmail. It's a pretty sorry mess, Chuck, don't you think?"

"I was foolish. But we can overlook that, can't we, Ben? I mean, start over."

"Tempting," I mused. "The aids are disposed of. The patients are account-ed for. We take the implants and destroy them. Or, better yet, we could say there's been a malfunction in the circuitry. A public disclaimer and it's all over. You lose your money, but retain your public image. Not bad for cutting your losses, huh?"

"Now you're thinking like a businessman, Ben."

"There's just one tiny impediment."

Thornton seemed relaxed now. Almost ready to reach for the checkbook. "What's that?"

"Jimmy Scotten. In the end it failed because of Jimmy Scotten. He was on to you. He was a smart kid who got involved in his problem. Jimmy's brother showed me a piece of paper Jimmy had written. He figured out what had hap-pened and contacted you. Didn't he?"

Thornton ignored my question. "Forget about the boy, Ben. It was a rare coincidence. I can clear you of that." He snapped his fingers as if to emphasize the ease of doing it.

"I've racked my brain for five years trying to figure out how a surgeon who's performed the same operation for two decades without a problem suddenly, unaccountably, does something as stupid as operating on the wrong patient. And leaves a sponge in the wound to boot. Doesn't make sense, does it, Chuck?" I could feel my pulse rate increase, my face start to flush. *Easy, Dailey, don't lose it now.*

"After all," I continued, "I was one of the most careful surgeons on the staff. I didn't make mistakes like that."

Thornton was sweating now. His eyes furtively danced around the room.

"It was Chip that planted the sponge," I said defiantly. As I spoke, I looked over at his son. His face had now gone pale, his eyes glittered with fear. "It was perfect. The Chief of Surgery at your hospital would never be suspected. He was beyond reproach. Harvard, the Brigham. It was all bullshit. It was you and your son that conspired to do this. All in the name of money."

"No, no," Thornton protested.

I continued. "Chip planted that sponge during the surgery when the scrub nurses changed. But he outsmarted himself. He used a plain sponge, figuring no one would know the difference, didn't he?" I yelled, with an anger I had never before felt.

"Chip told me he would take care of it. Said he had a way to raise a rumpus and get rid of you. I never questioned him."

I looked over at Chip, now sitting in the chair next to his father. The only thing left was the smugness of a privileged kid who always got his way, and if he couldn't, his daddy would fix it for him. My rage was consuming me. "It was Chipper, old boy, who always did the dirty work. He went over to see Jimmy, tried to talk some sense into him. It didn't work—he wouldn't agree to your plan. Isn't that right, Chip ol' boy?"

No answer.

"Isn't that right? I yelled, this time slamming my fist against the desk, knocking Thornton's Tiffany inkwell over, spilling black ink onto the floor.

"You can't prove anything, Dailey," Chip Thornton groaned from the chair.

"Can't I? How about the tape plug his brother found in the house, just big enough to fit into a number six trach tube? It would be easy for you to get into the house. You were friends with his father, maybe even his business partner. You were twice as big as Jimmy. Just hold him down, plug his trach with the tape plug, and watch him die. Then hang him with a cord to make it look like a suicide. Simple as that. No one would suspect anything. Except you left the plug behind."

Thornton looked at the stain spreading out on the Berber rug as Chip mumbled something. I moved over to Chip, grabbed him by his cashmere sport coat lapel, and lifted him off the chair. His face turned pale and his eyes began to water.

"What was that, Chip? I didn't hear you."

Chip just hung his head down and started to weep. I threw him back into the chair in disgust.

"Shut up, Chip," his father said. "I'll handle this, just like I handled that girl from Cranbrook." Then he looked back at me. His eyes had turned hard. He had his business face on.

"That's behind us now, Ben. Let's move forward." He had the checkbook open now.

I moved closer to Thornton, so close I could smell his hundred-dollar cologne. "I don't think so, Chuck. You see, I believe in Hippocrates, in good and evil, that kind of boring stuff," I said courteously, lifting him by the lapels of his custom suit and slamming him back down into his chair.

Fear swelled his face as he sagged backwards. "Calm down, Ben, calm down!"

"Tell that to Jimmy Scotten!" I yelled. "You tell that to me, as if it will change the five years of hell I've been through or bring back that dead boy? I've got a better idea, Chuckie, why don't you tell that to the police? They're much better at handling this sort of thing than I am."

Thornton smiled and shrugged his shoulders, like a poker player pulling out his last ace. "Ah, you are the master detective, aren't you?" he snarled. "Well, I have all the necessary documents signed, sealed, and delivered from Panatone, absolving me of any knowledge of the implant program and any fallout associated with it. When Pennington started this whole business, I had my lawyers draw up the papers. So you'll be spending a long time in the courtroom trying to nail me." His face was filled with a smugness built on years of deception and legal maneuvering.

"Maybe. But this tape in my pocket will go a long way to persuading a jury." I pulled out the cassette recorder that I had bought downstairs in the stationery shop. I watched as Thornton's face lost whatever color it had in it. "Would you like me to play it back for you?"

"You really are going to push me, aren't you?" he shouted. From the corner of my eye I saw Chip Thornton get up from the couch and move to the door. I moved closer to him, taking him by the hair and pushing him back into the chair.

"Stay where you are, Chip. I'm not going to do anything with either of you. I have a hunch you're going to do it to yourself. In fact, I'm going to walk out of here right now and never come back. The truth has set me free, as they say."

Thornton shrugged and reached into the top drawer of his desk, as if looking for a pen. When he pulled his hand out, he was holding the blue steel of a Smith & Wesson 45.

"I guess I'm going to have to do what I should have done in the first place. I was hoping I could put you in your place by the malpractice suit, but it wasn't enough." He brought the gun up, flipped off the safety and pointed it at my heart.

"In case you don't think I'll use this, guess again. It's perfect self-defense. You barged into my office and threatened my son and me. We had a history of personal differences. You wanted revenge."

"It'll never work, Thornton. Pennington is here. Are you going to kill him?"

"Phil won't say anything, will you?"

I looked over at the deflated bag of wind. He just sagged in his chair and said nothing.

At that point Thornton raised his gun toward my head. I ducked down behind the desk as the gun exploded. I heard a scream behind me. I looked back at Chip, blood erupting from his neck. Charles Thornton's face went blank as he watched his son slump to the floor, blood dripping onto the carpet.

Thornton fired again, but the bullet missed, hitting the wall behind me. I circled toward the end of the desk. There was another shot. This time I felt a pain in my left arm. I wanted to yell, but I couldn't. The pain was searing, mind bending. I could feel a warm liquid running down my arm. I knew I had been shot.

Somehow I had to stop Thornton before he got away. I crawled along the floor toward the side of the desk. I heard Thornton move to the other side.

"I'll get you, Dailey, if it's the last thing I do."

I saw his feet beneath the desk. I was getting dizzy from the blood loss. I had only one chance to get him. I leaned against the desk and lifted up on the overhanging edge. In one violent motion I heaved upward, standing the desk upright. Thornton fired at the desktop, but the wood was too thick. I leaned into it once more, hoping to topple it on Thornton.

There was a sound from the door as it crashed open.

"Drop your weapon and put your hands behind your head." It was Sennett's voice.

I pushed on the desk and felt it topple. There was a scream and another shot. Then nothing.

CHAPTER 35

Like a cold machine, long since dormant, I could feel myself begin to move. Slow and creaking at first. The engine started, and the dark haze of unconsciousness started to lift. Light intensified in my eyes. My brain started to identify the aroma in my nose. Pungent, clean, antiseptic. Another sensation: noise, high-pitched and whining. My ears. Could I hear? Then there was another sound, one I had heard many times before. High-pitched beeping. Slowly my surroundings came into focus. Faces hovered over me. One or two I recognized. I blinked my eyes.

"Where am I?" I croaked.

"St. Vincent's," a voice penetrated from the haze.

"Jordan, where is she?"

I felt a hand squeeze mine. "I'm right here, Ben."

My eyes squinted against the light, but her face began to come into focus. More light, the motor running better now.

"What time is it?" I asked groggily.

"Ten thirty in the morning," Jordan's voice replied.

"What about yesterday?" I said weakly, becoming more aware.

"It's all over. The nightmare is over," she soothed, rubbing my hand.

My body started stirring, and I struggled to sit up. "The tape, did you find the tape?"

"Everything. Including Thornton's confession," she said.

By this time all my central systems were functioning. All that remained to ascertain was whether my body was whole, or did the gunshot damage my arm? I moved my fingers. So far, so good. Pain. I could feel it, a throbbing in my arm. "Am I all right?"

"You are a very lucky man," Jordan said. "The bullet went through your arm. It tore one of the blood vessels. They were able to repair it, but you lost a lot of blood. You had us worried for a while."

"Do us a favor, doc. Next time let us do the work." I focused my eyes at the end of the bed. There was Sennett's face. A smile had finally creased the corners of his mouth, and he actually looked pleasant.

"There's not going to be a next time. I'm done with the detective business. I need to practice medicine," I mumbled.

"Now that the truth has come out, I'm sure St. Vincent's is going to be very anxious to have you back."

"What about Thornton?" I asked.

Jordan held the front page up to me. "Check the paper."

My eyes focused on the photo of a cuffed, silver-haired man doing the perp walk, his head partially hidden by his overcoat. The headline read "Prominent businessman, Charles Thornton, arrested after shooting."

I turned to Jordan. "Maybe there is some real justice after all." I tried sitting up. "I need to get out of here." Every muscle in my body seemed to ache; suddenly, I slumped back down.

"Why?" Jordan's voice asked.

I started to get up again and swing my legs over the edge of the hospital bed, but I didn't make it. My head was killing me. "Gotta get out of here," I could hear myself speaking. Then my head fell back and I was out.

The next thing I knew, the sun had begun its customary descent. With this bout of consciousness, I was a little less dazed. Better yet, the ringing was gone from my ears. I looked around. Jordan was sleeping in the chair in the corner. Struggling upright, this time I managed to swing my feet over the bedside.

I was about to move away from the bed when I felt a tug on my left arm. I looked down. There was the I.V. line, plugged in and working. Detaching the bottle from its stand, I carried it in my hand as I walked over to the corner closet. I was still dizzy, but at least the animal was functioning.

I found my clothes in the closet. Someone had been nice enough to wash and fold them neatly. I put them on, all except my shirt, which I left until I could get rid of the I.V. Every now and then I would glance over at Jordan. The pale light was streaming through her auburn hair and onto her angelic face. I didn't think I had ever seen anyone more beautiful in my life.

I turned to call the nurse and ask her to help me with the I.V., but I stumbled against the wall, knocking over the wastepaper basket. The sound woke Jordan.

She looked startled at seeing me out of bed. "Where do you think you're going?" she asked.

"I've got to get out of here," I said.

"Why?" she asked tartly.

"Two good reasons. First, I have no health insurance and, second, I need to find a place to live."

"Oh, grow up, Ben. The hospital is picking up the tab. It's the least they can do for you. As far as a place to live, you're going to come back to my house. You'll stay there until we can get you situated." There was a tone of finality in her voice, the kind of finality that told me it was now officially useless to argue. "Now maybe you should get back in bed until your doctor decides you're ready to get out of here."

I was beaten and I knew it. I humbled myself, retreated to the bed, and sat on the edge. "You know that I'm not good at taking orders, don't you?"

"Think of them as friendly suggestions. They're easier to swallow."

"When is my expected departure?" I asked.

"The doctor said he would stop in this afternoon. All your tests are fine. They say your arm will be as good as new."

"I can't wait. I hate hospitals."

"Coming from a doctor, that's strange."

"Are you kidding? Doctors are the worst patients of all. They're always afraid they're going to catch something." I fiddled with the I.V., trying to get myself comfortable.

Just about the time I finished getting it right, the door opened and in walked the surgeon. When he saw me, he smiled. "Looks like the patient is doing just fine. Ready to go home?"

I looked at Jordan. A smile flashed across her face. The lines of worry had evaporated.

"Okay, doctor, lead the way. I'm out of here."

IN MY CASE IT HAD BEEN A LOT EASIER getting into the hospital than it was getting out. Paperwork, nurse's instructions, more paperwork, and, finally, I got into Jordan's car at the turn-around at the front entrance.

"Nice car," I said jokingly. "It looks like something an undercover cop would use in one of those police movies, the ones with the chase scenes."

"A chicken in every pot and a car in every garage," she responded.

By this time Jordan was opening the door and trying to help me in. I was weaker than I'd thought, but I made it.

It wasn't a long drive back to her house. The streets were now mostly cleared, and the traffic was light. It seemed strange to pull up to her townhouse under such different circumstances. I still had a feeling of anxiety, but I was having a hard time bringing it to the surface.

It wasn't until I reached the front steps of her townhouse that I realized what was bothering me. What the hell was I doing here, the house guest of this attractive woman? *Look at me, a broken-down, on the fringe doctor. Yeah, everyone will tell you that I can start over, but it isn't that easy. New patient lists, restoring referrals, setting up an office. It's not that easy. Hell, I don't even have a home.*

And now what do I say, when I get inside? Excuse me, Jordan, but I'm going up to my room. Maybe she has something else in mind. Talk about feeling uncomfortable. Forget it, Dailey. Don't make a jerk of yourself. You're too old and too naive. It's not going to work.

We walked inside the brightly lit foyer. Mahogany table, gentlemen's stand in the corner, and a Kilim rug over the white Mexican tile. She took off her coat, hung it up in the closet, and then turned to look at me, her cheeks flushed red in the light of the hall.

"You don't want to stay, do you?" she asked. I should have known she wouldn't beat around the bush.

My mind was alert. The pain inflicted from my ordeal vanished as I looked at her. "'Want' is a funny word. I don't think it applies here. It's just that . . ."

"Can I tell you something?" she interrupted.

I nodded.

"I've thought a lot about you." Her lips parted when she spoke, and she held my hand in hers. Electricity went through me.

"I hate when people feel sorry for me. Taking in the stray dog," I said defensively.

"No, hear me out, Ben. I know you can take care of yourself. Maybe that's why I've admired you from a distance for a long time." *Admire.* And here I was, hoping for more.

"It's just been a couple weeks. That's not very long, you know." Her hand was caressing mine, and it felt good.

"Can I confess something?" she asked.

"Sure."

"I had a crush on you from the first time I saw you play. You weren't exactly the usual guy working out at the Pipeline."

"What could you possibly see in someone like me?" I asked quickly.

"Character, integrity. Besides, for an old man, you still have a good body." She laughed gently.

"Jordan, I'm not what you think. I've got no future, I've . . ."

"Shh. You talk too much," she whispered, first putting her forefinger on my mouth, then reaching her hand behind my head to bring my lips to hers.

I stood there, the warmth of her body pressed close to me, infusing my tired soul with a strange and forgotten feeling. This wasn't just lust. Through the mist in my eyes, I slowly began to recognize it. It was the powerful medicine of love, a potion to which I had long ago thought I was immune to.

Jordan led me up the stairs. At the top of the landing I looked down the hall at the spare room. Jordan tugged at my sleeve.

"Come this way, Ben," she said seductively. "That room is for guests."

EPILOGUE

I MAY HAVE UNRAVELED THE MURDER of Faye Donaldson and exposed Charles Thornton for his crimes, but there were still unanswered questions. Someone had torched my boat and tried to kill me at the lab in Ann Arbor. It was unnerving that the person—or persons—who had committed the crimes were still unaccounted for.

My anxiety was settled a couple of weeks later. Sennett called and told me Terry Scotten and two of his bodyguards were arrested for attempted murder. The forensic guys found Scotten's prints on the cocktail stirrer, but they didn't have enough to charge him with the fire on my boat. Sennett brought him down to police headquarters and, in his terms, "interrogated him hard." He guessed that Scotten's conscience got the better of him, because after an hour he broke down and confessed everything. Scotten said he couldn't live with himself anymore.

The lieutenant said that two bouncers that worked at his club were responsible for both the fire and the shooting. Scotten admitted that he masterminded both crimes. When I described the two guys with whom I had a run-in at the Plain View, Sennett said that my description fit them to a tee.

There was something else. In Scotten's statement to the police, he explained everything that had happened to his son. Apparently, after the mistake on Jimmy's original surgery, Charles Thornton had approached him with a huge settlement from St. Vincent's. Scotten had gambling debts and needed the dough, so he took the money, and then, to cover his own guilt, went after me.

Scotten admitted that after he found out what the Thorntons had done to his son, he realized how displaced his actions had been. He even said he was sorry about what happened to me. As much as I felt for his son, I had a hard time feeling the same for his father.

Scotten's confession was just part of a continuing buzz that wouldn't stop. My story was all over the local and national newspapers, most of it media sensationalism. I wondered what the hell was the matter with these people. I even got a call from the *Today* program, which I politely declined. I'm a doctor, not some kind of gumshoe. I didn't like it. To me, the whole sordid deal sounded like another blight on the city I loved.

Then I started getting calls from "friends" that I hadn't heard from over the past five years. I wondered where they were when I needed them. I even got a call from my ex, wondering if I wanted to go out to lunch. Apparently things weren't so good with the CEO of one of Detroit's largest banks. I not so politely told her to go fuck herself.

Aside from proving my innocence, two other positive events occurred. First, I got a call from St. Vincent's. They wanted me back and were willing to pay me restitution. After talking with Jordan, I told them I would accept the money. I didn't want a public legal battle, and in reality it was Charles Thornton, not the hospital, that had caused my problem. They thought they were doing the right thing. The money turned out to be a significant amount. I set aside enough to make up for what I had lost over the past five years, including a new boat, and gave the rest to charity.

The other was my relationship with Jordan. I never thought I could feel this way again. I had finally found what I was looking for, and I was never going to let that slip away. No meeting, no patient, no hospital committee would ever get in the way of my relationship with her. Insecurity would never grip me in its vice again. I knew she felt the same about me.

Gradually, there was no more fuel to keep the fire alive, and the story started to die out, enough so that I could regain some kind of normality in my life. After about a month after getting out of the hospital, Sennett called me. He said he wanted to meet me at the Pipeline. I arranged to meet him on Thursday before my set.

The weather had settled into a mid-winter doldrums; a little snow, lots of pale, gray days, and temperatures hovering around freezing. It was around five o'clock and the sun was just setting across the ice floes of the Detroit River. I drove up to the Pipeline and parked in the rear. William was still at his post.

Sennett was waiting for me at a table near one of the windows. When he saw me, he stood up, smiled, and then gave me a hug that that only he could deliver. We sat down at the table, ordered a couple of Labatts, and chatted for a while about all of the unwanted publicity. While he sat talking, he kept fidgeting inside his coat, like he was adjusting his holster. It made me nervous.

"What's the matter, Lieutenant, got an itch, or are you expecting some trouble?"

The lieutenant sat quietly for a moment, then took a pull from the bottle. "I guess I got to be ready. You never know when something is going to happen around you. You know, the type of guy that attracts attention." As he spoke, he winked over at Charlie.

"That kind of attention I can do without."

Sennett reached inside his coat pocket again and this time extracted a small leather case. His face looked serious. "Talking about the press isn't why I really came down here. The chief called me into his office this morning and said he wanted to give this to you." I heard some noise behind me and looked around. There was Charlie, Sid, and Jordan. They were all beaming. I wondered what the hell was going on.

I took the leather case and opened it slowly. There was a gold, metal object inside. I pulled it open and looked at it. It said, "Detroit Police Department— Police Surgeon." I turned it around and showed the badge to everyone. They all began yelling and clapping their hands. I stared at the badge again and studied it for a few moments. Then I started to laugh. It was a deep laugh, one that I hadn't felt for a long, long time. Maybe I was a detective after all.

GENE RONTAL is a head and neck surgeon. Born in Detroit, he attended the University of Michigan, where he received his medical degree. After completing a residency at the University of Minnesota, he went into private practice in the Detroit area and began teaching at the University of Michigan Medical School. He is currently a professor in the Department of Otolaryngology/Head and Neck Surgery. His writing career started twenty years ago when he published his first novel, *Sterile Justice*. Since then he has three other books in print (*A Lethal Dose*, *The Cruelest Cut*, and *The Police Surgeon*) and has participated in promoting them with book signings and radio and newspaper interviews. In addition to his mystery writing, Gene Rontal has published over fifty scientific articles, authored chapters in medical textbooks, and has been quoted in a number of lay publications, including *Time*, *Science*, *National Geographic*, and the *Wall Street Journal*. Doctor Rontal and his wife, Ellen, enjoy skiing, traveling, and spending time with their family.

www.ingramcontent.com/pod-product-compliance
Lightning Source LLC
Chambersburg PA
CBHW011118100726
47898CB00011B/3140